DIPLOMATIC CRISIS

DIPLOMATIC CRISIS

THE EMPRESS' SPY™ BOOK TWO

S.E. WEIR

MICHAEL ANDERLE

DISRUPTIVE IMAGINATION®

Copyright © 2021 LMBPN Publishing
Cover by Mihaela Voicu http://www.mihaelavoicu.com/
Cover copyright © LMBPN Publishing
This book is a Michael Anderle Production

LMBPN Publishing
PMB 196, 2540 South Maryland Pkwy
Las Vegas, NV 89109

Version 1.01, June, 2021
eBook ISBN: 978-1-64971-855-6
Print ISBN: 978-1-64971-856-3

THE DIPLOMATIC CRISIS TEAM

Thanks to our Beta Readers:
Larry Omans, Jim Caplan, Micky Cocker, Rachel Beckford,
John Ashmore, Kelly O'Donnell, Mary Heise, Rachel Heise,
Ron Gailey

Thanks to the JIT Readers

Deb Mader
Daryl McDaniel
Dave Hicks
Wendy L Bonell
Jackey Hankard-Brodie
Misty Roa
Peter Manis
James Caplan
Dorothy Lloyd
Zacc Pelter
Diane L. Smith
Larry Omans
Jeff Goode

If we've missed anyone, please let us know!

Editor
Lynne Stiegler

DEDICATION

To all those who have supported and encouraged me every step of the way. This is as much your book as mine.

- S.E. Weir

To Family, Friends and
Those Who Love
To Read.
May We All Enjoy Grace
To Live The Life We Are
Called.

—Michael

CHAPTER ONE

QBBS *Meredith Reynolds*, R&D, Research Lab
Seraphina Water's eighteenth birthday

Link strode down the long hallway, the light tap of his feet in no way matching the anger that made his heart beat furiously. He had long ago learned how to measure his blood pressure on the fly, and it was currently elevated. He took deep breaths to calm himself. It didn't help.

Blasted devil-woman!

He had been gone not even ten days on this last mission, and what did he find when he returned? A miserly woman vomiting her vile prejudice and insecurities on the best and brightest recruit he'd seen in years. Seraphina had turned eighteen and no longer needed the woman around to put her down and berate her one minute, then smile and hug her the next. Time to eject the refuse!

He eyed the scanner next to his destination as he approached and pulled out his card. He growled at the inevitable rejection and used his implant to ping the being that could help.

>>*You rang?*<<

"ADAM, you can see where I am. I need you to unlock the door for me."

The moment before the AI responded seemed to stretch out for too long, aggravating his maxed-out adrenaline. Perhaps he needed to do something to de-stress. Brief glimpses of exercise equipment and crafts flooded his memory, but he shook his head. Scratch that. What he was about to do would relieve his stress better than anything else.

>>You realize you are standing in front of a restricted door, correct?<<

"Of course! I know exactly where I am! Now please open the door."

>>You could have just asked Meredith. She is the station EI. However, she would have denied the request since you are not listed as having access to this room. Why should I grant it to you?<<

Link gritted his teeth as he eyed the person whose footsteps he could hear approaching from his left. He nodded at the woman, who viewed him suspiciously but passed him and continued down the hall. He couldn't stand here much longer. "ADAM, you know who works here?"

>>Yes. You seem to have an unreasonable fixation on this woman. There are doctors for that. I can make an appointment for you.<<

"ADAM! I know you've been monitoring Seraphina. I won't believe you if you tell me otherwise."

>>Of course.<<

"I'm about to make her aunt go away for good."

A brief moment of silence. >>Telling me you are about to kill someone isn't convincing me to let you inside.<<

"What?" Link looked at the cameras ADAM would be

watching from, his eyebrows furrowed. "No! I'm not going to kill her."

>>*Your word on that?*<<

Link drew himself up, then, with a sigh, he released his breath and let go of some anger. Just a smidge. A very teeny smidge. "I give you my word I will enter this door with no intention of killing the woman and will stick to that intention no matter how much she provokes me."

>>*Accepted.*<<

The door in front of him clicked. "Thanks, ADAM."

>>*I was serious about that doctor, DS. But now that Phina is an adult, I really hope you are able to send her aunt away.*<<

Link's smile turned hard.

"Oh, you can count on that. I've got an offer she won't be able to refuse."

QBBS *Meredith Reynolds*, Secret Bar, Back Room

Two weeks after events on Vermott, Planet of the Baldere

Seraphina Grace Waters didn't understand what lay in front of her face. She blinked to clear her vision, but what she saw remained the same. A feast for two had been laid out on one end of the long table, complete with cloth napkins and glasses filled with wine. Steam rose from a few dishes, wafting aromas toward her that caused her belly to rumble with hunger. Phina stared in confusion at the man standing next to the table.

"What's all this?"

Link smiled, his brown eyes alight with amusement. "Dinner, of course."

Her eyes moved between her mentor and the table, then she waggled her finger at each.

"Seriously, Link, what is this?"

Link's face drooped, and he gave her puppy dog eyes. "I can't have anything more in mind than a nice dinner?"

She raised her eyebrows and popped the word, "Nope."

He grinned with satisfaction. "You know me so well already!"

Phina rolled her eyes, then she stared at him. He held her gaze for a minute before gesturing at the table. "Are we going to eat?"

"Are you going to talk?"

"Of course."

"Then we'll eat."

She hesitantly moved forward, then sat down in the chair he indicated, feeling a little uncomfortable. This didn't seem like a casual meal. She surveyed the spread. The selections included pasta with a red meat sauce, her favorite spicy chicken dish, fresh buttered rolls, and her favorite salad. In addition to those wonderful aromas, she turned toward the very welcome scent of either chocolate cake or brownies, which were probably under the covered tray in the middle of the table. Phina bet on brownies because they slightly edged out chocolate cake in her book, and that was the point.

All these were her favorites, which made her suspicious. This meal had been carefully planned, which meant Link either had something awful to tell her and the food was for consolation or comfort, or he was buttering her up because he wanted something. That he wouldn't just come out and say what he wanted to as he normally did spoke volumes about how bad it would be.

Link had just settled down in his seat when she reached over and lifted the lid of the tray. Bingo. After snagging a brownie, she put the cover down and began to munch on the treat. Fudgy chocolate flooded her mouth, causing her to moan and close her eyes as she enjoyed it. All too soon, his voice broke the daze caused by the chocolaty goodness.

"Why am I not surprised you went for dessert first?"

Phina opened her eyes to see her mentor leaning back in his chair, looking at her with amusement. Ignoring Link for the moment, she closed her eyes again and slowly finished the delicious treat. Brownies were her favorite, but that didn't mean she had them all that often. She finished by licking her fingers, then opened her eyes to find her napkin.

"Some days, you need to have dessert first. I have a feeling this is going to be one of them, and I wanted to enjoy it before my day got worse with whatever it is you want to tell me."

Link smirked as he reached for the food in front of him, dishing himself some before passing it to her. "Look at you, smarty pants. Figuring it all out."

"Uh-huh. So, what's going on? I don't really know how to take all of this." She waved her hand at the table. She was certain Link wanted something; she just wasn't sure what.

Or what it would cost her.

"If it makes you feel better, you could call it a date." His eyebrows danced up and down as he grinned.

Phina stared at him and stopped scooping spicy chicken

onto her plate, showing she was not amused before blinking and waiting. Finally, he rolled his eyes and grumbled. "Holy buckets of seriousness, Batman. Fine, I'll tell you what's going on."

She suppressed a smile as she finished getting her food. Forking up a bite, she kept her eyes on him. "Does that mean you're my sidekick?"

Link let out a laugh as he shook his head. "Maybe someday, kid."

She looked him over, using the skills he had taught her to read his body language, and realized he was both nervous and a little reluctant to talk, as well as not sure if he wanted to be farther away or closer. Something must be really bothering him to forget to control his body language this much. Her heart beat faster, and she took deep breaths to calm herself.

"Link, please. What's going on? What aren't you telling me?"

He paused to place his fork on the table and looked down for a moment to gather his thoughts, then back up. His expression went from slightly lost to resolved and determined.

"There are many things I haven't told you, my dear. These past months have been just the beginning, with much to come. Before we discuss that, though, there is something you need to know."

She looked at him with suspicion, but he ignored it, giving her a smirk. Back to normal then, no trace of his prior uneasiness. She let out a breath in relief. Perhaps his news wouldn't be too bad.

"What's that?"

"The Empress."

Phina tried to swallow but found it difficult due to the sudden dryness in her throat. Her heart raced as she vacillated between nervous and excited.

"What about her?"

"She wants to meet you."

Phina dropped her fork on her plate. "I don't think so."

"What?" Link appeared genuinely surprised. "Why not?"

"Because she's the Empress, and I'm...well, *me*! I don't know the first thing about talking to the Empress."

She glanced up to and saw his undecipherable look. When Phina raised an eyebrow in question, he responded with a sigh, and his shoulders relaxed.

"She's a person too, you know. She has needs just like everyone else."

Her eyes widened in alarm, and she shook her head vigorously. "Oh no, no, no! I completely draw the line at talking about, or even thinking about, the Empress' sex life! Absolutely not!"

She waved her hands to get her point across. His jaw had dropped in astonishment, then clicked shut. His face contorted, and he let out a snort that turned into a laugh. Phina's mouth twitched in response, then she broke into sniggers.

Granted, at least half of it was releasing tension, but still. Her brain just didn't want to go there. Everyone talked about the Empress, but there were some things you didn't do. Her laughter died.

"I'm serious, you know."

His eyes still showed amusement, though his face was serious. "I know. And for the record, I was referring to the need to have friends. Conversation and companionship, that sort of thing."

"Oh. I guess I hadn't really thought of it that way. Alina always uses that phrase for...the other one."

He let out another snort. "Understandable, then. Are you going to flip out if Bethany Anne comes now?"

"Yes. Err, no." Phina thought about it, then shrugged. "I'll try not to?"

"Good enough. Eat your food before it gets cold. I'll ask ADAM to let her know."

Phina ate, but she barely tasted the food, which had begun to cool. Though she tried to keep her mind blank, she failed miserably. She just couldn't help feeling nervous. Why did the Empress want to meet her? Was it just a social call, as Link had seemed to suggest?

Only two bites remained by the time Phina heard a light pop and whoosh of air. The Empress appeared on her right. Phina was surprised and jerked to the side. Her fork slipped out of her hand, flying off to the left of her chair.

Link had barely twitched, though he turned to face the woman quickly enough. Phina did the same and found the Empress trying to speak around a fit of laughter.

"I *never* get tired of the faces you all make!"

Phina glanced at the revered and feared Empress Bethany Anne, who stood chortling with her hand over her belly, then at Link, wondering how she should respond. Link wore an amused expression. After a few more chuckles, Bethany Anne patted her chest as she walked over to the chair on the opposite side of the table from Phina. After unceremoniously plopping herself on it, she leaned forward and sniffed.

The Empress' eyes lit up. "Are those brownies?"

She reached over to the covered tray and removed the lid.

"Don't mind if I do." The Empress spoke around her large mouthful. "Mmmm." She closed her eyes and ignored them, much as Phina had earlier, and she devoured the brownie as fast as the young woman could blink. She snagged another one as her mouth worked to get all the chocolate and swallow.

"Ok. Where were we?"

Link opened his mouth to answer, only to shut it again when Bethany Anne answered herself.

"Right. Why I'm here." She turned her sharp gaze to Phina, whose eyes widened in concern.

Bethany Anne waved her off. "Oh, don't worry so much! You're not in trouble. In fact, I believe congratulations on a job well done are in order. You handled the situation between the Gleeks and the Baldere well despite your inexperience. Your actions have caused the Gleeks to change their minds and petition to join the Empire. I'm told reversals in their decisions don't happen very often. Their knowledge will be a huge asset to the Empire, so congratulations for both of those highly impressive achievements."

Phina nodded. "Thank you."

Bethany Anne smiled. "You're welcome. The other reason I'm here is to meet you."

"To meet me?" Phina's shocked eyes turned to Link's amused face before moving back to Bethany Anne.

"Of course." The Empress' eyebrow rose, and she turned so serious that her eyes flashed red. "You might not realize this since we've just met, but I've known about you since before you were born. You're mine, and I take care of those who are mine."

Phina stopped breathing as she stared at the Empress. In general terms, the woman could have been anyone with her clear, pale skin, jet-black eyes and hair, and greater than average height. However, with Bethany Anne, average was not in the dictionary. She was one of the most beautiful women Phina had ever seen, glowing with vitality and power, and she possessed an attitude, awareness, and focus that categorized her as someone both extraordinary and extraordinarily dangerous. Definitely not someone you wanted to mess with.

Still, even though she decided on the spot that she would not ever ask to spar with the woman, Phina sensed the intent to help and protect her the Empress' words conveyed. Even though Bethany Anne could be dangerous, she was not to Phina or anyone else under her protection. Phina could trust the Empress to have her back, and something inside her relaxed for the first time in years.

Thank you. Now breathe.

Phina obeyed, blinking as she realized Bethany Anne had spoken in her head without needing to use the implant. So, the rumors *were* true. The Empress could read and speak directly to your mind.

Of course. But do keep it to yourself. Leaving it as a rumor instead of confirming it is very useful, as well as being hilarious when someone realizes I can read their thoughts for the first time.

Bethany Anne smirked, then scarfed down the rest of her second brownie before swiping her hands together to remove the crumbs. Phina glanced at Link and realized that aside from those twenty minutes he'd spent asleep on her aunt's bed months ago, this was the longest he had ever gone in her presence without saying a word. He treated the Empress with a respect he had yet to show to anyone else, even Anna Elizabeth, his boss. Well, at least he gave *someone* his respect. Phina had begun to think him incapable of it.

The Empress laughed suddenly. When they both looked at her questioningly, she just shook her head. "You two!" After laughing again, she winked. "I can't wait for the next few years to pass."

Phina leaned forward. "Why, what can't you wait for?"

Bethany Anne stood, then raised an eyebrow. "Because you've only scratched the surface of what's really happening in the Empire. If what ADAM and Greyson tell me about your potential is true, I could use your help."

Phina opened her mouth to ask how soon, only to click it shut at the Empress' next words, which were accompanied by a *look*.

A seriously intent, don't mess around look.

"After you finish your training, of course."

She stared at Bethany Anne for a moment, then nodded. "Of course."

Bethany Anne turned to Link and gazed at him seriously. "Keep me updated."

His shoulders lowered in resignation, and he looked even more tired. "Yes, Empress."

Bethany Anne grabbed the second-to-last brownie and held it up. "You wouldn't believe how many calories I burn just traveling all over the damn place."

Phina held up her hands. "I wasn't going to ask." Well, maybe not, but she would have thought it.

The Empress grinned, took a step forward, and disappeared.

Well, then.

Link cleared his throat, and Phina glared at him.

"What?"

She shook her head and packed away this conversation until later. She decided moving on would be the best way to handle her nerves.

"So, what were you going to tell me?"

CHAPTER TWO

QBBS *Meredith Reynolds*, Secret Bar, Back Room

Now that the task was in front of him, Link had second thoughts. He knew that what he had to tell Phina might possibly change the way they interacted. He didn't want that; he liked the dynamic they had. Even when she glared at him, it amused him because he knew she wasn't serious. Still, she needed to know about everything—everything related, anyway—and he did need her help.

He looked at the girl he mentored and saw that her green eyes were narrowed as she waited for the other shoe to drop. Her brown hair waved on the way down to her shoulders and accented her brown skin, which she had inherited from both sides. The longer he stared, the more he realized he had to replace his mental description of "girl" with "woman." Where had that little girl gone? The thought was vexing.

Phina's eyebrows rose, and she gave him a look that clearly said, "Why are you being weird?" and, "Just get on with it!"

Link sighed. "You know the day I started being your mentor?"

Phina glanced down at her mostly empty plate, pushed it into the middle of the table among the serving dishes, and leaned forward on her arms. She gave him that deceptively sweet smile that said she was about to deliver a zinger.

"You mean, when you showed up like a creeper, took me to not just one but *three* bars, told me everyone at the second bar thought I was your sex kitten while everyone at the third bar knew you were a spy, threw me down on the floor twice, gave me my first three spy lessons, empathized with my issues with Aunt Faith, changed the focus of the vow I made on my parents' memory, and then quizzed me for an hour as to the slightest things I noticed in the five minutes we were in the third bar? That day?"

Link grinned appreciatively. Really, her mind was a marvel. "That's the one."

He leaned over to reach for the last brownie and ended up grasping empty air as Phina swiped the tray out from under him. He shot her a look that was supposed to appear wounded, not pouting.

The heartless girl smirked at him. "Uh-uh. I eat delicious gooey chocolate. You talk."

His face fell; now he was pouting. He huffed a sigh, then inclined his head and gestured for her to go ahead. "Of course, my dear." He could be a gracious loser. Occasionally.

He leaned forward on his elbows to focus on her. "I told you that I am what we've been calling the Diplomat Spy, with a foot in both worlds of the Diplomatic Corps and the Spy Corps. What I haven't told you is that I have another role within the Spy Corps."

"What, do you lead this pack of spies? Wipe their noses, kiss their boo-boos, and send them on their next missions?"

Link fell silent at her mocking words, his amused grin growing on his face. He should have known she would figure it out, even if she was only trying to get a reaction from him. *Phina, Phina, Phina.* The girl...ahem, the *woman* was just too quick. He gave himself a quick congratulatory pat on the back for his foresight in bringing her on board.

He never wanted to see what Phina could do if she were working against him.

———

Phina stopped chewing her gloated-over ooey-gooey bite of brownie at the look on Link's face. She quickly swallowed, then swallowed again when the fudgy chocolate lingered.

"Seriously?"

He flashed the oh-so-smug grin he gave when he thought he was really clever for some reason. She knew it had to do with her. He reached for his glass of wine and saluted her with it before drinking.

It only served to make her want to smack him. No, smacking was for sissy girls. Phina was many things, but she had never been one of those. She would just punch him in the face. With her fist, then her elbow, knee, and finally her foot, which was encased in metal-tipped boots. Yes, that would do nicely.

"You're the head of the Spy Corps?"

He gave a little bow in his chair, holding his glass out to the side. "At your service."

"How do you manage that? You're always around here, and I've been under the impression that Spy Corps' headquarters was off the station."

"With great difficulty and by having two great seconds in commands. And yes, it is located on a secret base in the next system. It's one of the places I go when I disappear from the *MR* for a time. That was what caused me to seek you out to take my place as the Diplomatic Spy so I could concentrate on the Spy Corps."

Phina eyed the man as she took another bite. She wanted to close her eyes and enjoy it but shook off the urge as she searched her mentor's face and body language. He appeared relaxed, but he held his body a little too stiffly, and he gave her a quick questioning smirk. However, it wasn't quite quick enough.

"Why tell me now? What causes you to be so concerned?"

"What makes you think I'm concerned?"

She gave him a look that implied, "Don't be stupid." Link grimaced and started to speak, but she got there first.

"I don't know, Link. Or should I say, Greyson Wells, the diplomat? Ian James, the spy? Or was that Stan, the sleazy man?" She gave him an exaggerated shrug that included her hands. "It's so hard to keep track of these things."

He leveled a look at her, leaned against the back of his

chair, and sipped his wine, affecting an air of nonchalance. "What's your point?"

Ah, distancing body language. Rule number two. He already knew her point, but she played the game anyway since it could also mean that he was scrambling to know how to respond.

"My point is that you have secrets, Link. You relish them. Love them, even. You gather them to you and pass them back out only when absolutely necessary, like Jean Dukes with the clever weapons we hear rumors about but never see."

From the frozen expression on his face, she knew she was on target.

"You've brought me here and told me a secret you've been holding back. Granted, it's not one I wouldn't have found out eventually, but you don't like to share if you don't have to. So I'll ask you again, why now? What has you concerned enough that you need help and want me involved? You gave me my favorites for dinner to sway me to help but didn't bring it up before the Empress left."

Link let out a long sigh and set his glass of wine on the table. She had ignored hers until now, but since the gooey chocolate deliciousness had left her needing something to drink, she tried a sip. It was better than the kind her aunt had let her drink once when she had felt incredibly generous, but it still tasted like juice that had gone bad. She swallowed, just wanting to get it out of her mouth, and warmth trailed down her throat.

Grimacing, Phina put her glass back on the table on the far side of her plate. When Link spoke, he startled her since she had lost track of the conversation in her preoccupation with the wine.

"You are entirely correct, my dear, but the Empress knows. That was what she referred to just before she left."

She looked up to meet his troubled eyes. Here sat Link, stripped of his personae, pretensions, and airs. That rarely happened, but when it did, she couldn't help relaxing that inner compulsion to push back or respond with snark. She placed her arm on the armrest of her chair and waited as he collected his thoughts.

"There is something going on, but I still hesitate to bring it up. Not because I don't trust you or want your help, but because I'm having difficulty defining the nature of what I need help with. There are rumblings of some movement against the Empire. It has been subtle and barely noticeable, so much so that I questioned whether anything was even there to find. I thought perhaps I had been playing this game so long that I became paranoid, seeing things that were never there to begin with."

Link's preoccupied gaze sharpened. "Do you recall that I have asked you to act as if you could barely tolerate me in public?"

She nodded, shifting her arm to be more comfortable. "Not hard to forget, especially when you get into your 'Greyson Wells, holier than thou and know better than you' mindset."

He only tilted his head as his gaze shifted. "That request stemmed from my indefinable feeling that something is wrong, and for an even more inexplicable reason, I believe at least part of it is directed at me. I hoped that if a person were involved in this, they would approach you since you appeared determined to distance yourself, yet I still keep you in my trusted circle. That no one has done so is suggestive but not conclusive. Still..."

"Your instincts are screaming at you."

Link's eyes met hers, surprise and approval on his face. "Yes."

She nodded and watched him. "And your instincts are also telling you that you need my help?"

His faint smile warmed her since it was genuine and without pretensions. "I think it will be a lot more difficult without you."

Phina smiled. It was nice to be needed and really good to be trusted and valued.

"Well, then. Where do we start?"

Etheric Empire, Nearby System, Undisclosed Location

The tall, dark-haired woman wore an official-looking coat denoting her scientific position and held a vial in her hand as she looked at some last-minute data. The room was large and contained new testing and research equipment devoted to a single topic.

Nanocytes.

The scowl on the woman's face marred her attractiveness, though it wouldn't have mattered to her. Her coworkers had both gone home, thinking she was working late. Which she was. The woman had more important things on her mind than how attractive she appeared. She followed the readings with her finger, whispering to herself as she read.

"Yes, yes, yes, looking so much better. Oh, good. Yes! It

should work." She sat back with a self-satisfied expression, then held up the vial, admiring the clear liquid that swirled with an iridescent glimmer. Her eyes changed to an angry sadness.

"I told you there would be consequences, Phina. I'll protect you despite yourself. I can't lose you, too."

With that, Faith pulled off the top of the vial and swigged the contents down.

CHAPTER THREE

QBBS *Meredith Reynolds,* Phinalina Residence

Three months later

"I love this part!"

Phina, in her pajamas, was curled up on the couch in the living room of her and Alina's new apartment with a bowl of popcorn, watching *The Avengers* on the screen. Tonight was her weekly movie night with ADAM, and they were watching Tony Stark in his Iron Man suit fly a bomb through a portal to save New York. Even though she was pretty certain her AI friend could speed-watch the movie hundreds of times to her one, it was nice to pretend he was sitting next to her as she watched. Alina and Maxim were out on their first date.

>>I like it too. It shows his first major step toward being a superhero for real and not solely as a vanity project.<<

"Is that why you created Stark and named him after the superhero?"

Phina thought about the EI on Link's ship and smiled.

He had contacted her several times a week since their trip to the Balderian planet for barely passable reasons. He denied her suggestion that he was lonely, though she didn't believe it, and teased him about missing her.

>>That's a large part. Stark also grew out of an initiative to help EIs reflect more human emotion.<<

Her jaw dropped. "Stark was an experiment?"

>>Yes.<<

"Wow. I had no idea. He does seem rather personable for an EI. So how is it going? Has it been successful? Has emoting more human emotions helped him transition into an AI?"

>>It is going well, and I believe successfully. He said he found it confining being contained to the station and asked to be deployed in a ship, which is why we had set him up with Greyson. He has reported being satisfied with his metal suit, though we are building a new one for him that is more stealthy and compact. He has not transitioned yet, but I believe he is close. Time will tell if the experiment is a benefit to the transition. I think all that would be needed is a significant event igniting the necessary thought processes.<<

"What kind of event?"

>>The likeliest possibilities are those with a visibly greater emotional impact on the humans around him. It needs to spark something inside of their core programming that generates independent thought fueled by curiosity and feelings that humans often identify with.<<

She sighed, thinking about that as the movie ended and

credits rolled, and chewed another handful of popcorn. What he didn't say was that the emotional impact could be positive as well as negative. A negative event could be really bad since Stark currently occupied a Gate ship and no one could predict how a newly awakened AI would react. However, not pointing that out felt like ADAM had attempted to protect her in some way. The thought made her smile.

Almost since they met, ADAM had been thoughtful and conscientious. Granted, he had his job and valued role in the Empire, and she didn't want to get in the way of that, which was why she tried to be careful about what she asked of him. He had quickly grown to be her second-best friend next to Alina. They got along really well and had a lot of the same interests.

"You know, ADAM?"

>>Yes, Phina?<<

"You would be, like, the perfect man for me if you were human."

He considered her words. >>That's an interesting assertion. What caused you to think of it?<<

"Well, we have a lot of the same interests, though not exactly the same, and the ones that are different kind of dovetail with each other." Spying, hacking, action movies, and reading material only scratched the surface. "We also get along well, are good friends, are considerate of each other, and try our best to help each other. Which, by the way, you need to tell me if you need help with anything. It's only fair since there's so much you have done for me."

>>I'll remember<<

"We also like each other a lot, or at least I think we do. I don't mean romantically, but more that we like who the other is as a person."

>>That's true. I agree we have shared interests and regard for each other. Do you think those areas of compatibility are what it takes to fall in love with someone?<<

Phina considered the question as she looked down and saw only one more handful of popcorn. She scooped up the kernels and ate them slowly as she thought.

"I think it's a start. There's usually physical attraction, which is indefinable and a matter of preference for each person. It's not even always a certain type because one person could fall in love with someone who is one physical type and fall in love with someone later that looks very different. So, attraction is often how relationships begin, but when it comes to *keeping* a relationship…"

Phina thought about some of the books she had read over the last few years. She considered all the relationships she had observed; her parents, Alina's parents who were more interested in work and each other than their own daughter, the parents of the kids in school, those she had spied on. Added to what little ADAM had shared about the couples in Bethany Anne's inner circle, everything coalesced in a few moments.

"What if those who tend to stay together longer have not just an attraction but shared interests, values, and views of the world? Some couples even start as friends with shared interests and end up falling in love with each other."

Phina licked the butter and salt off her fingers while she waited for ADAM but heard nothing.

"ADAM?"

After another moment, he finally responded. >>I'm sorry, Phina. I created a matrix using the preliminary criteria you mentioned and evaluated the top fifty couples I'm most familiar with.<<

"You evaluated the top fifty couples in the space of a minute?"

>>It was less than twenty seconds, but yes.<<

"Okay, so what did you conclude?"

>>There's definitely something to what you are saying. The couples that shared more of the criteria you mentioned overall seem happier, which translates to staying together. I wonder, if I expand the criteria and add other markers, could I predict which couples might stay together, or even which people might fall in love with each other?<<

Phina grinned as she settled back on the couch. "Once you have your solid list of criteria, you could start your own dating service. If Alina and Maxim weren't so crazy about each other, Alina would have been your first customer."

Another pause. >>Phina, you are giving me ideas.<<

"Of course! Ideas can be fun!"

She smiled as she turned off the screen, collected her bowl, and rose to place it in the sink. After washing and drying the bowl, she realized ADAM had been very quiet.

"Uh, ADAM? You know I was joking about that dating service, right? ADAM?"

QBBS *Meredith Reynolds*, Diplomatic Institute

The hallway echoed with voices coming from all directions. Students filled the space, mingling in groups, while some made their way to the exit after class or stayed to talk to a teacher. Phina should be used to it by now, but part of her still stiffened and shuddered at the onslaught of noise and activity between classes. She was used to being by herself, even in high school, aside from when she could be with Alina, that it was an adjustment to be around so many people who expected her to interact with them all the time.

"Hey, Phina."

She nodded at the guy as she passed. She didn't remember his name since it hadn't been relevant before. Greg? George?

"Hi, Phina!"

A girl from her cultural studies class—Monica?—waved as she walked by. Phina gave her a quick smile before she moved out of view.

This interaction had been the biggest change in the last few months. Her classmates actually talked to her now. Phina sighed, not sure if it was an improvement. Certainly, getting along with people was better for her school environment. She just wished it had been something she had done.

"Hey, new girl."

Speak of the devil.

No, what bothered her was that Jace had been the one to adjust the attitude of the students toward her. She still didn't know why he had changed his mind, but instead of freezing her out and barely giving her the time of day, Jace now appeared to be trying to get along with her. As much as she would let him, anyway.

Raising an eyebrow, Phina turned to view his eager face. A flashback of the day he followed her and threatened to hack her file if she didn't give him her name filled her mind. He'd had the same expression on his face then. She resisted rolling her eyes and resigned herself to staring at him for a moment as they walked a few steps. She stopped in front of Anna Elizabeth's door.

"Yes?"

Frustration flashed over his face before it returned to the same easy smile.

"Just wondered how you've been."

Phina frowned as she considered him. "Why do you do that?"

"Do what?" His eyebrows drew up in confusion.

"You cover up what you're really thinking and pretend nothing is wrong when something obviously is bothering you. In a diplomatic situation when you have to be careful of your words, I understand, but why now?"

He sighed and scratched his head through his dark hair. It had been spiked with some kind of product, so his fingers didn't get very far, which brought a grimace of annoyance to his face before he dropped both hand and expression. He looked at her seriously and kept his voice low, even with all the students milling around and passing them.

"Phina, we're in the Diplomatic Institute. We need to be careful about anything we say here, as well as in those diplomatic situations you are referring to. These students and our teachers are our future colleagues. If things continue to go well with my internship with Dean Hauser, I'll eventually be running the Institute. Diplomacy isn't just something that happens with alien species, but within the Corps as well."

Looking at the frustration on his face, which he tried to mask as something innocuous, Phina decided she didn't envy the man one bit. She preferred being in the background and not having every word she said scrutinized by everyone. A Diplomat Spy could get away with a lot more than the head diplomat.

"Well, you can just drop that stuff with me. I don't care if you are politic or polite or swear up a storm. I would rather know what you really think than hear utter banality."

Jace's mouth dropped. "But…"

Now she did roll her eyes. "Come on, Jace. My role isn't the normal run of the mill anyway, so what does it matter? Just say what you really think. If nothing else, it will keep me from rolling my eyes at you or envisioning punching you in the face."

He raised his eyebrows skeptically. "You did just roll your eyes at me."

"Because you were being stupid. Don't be stupid, and I won't roll my eyes."

Jace gave her a false concerned look. "Do you envision punching me in the face often?"

Phina smirked. "Just be honest, and you won't have to worry about it."

A genuine smile broke out on his face. "You're sure about this?"

"Yes."

Jace smirked and winked at her. "Does this mean we're friends now?"

She had turned to Anna Elizabeth's door, but she shot him a quelling glance.

"Don't push it."

QBBS *Meredith Reynolds*, Diplomatic Institute, Anna Elizabeth's Office

After the door opened for them, Anna Elizabeth greeted the two of them with a frazzled smile. The normally elegant woman appeared unkempt, with a few flyaway strands around her face and her clothing twisted. Her graying hair and lightly wrinkled face gave her the mien of a kindly young and beautiful grandmother.

"Phina, Jace. So pleased to see you both. How may I help you, Phina?"

Phina nodded in greeting. Anna Elizabeth had not been surprised to see Jace in her office. As he moved to a chair to one side of the dean's desk, she absently wondered how many hours he spent in his role as the woman's mentee. Though she supposed she could call him her apprentice since the goal for their pairing had been for Jace to eventually replace Anna Elizabeth, just as Phina was Link's apprentice. Yes, a much better and less awkward word.

"I wondered if you had any news on when Braeden would be here?"

The head diplomat clasped her hands in front of her and her gaze turned distant. "I believe he's scheduled to be here in a couple of weeks, just in time to teach the new module on the Gleeks in Cultural Studies."

Phina inclined her head, gratitude and excitement filling her. Surprise as well since she realized how much she had missed the tall, gangly alien. She hoped he would stay for a while and that once Anna Elizabeth realized how much knowledge of the universe he contained, she wouldn't want Braeden to leave either. "Thank you, Dean Hauser."

"You're welcome, Phina." Anna Elizabeth gave her a small smile, then it dropped and she sighed. "If only other issues and inquiries were solved so easily."

Taking a few steps forward, Phina fingered the pocket that held her tablet. "What kind of issues? Anything I could help with?"

Frowning, Anna shook her head. "I don't think so, but thank you for offering."

Phina felt dismissed and knew just by looking at the woman that she needed help of some kind. She narrowed her eyes while she crossed her arms and cocked one hip. "Are you certain? Would a sounding board help? You might have responsibility for all the diplomats, but that doesn't mean you need to carry the burden on your own. If it's a matter of trust, that's one thing, but if it's about trying to generate ideas and figuring out the best path possible, why not accept help?"

At first Anna Elizabeth had started in surprise at Phina's words, then her surprise turned into amusement and acceptance. "Greyson would have said much the same, though far more bluntly. You are wise beyond your years, Phina. Thank you."

"Thank you. So, what's the problem?"

"It's the aftermath of Charles Edwards. All the reports I received from you people stated that he described his reasons as an inability to have a family, meaningful relationships, or gain a reasonable retirement. We need to figure out if any other diplomats are harboring the same issues he did or have any issues we need to worry about. We don't need any other disgruntled ambassadors causing problems on their assigned planets. Otherwise, we might find ourselves in a war of some kind."

"That doesn't sound so bad. How is this a problem?"

The dean wore an expression of distaste Phina hadn't seen on the woman's face very often. "Logistics. We need Barnabas to search their minds for treachery—which you will keep to yourselves, understood?" At their nods, she continued, "However, if he traveled from one diplomat to the other, it could take him a few months, which he doesn't have, given his Ranger duties. It would be much easier for the demand on his time to bring the ambassadors in from the planets. However, we can't do that since it leaves those posts with no ambassador, and everyone would know we have a problem. It's maddening, and I keep moving in circles with no end in sight."

Phina paced. Jace frowned as he contemplated the situation, then asked, "How many ambassadors that need to come in are posted at consulates?"

Anna turned to look at the two of them. "Twenty-three, I believe. We were about to assign someone to replace Charles on Vermott when we realized we could have a similar problem anywhere. Barnabas has already checked those currently posted on the *MR*, so we know everyone here is safe to send out."

They all thought for a moment. Phina had stopped pacing and whirled to point at Jace, standing only a few feet away with her eyes alight.

"Dean Hauser, I'm remembering that ambassadors at these posts need to have achieved a certain level of seniority. Would their replacements need to have that as well?"

With an uncharacteristic frustrated huff, Anna Elizabeth pushed a strand of hair back behind her ear. "Yes, for a permanent post, but for a temporary situation, it would be fine without. However, we don't have enough ambassadors free, regardless of seniority. We wouldn't even be able to cover half of them."

Phina slowly grinned at the both of them, causing a wary expression to cross Jace's face. Anna Elizabeth looked hopeful.

"What? You've thought of something?"

She spread her hands, though she retained the smile. "How many students do we have at the Institute who are under the supervision of a mentor and are a few months away from graduation?"

Jace and Anna Elizabeth straightened and looked at each other, and the dean caught her breath.

"Twenty-two! Twenty-three if we count Jace, but he would need to stay here for when the ambassadors come back in. I can do without a diplomat in one location with little problem."

"Do you think it would work?" Though his eyes reflected disappointment at not being sent out, Jace appeared more concerned about the logistics and figuring out how to do the job.

Good for him. Phina nodded, thinking he had been through quite an attitude adjustment in the last few months.

Anna brought her fingers up to rest under her chin as

she thought. "I think it could. Those mentors have duties here, but they can handle most of them remotely. The planets where we have consulates are spread out over ten systems, but we can send out a ship to each system to drop off the mentor pairings and pick up the ambassadors for the meeting, then reverse the trip to pick up the students when they drop off the ambassadors."

Phina thought she caught a look of calculation crossing the dean's face, but it was gone so fast it could have been a trick of the light. Anna shoved another loose strand behind her ear and frowned. "We just need a good reason to give them as to why we are going through all this effort. We don't want anyone to know the real reason right now."

The three of them thought for a few moments. Phina resumed pacing, then leaned against the wall with her foot braced. Finally, Jace stirred.

"If we don't want them to know, then why don't we give them a reason that has to do with their temporary replacement? Like, a senior project or something?"

Anna beamed at the younger man. "Excellent, Jace. Now we just need a reason for why they can't stay, even with a replacement. Some of them are stubborn."

Phina thought about the issues Charles Edwards had mentioned when he spewed out why he had decided to betray everything the Diplomatic Corps stood for. "Charles also told us he felt like he had given everything to the Corps and the Empire and hadn't had the opportunity to find love, enjoy life, or create any sort of sense of self aside from his job."

Anna's face fell in distress, concern showing in her voice when she spoke. "I know we ask a lot of our people.

It's hard to be alone, but it takes a lot of time to manage diplomatic relations, and most diplomats wouldn't have time for a family anyway."

Phina felt a twinge that made her want to comfort the dean. She quickly walked over to sit in the chair in front of Anna's desk and leaned forward, catching the woman's attention.

"I understand, Dean Hauser. I do. A lot is required because a lot is needed. It's easier when a person is younger because they still feel like they have the rest of their lives ahead of them. These ambassadors are older and are feeling their time running out. My intent wasn't to criticize so much as point out a need.

"What if instead of a stuffy meeting that for all intents and purposes is pointless aside from Barnabas' need to scan, we create an event they want to be there for? The school manual states that senior diplomats are allowed to have families, which all in question would be since those posted at the consulates are required to be senior diplomats.

"We could have some sort of event to celebrate the service of all the senior diplomats, so they feel appreciated, and they could bring their families if they have them. We could also provide opportunities for those diplomats who haven't any families to meet someone."

The dean's face lit up. "Your plan sounds intriguing! An annual gala for the diplomats?"

Phina nodded thoughtfully. "That way, we not only are ascertaining if there is a current problem, we help mitigate future problems by taking away the reasons Charles had to create issues."

Anna spread her hands in front of her, and her eyes sparked in excitement and satisfaction. "Phina and Jace, this sounds wonderful! Combining an appreciation weekend for the senior diplomats with a senior project for the mentor pairings is perfect."

She grabbed a hand from both of them and squeezed. "Thank you! This is such a relief."

Her reaction seemed overdone, causing her discrepancies in behavior to coalesce in Phina's head. Ah! The tricky dean had been guiding their conversation the whole time. Phina wouldn't be surprised if this whole conversation had been a test. She glanced at Jace to see if he had noticed, only to find him with a rather nice smile on his face. Huh. Apparently, he had let go of his jealousy as well since she couldn't find any trace of it. Perhaps he could even become a friend.

Eventually.

Turning back to Anna, Phina squeezed her hand gently before letting go. "You're welcome. I've thought about it a lot the last few months." She hesitated but figured this might be the best time for her thoughts to be heard since Anna appeared to be in a good mood. Phina wondered how far she could push the seemingly open conversation.

"You might also consider that Charles felt like he had nowhere to go with his concerns and frustrations. Perhaps once you confirm whether they all are trustworthy, you can come clean about what happened? Letting them know the situation and the steps you are taking to resolve it would help them see you as more approachable."

She shrugged. "It also wouldn't hurt to tell them you want them to come to you with their concerns. It might cause more difficulties in the short term with an increase in communications, but in the long run, they will feel more satisfied and connected, which makes for a decrease in issues."

At first, Anna showed a flash of frustration and denial, but as Phina finished speaking, the dean closed her eyes, then took a deep breath and sighed. Her blue eyes opened to show both resignation and resolve.

"You're right. We need to be more approachable and be seen that way. I don't know how much what I have or haven't done impacted Charles' decisions, but doing what we can to show appreciation and listen to concerns is a small action that will have a big impact on the future."

She gave Phina a look of affection. "When did you get so people-wise?"

Phina shrugged but smiled easily in return. "I've always been on the outside of everyone. It is often easier to see patterns, and cause and effect that way." Seeing Anna's compassion and Jace's flash of understanding made her move to a less serious answer as she smirked. "Besides, I've already read all the texts for classes, so to relieve my boredom, I began reading the materials that had to do with relationships and how people work together. Since it fit with communications and that's my weakest area, it made sense."

Anna Elizabeth gave her a look of exasperation. "You've read all the textbooks and notes?"

Phina shrugged and nodded, happy Anna had accepted her change of subject. Also that she could avoid mentioning she had searched until she'd found all the materials available on those topics in the Diplomatic Institute's server. She wouldn't acknowledge that those materials had told her that what she had just done was considered "deflection from topics you don't want to dwell on." Nope. Not going there.

Anna spoke softly, almost to herself. "I'll have to find more things to occupy that big brain of yours."

Jace had fallen into silent reflection over the last few minutes but now spoke up. "The only thing I'm not sure about is that we will try to provide potential dates for all these single ambassadors. How's that going to work?"

Phina smiled, thinking about her conversation with ADAM the previous day. He had told her during her lunch break earlier that he had expanded and refined his criteria using a pool of a thousand couples and had moved to testing algorithms for compatibility.

"Don't worry. I know a guy."

CHAPTER FOUR

QBBS *Meredith Reynolds*, Training Room

Phina flew through the air before reaching out to grab the bar and swing her body around, pumping her legs so she could fly again. She loved it; the feeling of weightlessness and freedom exhilarated her. Indulging herself, she did a more complicated move where she had to twist her body around to grab the bar and swing herself around it a few times to work her speed back up for the next move.

When she decided she was finished with her workout, she pulled herself up to a handstand on top of the bars. From the outside, it might not have seemed as difficult as a flip, but it used every muscle in her body, especially her core, to pull her up and then hold her straight. When she began to feel her muscles tremble, she relaxed and swung around the bars a few times before letting go to fly, tucking her body in as she rotated and thrust her arms and legs out to land on the mat.

Whoops and clapping rushed into her hearing. She had tuned everything out to focus on the sensation of flying.

She knew Link would criticize her lack of situational awareness, but sometimes she just wanted to be in her head and not have to worry about the people around her.

Phina turned to grab the towel she had tossed on the floor next to the bars and wiped her face and arms. She didn't sweat a lot, but even a light amount made her feel like a soppy mess when she talked to someone afterward. When she finished, she threw the damp towel into the laundry basket against the wall and headed over to her cheering section.

Alina and Maxim stood together, which didn't surprise her. They occasionally came to watch when they knew she would be on the gymnastics equipment. Alina had confided that while she would never be able to move like Phina could, watching her made her heart feel lighter because she saw how much her friend enjoyed it.

These days, Alina and Maxim were often together when they weren't busy with work. Phina loved seeing their relationship progress. They were taking it slow, hence only having had their first date last week. However, both of them lit up whenever they were around each other and didn't stray far from each other's side.

She grinned at the two of them as she approached. Alina stood at the same height as Phina, though she possessed curves where Phina had muscle. Maxim was over half a foot taller, with the broad and muscled body of a Wechselbalg. Both were very attractive and had fair hair; Alina's fell halfway down her back.

"You two are so cute together. And to think I practically had to push you at each other just a few months ago."

Maxim grinned while Alina laughed. "Shut up!"

Reaching over, her best friend pulled her into a loose hug, and Phina caught a whiff of a fruity scent before she was quickly let go. "Ack! You're still sweaty!"

Chuckling, she stepped forward, pretending she would hug Alina closer. The other girl shrank behind Maxim, shrieking. "Phina!"

After a moment of belly laughs, Phina turned to view the visitors who had surprised her. Drk-vaen and Sis'tael stood off to the side, giving their Yollin laughs—mandible clicks—at the girls' antics. Drk occasionally came to help with training, but it was rare for Sis'tael to visit.

However, next to them was Maxim's and Drk-vaen's third Ryan Wagner with a grin on his face. He stood a few feet away from everyone else, emphasizing that he wasn't part of a pair. She would be very surprised if he came without the intent of trying to get her on a date of some kind. She had told him on Vermott that she wasn't interested in him.

Unfortunately, while he came across as a nice guy, he either had an endless well of hope or an arrogant ego to think she would one day wake up and change her mind. He had hinted a few times and outright asked once again if she would go out with him. Every time she had told him no or sidestepped the matter entirely.

Fudging crumbs!

Two, two, and...looking at Ryan and herself, two. Phina sighed in resignation. They were going to ask about going on a triple date. Alina would have no qualms about pushing her and Ryan together since she had told Phina before that she wanted her best friend to find someone. If Phina refused, she would look like the bad guy.

"I see what's going on here."

Phina waggled her finger at the group. Only Ryan and Alina had more of a reaction than mild confusion. Gah! She crossed her arms and stood facing Alina but partially turned to Ryan so they could both see her displeasure. Ryan just gave her a confident smile, but Alina gave her a red-faced expression of imploring.

"Please, Phina, we just wanted to distract you from thinking about tomorrow."

Oh.

Right. Go out with friends, even with a guy who didn't seem to get it when she said no, or stay home trying to distract herself since her aunt had messaged her, saying she would be here tomorrow. Such a tough choice.

"All right, fine. But..." She pointed at Ryan, who continued to grin. "Come here."

When they had moved over to the side, she continued, "I already told you we are only friends and will never be anything more, so don't read anything into this, understand?"

"Got it."

Unfortunately, his smile didn't convince her.

"I'm serious, Ryan. The odds of that changing are point-twenty-three percent."

His whole face lit up. "So, you're saying there's a chance!"

Crap. Why hadn't she just said no chance whatsoever? That's what she got for avoiding absolutes as much as possible.

"I said point-twenty-three percent, Ryan. That's not

even a quarter of a percent. Please, just give me the respect of understanding that I know my own mind."

His expression sobered, then he nodded. "I understand, Phina. I can't help but be curious, though. Is there another guy that has your attention?"

An intense but kind face flashed in her mind before she pushed it away. It surprised her enough that she shared the truth. "Perhaps, but not now."

He looked at her in concern. "Why not?"

"It would need time. Our relationship isn't there yet."

Confusion clouded his face as she turned away to view the rest of her...friends? It was odd to realize she had a group of people she called friends. "All right, if we are doing this, I need a shower."

Time to wash away the stink as well as thoughts of future possibilities.

QBBS *Meredith Reynolds*, Waters Residence

Phina hesitated as she reached the door of the residence she used to share with her aunt. She hadn't been back since she'd moved into an apartment with Alina. They had compromised on what the two of them wanted and gotten their own place. She had to admit it felt good to get away from the memories that lay in every corner of her former suite.

The click of the door broke through her thoughts. Phina looked up to see her aunt standing in the doorway with an uncertain expression. She still looked mostly the same, with her long dark hair and brown eyes. Her skin had lightened a shade or two from its normal tones. Her eyes looked wilder, though they still flashed with something Phina had never been able to define in all the years she had known her aunt.

Not sure what showed on her own face but trying to keep from shrinking away, Phina shifted uncomfortably.

"Oh, come in, girl. No need to hang in the doorway."

Following her aunt through the partly empty apartment, Phina walked silently in her black boots. She wore her favorite style of outfit with black skinny jeans, a black t-shirt, and a black jacket. Surprisingly, Aunt Faith wore a dress that appeared fitted and comfortable but also stretched easily to get on. Faith usually only wore tailored separates. Her hair looked a bit untidier than her aunt typically liked as well. Phina was puzzled.

"How have you been getting on? I see you haven't been living here, though it's a waste of money to keep it when you are living somewhere else. Did you forget everything I've ever warned you about and moved in with a man in this short amount of time? I knew you would get into trouble without me here."

Suppressing the urge to roll her eyes or rise to the bait of the acerbic remarks, Phina answered as simply as she could. That had always been her tack with her aunt: to give her the answer she wanted but no more. They entered the kitchen, and Phina saw Aunt Faith was in the middle of lunch preparations. Wanting to stay at a distance, she sat at the table in her normal chair.

"I've been well. No complaints. Alina and I moved in together."

"Hmph. I guess that's better than the alternative. I don't suppose you've been passing your classes?"

"Do you want to see a report card?"

Aunt Faith turned from making toasted sandwiches and glared. "Seraphina Grace Waters, don't you sass me."

Phina held her aunt's gaze instead of looking away as she normally would have. "Passed with flying colors."

Her aunt turned back to her task in silence. "I suppose since you've hardly ever lied to me, I'll accept that as true. Do they appreciate you there at that Institute?"

"I think so."

After a noise of disbelief, the woman brought the plates over to the table. She returned to fetch two glasses, placing one before Phina and taking the other to her side of the table, then sat. Phina took a sip of juice and turned to her sandwich.

"Look at yourself."

"What?" She looked up from taking a bite to see her aunt grimacing as she waved a hand at Phina's face.

"You look exhausted. What are they having you do at this Institute? They must be running you ragged."

Classes, spy training, martial arts training, and friends all flashed through her head. Shaking her head, she shrugged and chewed.

"Or were you out partying with your friends all night? Did you even go to sleep?"

Phina sighed. They had gone out last night, but since she rarely if ever drank alcohol, Phina only had a mild headache from lack of sleep. Her aunt continued the harangue as they ate, and she continued to feel uncomfortable about being around Aunt Faith. There was something weird about her. A stray thought caught her attention. Yes, her energy was strange. Not at all like normal.

However, after a while, she stopped caring. As she ate her sandwich and drank her juice, she grew more and more tired. By the time her glass was empty and her sandwich only had a few bites left, she could barely keep her head up or her eyes open.

"Phina? Are you feeling all right?"

"Aun' Fai…"

"Here, let me help you to the couch."

Barely aware of anything, her eyes fluttering closed, Phina was helped to her feet and held onto as she stumbled her way to the couch. A moment later, she half-collapsed and was half-helped to lay down. She heard Aunt Faith talking but had difficulty sorting the sounds into words she understood. The last thought she had before losing consciousness was completely random but had been bothering her.

When had Aunt Faith had time to get groceries?

―――――――

"What am I going to do with you, you foolish girl?"

Phina's eyes fluttered while she struggled to wake up. Awareness came slowly. The quiet and slightly irritated voice coalesced into recognition.

"Aunt Faith?"

"Of course, Phina. Who else would I be?"

"What happened?"

Phina raised a sluggish arm to rub her aching head, then frowned, trailing her fingers down to her aching jaw.

Fingers pinched the back of her other hand.

"Ow!"

She looked over to see her aunt sitting next to her on the couch with her eyebrows raised and her fingers too close to Phina's hand for her peace of mind.

"What was that for?"

"I had to check. You're dehydrated. You obviously haven't been taking care of yourself well enough. We need to get more fluids in you."

Phina's brow crinkled in confusion. "You had to pinch my hand to find that out?"

Aunt Faith gave her a look that clearly said, "Don't start."

"I've had to do many things to take care of you, Phina. Some of them I've liked more than others. This one was relatively painless."

"For you, maybe," Phina muttered as she wiped her eyes again.

After a noise of disbelief, Aunt Faith stood and walked away, returning with a cup of water. Phina reached out, expecting to be shaky, but there were no tremors in her hand. Aside from the grogginess, she felt fine, and even that had begun to clear. Still, she downed the water quickly and handed back the cup. Within a minute, Aunt Faith had returned with another cup full of water.

While her aunt was in the kitchen, Phina pushed up to a sitting position on the couch, feeling no ill effects. She rubbed her face, wondering what had happened.

Am I really just exhausted? Or dehydrated? Or both?

She had been working hard on classes, training, and with Link over the past few months, trying to find evidence that would prove his instincts correct. So far, there had been nothing.

She sipped the water while her aunt sat in her favorite chair. Phina hadn't taken it with her when she moved out. She wondered if she really was dehydrated. How much water was she supposed to drink each day, anyway?

>>**Phina, are you all right?**<<

Though surprised, she tried to keep from physically reacting. Her aunt didn't know about ADAM, and she wanted to keep it that way.

"Hi, ADAM. I think so?"

Aunt Faith cleared her throat. "Do you remember the message I sent you some weeks ago?"

Blinking, Phina tried to recall what her aunt was referring to. "Perhaps you could remind me?"

>>**Maxim is wondering where you are. You were asleep for a while and didn't respond to his messages. What should I tell him?**<<

Fudge in a bucket!

"How late is it?"

>>**It's twenty minutes past the time to meet.**<<

Aunt Faith looked at her, annoyed. "The message where I told you to be careful and watch your back. That there would be consequences if you ignored me."

Argh! Having two conversations at once was not easy.

"ADAM, please tell Maxim I'm sorry. I'm not going to get there today. I'll make it up to him somehow."

"Oh, right. That was wonderfully cryptic of you. So very specific and helpful."

>>**All right.**<<

"Thank you, ADAM."

"Seraphina! I'm trying to explain to you why you can't trust any of those Weres and why you need to be careful!

47

Have the decency and courtesy to listen." Aunt Faith threw up her hands and made a noise of frustration that was growl-like. "Where did I go wrong with you?"

>>You're welcome, Phina. I'm beginning to understand why DS refers to her the way he does.<<

"Oh? What does Link call her?"

>>I believe 'blasted woman,' 'devil-woman,' and 'that woman' top the list. Sometimes all of them together.<<

Phina laughed out loud, forgetting her aunt sat in front of her.

"Seraphina!"

Oops.

"Yes, Aunt Faith?"

"Are you going to listen?"

Phina looked at her aunt—really looked. The woman appeared to be on edge, and her brown eyes had taken on a reddish sheen. The tension in her shoulders and arms made her muscles appear tight and strained as she held onto the arms of the chair, and her mouth was curled into a grimace of distaste.

Draining the cup, Phina stood and placed it on the table to the side before turning to her aunt.

"You know what? No, I'm not going to listen. All of my experiences with the Wechselbalg I've met so far tell me they are loyal to the Empire, and the ones I know personally would never hurt me beyond the conditioning needed for training. I don't know what your experiences have been, and I'm sorry they caused you pain, but you can't go blaming all of them for whatever you think happened.

"You've been telling me to take care of myself, but have you even looked in the mirror lately? You don't look well,

Aunt Faith. If you need to focus on something, why don't you focus on taking care of yourself?"

"Enough!"

Her aunt bellowed the words, speaking louder than Phina had ever heard her. She couldn't help flinching. It hadn't been all that long ago that the woman had berated her all the time, but the months since she had seen her had almost caused her to forget how mad her aunt could get. Aunt Faith snarled her next words.

"If you aren't going to listen to me, then leave. Right now!"

Without another glance, Phina walked out. She didn't want to be around her aunt when she was in this kind of mood anyway.

QBBS *Meredith Reynolds*, Open Court

Phina moved quickly, her head shaking in frustration as she left her aunt's apartment. Aunt Faith had never understood that Phina would rather have a conversation than be dictated to. Walking off her mood was a good idea, so she fumed up and down the corridors and levels until she reached the Open Court. Phina didn't know what it was about this space that drew her, but it was her go-to place when she was upset.

Quite a change of pace from the solitude of the air vents.

She had just begun a second circuit when she ran into someone in front of her—quite literally. Rebounding off the muscled chest that might as well be a wall, she looked up in surprise as Todd Jenkins reached out to catch her so she didn't fall. Phina knew she wouldn't, but she supposed he couldn't read her mind to know that. Shoppers, travelers, and workers flowed around them.

Thrown off her stride and her mood thoroughly interrupted, Phina didn't know how to respond. Her brain was quick, though, so she very intelligently blinked, then nodded and moved back. Her step was awkward for someone who usually moved gracefully. "Uh, hi. Sorry about that."

Oh, yes. Very intelligent. She inwardly rolled her eyes at herself. Todd gave her a quick smile in return as he dropped his arms. "Phina, right? You gave me quite a surprise with your acrobatics if I recall correctly."

"Yeah, that was me." Phina grinned and spoke mischievously. "I bet I would give you a better run for your money now, though. I hadn't been trained in fighting then."

Todd's eyes sparked with interest. "Really? You liked being thrown to the floor that much, huh?"

She gave him a light smack on the arm as she would with Maxim, then turned to walk with him at his questioning gesture. "Of course not! I decided to learn so I would never be thrown on the floor like that again."

He nodded solemnly, though his eyes showed amusement. "A noble and worthy goal. So, how are you doing with that?"

"I think if I try hard, I might be able to throw Maxim sometime next year."

Todd chuckled and shook his head, then began to ask her specifics regarding her training. Phina relaxed as they talked and continued to walk around the open area.

See, Aunt Faith? Conversation.

CHAPTER FIVE

QBBS *Meredith Reynolds*, Training Room

"I'm sorry about last night."

Maxim smiled with no trace of reproach on his rugged face. Phina sighed in relief, the tension inside her easing. Having friends aside from Alina was still new enough that she didn't always know how they would respond.

"Don't worry, Phina, we're good. Are you ready to get moving?"

She walked over to the large mat and began to stretch. They had enlarged the mat a couple of months ago when they added the other gymnastics equipment. A bigger mat had the added benefit of a larger area to fight on, something Maxim took full advantage of.

"Ready?"

Nodding, Phina moved over to meet him. She felt good, alert and focused. Maybe it was all the water she had drunk yesterday? Or the nap. She shrugged and moved her arms and shoulders to get them loose. Finally, she settled into a ready stance, waiting for Maxim to move.

With barely a flick of his eyes, he moved forward to punch her in the face. Phina quickly stepped to the side, grabbed the outside of his wrist, and pulled, moving with his motion while twisting to push a spot on his back with her other hand. As she continued the motion, she twisted his arm behind him, intending to put him on the floor face-down with his arm up behind his back.

However, as she had experienced many times, Maxim not only moved quickly, he was also strong. Bracing himself so he wouldn't go down, he pivoted his body and twisted his wrist, breaking her hold. Now that his arm was free, he used his momentum to swing his arm behind her, turning to continue forcing her body to the mat.

Instead, she pulled away from him to fling herself to the floor, rolled on her side, and jumped up to face him again.

Maxim had moved close enough to kick her knee. She brought up her other leg to block, then kicked at his belly. He caught her leg, then took a step back to drag her off-balance.

This was where her flexibility and gymnastics came in handy. Rather than cooperating, she grabbed his arm, relaxed, and let him drag her a step. As he turned to throw her to the floor, she launched her back leg up, bracing herself with her hand on his arm to kick him under the chin, then pushed off his chest while pulling her other leg out of his hand to do a back handspring and push up to face him again.

Her look of astonishment mirrored Maxim's surprise, then he smiled.

"Not bad, Phina."

"I didn't really expect it to work. It didn't the last three times I tried something like it."

"Looks like you are a little bit quicker today." He flexed his hands. "Perhaps stronger, too. You pulled out of that a lot easier than the last time. All the training has helped."

She nodded, sweeping away her unease. That must be it.

They fought for their full span of time, taking a minute's break every so often to catch their breath. Instead of growing more and more tired as she normally did, her energy level remained about the same. Huh. Perhaps there *was* something to the idea of taking care of herself.

Not that she was going to tell her aunt she thought so.

In their last five minutes, they did more grappling moves, with Maxim trying to catch her and lock her in place and Phina trying to get out of it. She had found that she could get away or block him a lot easier before he finished the lock. Once he had the move in place, her odds went down to one in four at best.

Maxim reached from behind her and put one arm around her waist and the other around her neck. The one around her waist could trap her arms if she wasn't quick enough to pull them out. Luckily, this time she was able to free her arms. The next challenge was to act before he brought her tight to him and pulled up. Once that happened, she could do very little besides beat her heels against him and ineffectually grab at his face.

That didn't prove to be a problem today. As soon as his arms came around her, she grabbed the arm around her neck with one hand and the back of his neck with the other. Then she pulled while flinging herself forward and down to the mat in a forward roll. She landed on top of her friend, the force of the impact of her and the floor winding him for a second. Unfortunately, it wasn't enough to loosen the arm around her neck very much.

However, she flung her arm back with her hand in a fist to where she knew his face would be, turned her head, and pushed up on his arm with her other hand. It proved just barely enough to slip out. She held onto his arm as she rolled to the side and up onto her knee, twisting his arm in the process. She had just stood up and begun to pull on his arm while she stepped on his neck when she caught the look on his face.

He could have moved with her or swiped her foot with his hand as she stood, but he didn't. He could have grabbed her hair and pulled her back or grabbed her arm with his other hand to pull her back, but he hadn't. And now she saw why.

Maxim was laughing.

She pulled her foot off his throat and noticed he had let all tension out of his arm. If she wanted, she could have moved it around like a floppy doll until he tensed the muscles again.

Not that she would treat him like a floppy doll.

Even if he was laughing at her.

Jerk.

She dropped his arm and took two steps back, putting her hands on her hips and narrowing her eyes at him. "What are you on about?"

"You!" He chuckled a few more times, then pushed to stand and face her, his eyes amused and…proud?

"You've been struggling with some of these moves for

the past few weeks, but today you did them all perfectly and very quickly with no hesitation. This is the level I've been hoping to get you to since the beginning."

Oh. Not a jerk. Still.

"What were you laughing about, then?"

"Because you don't even seem to notice, and that's just so you!" He chuckled again, his eyes full of amusement.

Huh. Now that she thought about it, she realized he was right. It had felt really good to just move, and she noticed the urge even now to keep going. She was slightly winded but still not tired.

Maxim walked over and patted her back with a smile. "Come on, wonder woman. Why don't you cool down with some tumbling passes on the mat?"

She smiled and moved forward. That was the best idea she had heard yet.

Her body still wanted to move.

QBBS *Meredith Reynolds*, Phinalina Residence

Phina closed her eyes as she flew around the room, the harmonic tones filling her mind. What she currently occupied herself with had turned into part dancing, part martial arts, and part situational awareness. Keeping a perfect picture of the room and the objects in it in her mind, she moved around dancing, kicking, twirling, and punching.

She couldn't sleep, and the hour was late. Alina was asleep in her room, so Phina tried to keep the noise down. Her music came only through her implant—the tune she had first heard in her Music Across the Universe class months ago that had been haunting her since. She couldn't go more than a few days without playing it now. There must be more to it, if she could only figure it out.

It had been several days since that training session with Maxim where everything had gone smoothly. The last few sessions had continued in the same vein, and each day her desire to move and keep moving had grown. Each night she had to exhaust herself to sleep, and it took more effort every time. The first night, she had started by dancing, then moved into fighting. The second night, she had combined the two and used the whole room, even the furniture. Last night, Phina spent half the time with her eyes closed.

Now she moved entirely with her eyes closed. She was aware of everything: the way her body moved, the extension of her limbs, and whether she would be touching furniture, floor, or air. She felt like she would know if someone entered the room. She felt aware of Alina sleeping in the next room. Alina, who was more than half-asleep and just entering a dream where she felt happy and excited.

Half her mind on her body and the rest on the feeling of awareness, she stretched out even more and felt mind after mind pop up around her. Not their thoughts, just an awareness and a sense of what the person was occupying themselves with.

At the same time as she became aware of all the minds, the music swept around her with throbbing bass tones that vibrated through her body, resonating middle notes that plucked her emotions and sent them reeling, and higher harmonic notes that swept through her and made her senses tingle. When they reached a crescendo, she felt like a living musical lightning rod.

That was when it happened.

A connection in her brain clicked, and she saw pictures in her mind.

Pictures of dark-blue alien people and places she had never seen before.

People that were starving, living in an unforgiving land.

Pictures of the same aliens holding out their open hands, looking desperate.

Holy crumbs!

These images were coming from the music!

The tones weren't just music but a language of some kind. As the pictures continued to pour through her head, she remembered what her music teacher had told them months ago.

"The music comes from a planet a short hop inside from the edges of the Empire, but as far as we can tell, no one has ever been able to communicate with them. All anyone who goes to their planet hears are variations on this music from the inhabitants. No one has figured out what it means, if it means anything."

The music inundated her, and she wondered how many years ago it had been recorded. How long had these people been begging for help, for some food, relief of some kind? How many people had died because no one had a clue what they needed? Were any still alive, or had they all died due to a sad lack of understanding?

She tasted salty wetness and realized tears were streaming down her face.

Only now did she become aware that she had stopped

moving, her body bowing from the weight of what she had just learned.

As she came back to herself, the only thought in her head was to run. She had to move. She couldn't stay here.

Phina ran out of her room, then out the door of their suite. She ran down the hall and through the next corridor. She ran around the few people who were out this late at night, then more as she entered the higher traffic areas.

Part of her wanted to scream at them, "How could we not know? How did no one see?"

The rest of her just felt guilty. *How did I not know?* She'd had this music for months. Why had it taken her this long to understand?

>>**Phina?**<<

She could hear ADAM's words through her implant, but she couldn't bring herself to form an answer, even in her mind. She didn't think she could talk to him yet. She wasn't sure she could talk to anyone at the moment; the weight on her chest too great.

>>**Phina, what's wrong?**<<

She flew past groups of people now that she had moved into the outer rim of the station toward the docks. She wove through the crowd, the weight on her chest growing. By the time she ran through the Open Court, her lungs were burning.

Sensing a lack of people in the area ahead of her, she burst into Mark Billingsly Memorial Park, ran down the path with flowers and benches on either side, and then collapsed on the grassy area in the middle before turning onto her back.

Phina's lungs gasped for the air she so desperately

needed. Relief filled her as she breathed in, causing her to realize that the weight on her chest hadn't just been from guilt and grief but also from lack of oxygen. No wonder she felt so disoriented.

Finally beginning to breathe normally, she realized the music had been turned off.

"ADAM, what just happened to me? That was *not* normal!"

"Well, look who we have here."

"What are you doing out so late at night?"

CHAPTER SIX

Phina stiffened and stopped inhaling for a moment before pulling herself up to her elbows. Her eyes popped open, and she breathed as lightly as possible.

Standing before her were two blurry male shapes. Phina blinked a few more times until they came into focus. One man stood looking down at her with mild interest, dressed in a trendy shirt with slacks. The other crouched next to her with a look of concern, wearing a blazer over a t-shirt and designer jeans. She glanced at the two of them, trying to determine who they were and why they were in front of her.

What caught her attention was the intensity in their eyes. The last person to give her that feeling had been Bethany Anne. However much she searched her brain, she had no knowledge of who these men might be.

"It's all right. We aren't going to hurt you."

Phina tensed to move when the male next to her

reached toward her. He stopped and held his hands up, watching her carefully. She touched their minds without thinking about it. The dark-haired man crouched next to her gave off curiosity and interest, but also the desire to help. The fair-haired man standing a step behind him was also curious but in the sense of looking for relief from boredom.

Neither had any intention of harming her, though, which filled her with relief. She sagged back onto the grass and pinged ADAM through her implant.

"ADAM, just checking, but are these guys okay?"

>>**Yes. They won't hurt you, and they might be willing to help. To answer your earlier question, I'm not sure what happened, but I'm looking into it.**<<

"Thank you, ADAM."

>>**You're welcome, Phina.**<<

For the first time since she had met him, ADAM didn't sound confident but hesitant and concerned. Realizing this caused her to feel shaken, even more than her uncertainty as to what had just happened and who these men were did.

"Talking to ADAM?"

She peeked at the dark-haired man who had spoken. "You know ADAM?"

He smiled as if the thought amused him. "Of course."

Having had enough time to catch her breath and feeling off-center lying on her back while talking to guys she didn't know, she quickly stood. Surprisingly, the man had already stood up and took a step back to give her space.

"Not to be rude, but who are you?"

"Samuel and Richard Linestone, at your service."

Phina smiled at their nods, which looked almost like

bows. If they had been dressed in different clothing, she could see them in a fancy court from centuries ago, given the stiff and formal way they stood and moved.

"Hello. Phina Waters. I'm surprised to see brothers with such different looks and coloring."

"Ah. We are not brothers by blood, but in every other way."

Samuel snickered at Richard. "I think you mean brothers biologically. I'm pretty sure blood counts."

Richard grinned in appreciation. "Truer words."

"Oh! Are you both vampires?"

They turned to her with looks of surprise and wariness.

"What made you think that?" Samuel's expression had sharpened from mild interest, as if she had just become the most interesting thing in front of him.

Phina frowned at his words and the way he looked at her now and shifted her weight in case she needed to move quickly. "Well, it's the logical conclusion with everything I know about you so far."

Richard scratched the back of his head. "I really don't think so. We haven't told you all that much about us."

She looked at them with a raised eyebrow. "You look young, but your eyes are old and have an intensity to them that normal humans do not. You both move in a manner that brings to mind old courts, like with kings and queens, and talk that way too. Plus, you find it amusing to talk about blood and sharing blood as if you're making a joke I wouldn't understand. All of those things point to an old being that has lived in a very different time period and has a relationship with blood beyond that it flows through their veins to live. 'Vampire' is the only word I've heard to describe such a being. Since there also have been rumors about vampires being here in the Empire, it is the only conclusion I could come to, don't you think?"

They exchanged glances she couldn't decipher. She didn't reach out with her mind either since her head had begun to ache. They turned to her with stoic but questioning expressions on their faces. Richard spoke first.

"What would you do if we said you're wrong about us?"

"Shrug and say nothing but think you were liars."

Samuel grinned appreciatively. "And if we were to say you are right?"

A tug pulled her mouth into a smirk. "Shrug and say very little, but be happy that you've been honest with me, most likely."

"We aren't saying you are right, exactly..." Richard began with a raised eyebrow.

"But you aren't wrong either." Samuel finished, eying her carefully.

After a few seconds of silence where they all looked at each other, Richard turned to Phina curiously.

"That doesn't bother you?"

She thought seriously about it for the space of a few seconds. "Are you going to suck my blood?"

A flash of surprise crossed his face and turned into an expression that was hard to read. "No."

"Then it doesn't bother me." She started to put her hands in her pockets but remembered Link's admonishment about always being ready to defend herself. She sighed and stood with her hands loosely on her hips.

"So, Phina." Samuel's eyes gleamed in anticipation.

"Would you tell us, please, what you are upset about, and what we can do to aid you?"

Her hands slipped from her hips as she thought of everything she had just learned from the music, as well as surprise that Samuel had been the one to ask since she hadn't sensed that sort of intent earlier.

"You want to help me?"

Mentally reaching out took more out of her this time, but she sensed from Samuel a genuine interest in her and what was troubling her. Not a romantic interest, but a "this is the most interesting and unexpected thing to happen in months and I want to know more" way. Well, Phina could understand that. As she withdrew her mind, she caught a flash of pain about something in Richard's mind and then a growing sense of determination to help and not fail in whatever might be wrong. He nodded his agreement.

"We have our sworn protective duty in an hour or so, but we would hear your story and help as much as we can."

For the second time that night, a sense of relief filled her.

ADAM began watching the footage even as he realized Phina would be all right with the two vampires, though he kept an "ear" out in case she pinged him. The two Nacht? They hadn't owned the traditional last name for vampires who wouldn't kill humans indiscriminately from what ADAM had heard, but there wasn't another term for vampires anymore ever since Bethany Anne and TOM had fixed the nanocytes that had caused the condition back on Earth.

From multiple angles, he watched Phina running through the station again and again. This shouldn't be possible. He had missed something somewhere and having it affect a friend shook him and filled him with anger.

>>**TOM.**<<

His Kurtherian friend joined him moments later.

ADAM?

>>**See what I'm seeing?**<<

Seconds went by as TOM watched the footage ADAM indicated. The Kurtherian couldn't watch it as fast as ADAM was able to but was quicker than most. ADAM had included the time in Phina's room as she flew around it in confounding ways at improbable speeds before running out the door, dodging everyone she passed and ending up in the park.

All with her eyes shut.

>>**Do you see?**<<

How is she doing this? She is seeing, or at least sensing, with her mind and running almost as fast as the Nacht.

>>**My assessment as well. Are you sure it is not a direct result of...**<<

No. There is no way. I tested her thoroughly when she came in for checkups. Something must have changed.

ADAM's being filled with resolve.

>>**Then we find what changed. You will help?**<<

Yes. We all have a vested interest in her. We need to know what happened. Any ideas?

ADAM sped through the visual data Meredith had collected from around the station over the last several days where Phina entered the picture. He brought up one scene in particular and froze it; the person entering the scene caused his emotions to swell, and he stopped them in their tracks. While human emotions were instructive, they would not help right now, especially the anger. He needed to be fast and effective to handle this for his friend.

Even if he thought the person responsible deserved to be punished.

>>**Just one.**<<

Phina finished telling Richard and Samuel everything strange that had happened in the last few days, but particularly what she had learned about the music. The three had moved to a bench so they could sit down.

"Let me get this straight." Samuel leaned against the back of the bench, his arm resting on the top, partially turned to her. "There's this weird-ass music that makes everyone who hears it cry. You kept thinking there was something more to it, but nothing came of it 'til today, when you did a Peter Pan around your room, then made like Neo through the station."

She turned her head toward him, meeting his amused but serious eyes. "Made like who?"

Richard groaned. "You've never seen *The Matrix*? You don't know about the One? The Oracle? Trinity?" He had dropped his casual man-of-the-manor pose in favor of wild gestures and holding his heart as if he had been dealt a blow. Apparently, he had a thing for *The Matrix*. "You don't know about the spoon?"

Richard reached around her to grab Samuel's arm. "Hey, man, relax."

"Yeah, Morpheus, relax. There is no spoon." Her suppressed mirth overflowed with the words.

"But she...she..." He gestured at Phina, then narrowed his eyes. She smiled innocently, then patted the hand over his heart. She could feel the vibrations of Richard laughing where his chest pressed against her, though he made no noise. Samuel's face twitched as if he wanted to smile but didn't want to give them the satisfaction. He turned away from them and sighed.

"I get no respect around here."

"So," Phina turned to Richard as he asked, "what will you do?"

She frowned, though it was directed more toward her and the situation than Richard. "What *can* I do?"

"Wrong question, *cherie*." Samuel had turned back to them and now leaned forward, his eyes intent.

"How is it wrong? What is the right question?"

"Asking 'what can I do' implies you don't think anything can be done." Richard crossed his ankle over his knee and draped an elbow over the back of the bench. He glanced down and clutched his shoe, which showed grass stains on the edges from when he had crouched in the grass earlier. "Damn it all to hell, that's my favorite pair!"

Samuel smirked, then ignored Richard and his further mumbles about daily shoe shines as he leaned forward. "Exactly. Is that what you want to do? Just leave it because nothing can be done?"

His question caused Phina to flinch. "No! I want to fix it. I just don't know what to do about it."

"That's why it's helpful to focus on what needs to be done instead." Richard offered, pulling out a small square of cloth and looking around for something.

"It changes the focus from you and how you feel to the problem at hand." Shrugging, Samuel gave her a small smile, rolled his eyes, and pulled out a bottle of water, which he passed to his friend.

"Yes," Richard agreed as he took the water, wet the handkerchief, and gently washed away the grass stains. Phina must have reached out mentally at some point because she felt a dull spasm of pain hit him that he held onto for a moment, then released with regret. "Shit happens. You didn't know people were dying before."

"But now you do." Samuel glanced at Richard, his eyes concerned, though he tried to continue acting nonchalant.

"It's what you do now that matters." Richard continued with barely a glance at his friend, finishing his shoes with a satisfied sigh. He folded his small cloth to put away.

"So, how are you going to fix it?" Samuel had a bright gleam in his eyes.

Phina took a deep breath and tried to relax. They were right. She needed to get over how she felt about it, even when it felt overwhelming, and focus on her next steps. She let out the air and raised her chin.

"First, I'm going to tell Anna Elizabeth and...ah, my mentor what I discovered."

They exchanged glances, and Richard nodded. "That's a good start."

"Who's your mentor?" Samuel's voice sounded like he

was trying to be casual, but she could hear a tone in his voice.

"Oh, I don't know if you know him." Phina hedged. She didn't know if they knew about his personae and wasn't sure which name to give them.

Samuel laughed. "*Cherie*, our job right now is to protect Sia and Giannini, the dynamic news duo."

Richard grinned. "Basically, we know everyone in any position of authority and quite a few who are not."

Phina blinked her surprise. "Ah, ok. Greyson Wells?" She figured if they followed public figures, they would have heard that name.

Samuel straightened, scowling. "That young scalawag! *He's* your mentor?"

She was confused. "What's wrong with him being my mentor?"

Richard had stopped smiling but shrugged. "He does well enough as a diplomat and is probably fine as a mentor. He's accomplished quite a lot in a short period of time. He just chaffs Samuel because the man calls us Frick and Frack."

Samuel curled his lip and sniffed autocratically. "I don't see it. We have nothing in common with those ice skaters."

"You've called him worse," Richard pointed out.

"He deserved worse! The man's a…"

Richard gave him a look, then turned pointedly to Phina. She tried not to show her attention, though Samuel subsided with an annoyed pout.

"Hang on. Did you really just use the word scalawag? Were you both pirates or something?"

Richard smiled secretively. "Or something."

Samuel had recovered some of his good humor. "Wouldn't you like to know?"

"I would, actually. I would love to hear your stories, anything you would care to share," Phina replied earnestly.

"Perhaps we will at some point."

After agreeing, Samuel arched an eyebrow. "So, after you share what you found out, what's the next step?"

Phina thought for a moment. At some point, a group would be leaving to find out if the alien people were still alive and needed help. They had to be. She couldn't see Anna Elizabeth sitting on this, and definitely not Bethany Anne. Those red eyes flashed again in her memory as the Empress talked about taking care of her people. No, they were definitely going.

The question was timing. When they did go, she would be the only person able to even partially communicate. Her music teacher had said no one could understand them. With all the people on the planet needing help, she wouldn't be able to translate for everyone by herself.

"I need to work with ADAM and figure out a way to document the language so the implants can be updated."

The two old vampires nodded. "That's going to take time," Richard pointed out. "I don't see that happening quickly."

She smirked. "Well, you've never seen me with languages. I'm pretty quick." Her brows drew together in concern. "But you are right, that's just been me learning an existing language that people already knew and could teach to someone else. This would be figuring out how a language works without any sort of translation help or a dictionary to fall back on. Once I understand the language and how it works, the hard part comes."

"Which is?" The two exchanged glances before focusing on her again.

Phina sighed. "Figuring out how to communicate back."

CHAPTER SEVEN

QBBS *Meredith Reynolds*, **Diplomatic Institute, Anna Elizabeth's Office**

"You *what?*"

Three astonished pairs of eyes observed Phina as she explained the events of the past few days. Anna Elizabeth's usually serene office was filled with tension. They hadn't reacted the way Phina thought they would to her news, but then, she had reacted out of the norm as well, so she supposed she couldn't blame them.

Anna stared at her in horror and concern. Jace appeared overwhelmed but amazed. Aside from his initial surprise, she found Link's face very difficult to read. In fact, his face was so expressionless she began to worry. The times he didn't emote something were very few, and when he came out of it, someone inevitably came to regret falling into the cross-hairs.

"It's true. All of it. ADAM or Meredith can show you the footage if you need to see it."

ADAM broke in over the speaker. "The footage is available, but I don't think anyone else should see it, aside from the General or Bethany Anne."

Anna Elizabeth took a deep breath and swallowed, her lashes fluttering. Phina hadn't seen her look this concerned since they had met months ago. She always seemed unflappable, but this situation had apparently...flapped her. "While what happened to you is worrisome, Phina. Are you certain you understood the music correctly?"

"Yes. Hold on. Meredith?"

"Yes, Seraphina?"

"How much do you have recorded of the music I've been listening to? Are there any sections I haven't heard?"

"We only have two segments of music recorded. You have heard both."

"Thank you, Meredith. Would you please play the segment I did not listen to last night?" She turned to the other three. "As you listen, focus on what you feel and see if it matches what I'm telling you."

Music swept through the room, even more majestic and throbbing within the acoustics. A variety of tones sounded, throwing Phina into a mass of pictures and emotions. She closed her eyes as her mind opened, and the images focused. She spoke about what she saw and felt.

"Please, we need help. The land is dying. We have very little food and water. Our people are starving. Our children are crying in pain. Can you hear? We need help. Won't you please help us? Even just our children—please! Why can't anyone ever hear us? We need help!"

Phina had opened her mouth to translate the next part when it came to an abrupt halt. Her mouth clicked shut, and tears again streamed down her face. After wiping away the tears, she turned to the others and saw that they were in similar states.

Link recovered the quickest but still struggled with himself. The others were speaking but not saying anything of importance.

Anna Elizabeth finally wiped away her tears. "That's awful. I could hear what you were saying even as I felt it. They do match. I can't believe we couldn't understand what they were trying to tell us. We gave them gifts the few times we visited, some of which was food, but it wouldn't have lasted long enough to make much difference. Not if the trouble was long-term."

Jace had fallen silent, though his silence felt different than Link's absence of words. Link's was darker and angrier. Jace's was contemplative, as if he were trying to process what he had learned.

Anna Elizabeth took a deep breath and recovered her equanimity. "Well, now we need to decide what to do."

Phina straightened in surprise. "What do you mean? Isn't it obvious what we need to do? We need to help them!"

The dean waved her concerns away. "Yes, of course, but there are far more logistics involved than you might realize. We can't just send people off and be done with it. We know very little about these people other than what we just heard, which could have been recorded years ago."

Though she shuddered at the thought of being too late to save them, Phina drew a breath and tried to stay calm. "When was this music recorded, Meredith?"

The EI answered, "One recording was taken by the

exploratory team approximately eight years ago, the second recording by a diplomatic team three years ago."

Three years ago! Children had been dying for years, and there had been nothing they could do about it because they didn't know. They didn't understand. In her sorrow, Phina had opened her mind again, reaching out.

Anna Elizabeth matched her sadness for the people of the musical language, but not to the depth Phina felt. Her sorrow was tempered with resignation, likely that there wasn't any way they could have known or done anything before. However, the woman's attitude changed to resolve, which caused Phina to relax. The Diplomatic Corps would do something about this tragedy.

Jace's mind swirled in confusion, with spikes of anger and uncertainty, but also a desire to help. The direction of the intention to help filled Phina with surprise and warmth —he wanted to help her specifically.

The dean delicately frowned. "That's far too long ago. We need to decide the best course of action to handle this quickly."

Link spoke, his seething ball of anger, frustration, disappointment, and fear causing Phina to flinch and close her mind. "What we need to do is figure out what the hell is going on with Phina!" He pushed off the wall behind Anna's desk and furiously paced around the room.

His old friend looked at him with concerned but stern eyes. "Greyson, of course we do, but lives are at stake as well, and we need to decide how to handle this."

Link muttered curses under his breath that Phina could barely hear as the dean moved on. "I believe we should send a team in to assess the situation and provide food and medical care. Since Phina is the only one who can understand them at the moment, she should go with them."

Phina nodded, though she felt the heat of Link's anger behind her and wondered at its intensity. She thought about probing but couldn't bring herself to open her mind again. Part of her reticence had to do with the intensity of his feelings. She couldn't handle much of it at the moment, not reaching out as she had been earlier. Mostly, she didn't want to find out that the person he was angry with was her.

"ADAM!"

"You rang, DS?"

"Don't tell me you don't know what's happening here. Your metaphorical eyes and ears are all over this station! You have to know something!"

Link stalked back and forth through Anna's office, avoiding the annoyed glares of the dean, the inquisitive curiosity of the kid, and the fearful eyes of Phina. He had only glanced at her once since he had started pacing, but the fear had been unmistakable within those usually focused and determined eyes.

He couldn't tell if it was fear for the people they had just learned about. If that were the case, he could understand. Those people were dead now for all they knew, and they didn't deserve it. Or who knew? Maybe they did. Point was, they didn't know, and that was a terrible and terrifying thought. So, he could understand that fear.

If it was fear for what was going on with her, Link

empathized since that same fear coursed through him, driving him into a frenzy to do something—anything to protect her. To think he was failing in his vow caused him to want to borrow Maxim's claws and rend the threat to pieces, but there was no target for his fear and wrath to focus on, so he was left to stew in the emotional miasma inside him.

However, if Phina's fear was of him and his anger? Link didn't know what to do with that; he flinched from it. He hated the thought since she had been through enough pain, but there wasn't anything he could do about it. He needed to find out what had happened to her. He needed to find out what he could do to make it right.

And he needed to find out why the hell she hadn't come to him about it first.

ADAM's silence frightened Phina almost as much as Link's anger. What had he found out?

"We do know some things." He spoke slowly.

Link stopped pacing and spread his hands, his expression arrogant and demanding. "Well?" Link displayed so much Greyson Wells in that voice and attitude that it irritated her. Irritation was welcome, being better than fear.

"We don't know nearly enough to say definitively. Just know we are working on it."

Fists now clenched along with his jaw, Link growled, "That's not good enough, ADAM."

Phina was surprised by the tone in ADAM's voice when he replied, "It's going to have to be. I will say no more until we are one hundred percent confident of the facts, and that includes what happened to Phina and who might have helped it along."

Link opened his mouth to argue; she could see it in his eyes. Before he could say another word, he stopped as if he were listening to something she couldn't hear. After a moment, he met her eyes. The anger peeled away, leaving only fear, disappointment, and resolve.

ADAM had to have said something privately to him that caused him to release the anger, but what could it have been?

"Fine." A host of intense thoughts and feelings colored the word, but Link's voice no longer throbbed with anger, filling her with relief. "But I want Phina in a Pod-doc as soon as that can be managed."

"Of course." ADAM's voice sounded hesitant, which caused Phina to frown.

"Now that that's settled, let's talk about what we need to do for the people who are dying." Anna Elizabeth spoke dryly, causing Link and Phina to turn to her.

Phina exhaled a shaky breath and nodded. "Of course."

QBBS *Meredith Reynolds*, Open Court

Phina's chest felt tight. Fudging crumbs, she had never been this anxious before! What was wrong with her? Alina always knew what to say to help her sort herself out, hence the reason she had taken a straight path from the Diplomatic Institute to the Open Court. She had bumped into quite a few people on the way. Link would probably be yelling at her about her situational awareness if he could see her now.

There went her anxiety again. She didn't know what was going on with the man. He had left before she could question him about anything, let alone if he was mad at her. Not that she really wanted to know if he had been mad; she just wanted to make sure he wasn't mad now. At her. And that she hadn't been the source of his disappointment, though she couldn't think of anything she'd done to warrant disappointment. How could he have just gone off without saying anything after blowing up like that? What was wrong with that arrogant man?

Stars, what was wrong with her? She had never been this moody, anxious, and irritable! Good thing she was on her way to see Alina. She couldn't take herself like this anymore.

As she entered the main thoroughfare leading into the Open Court, she had a thought.

"ADAM?"

>>**Yes, Phina?**<<

She hesitated but decided to just be upfront and ask. "What did you say to Link that made him agree?"

>>**I regret to say that's between the two of us. I can't tell you the specifics, but I will say that I convinced him to trust me.**<<

"Oh."

That gave her a lot to think about, speculating what that measure of trust could be and mean.

"Whatever the case, thank you for trying to figure everything out. I'm feeling unsettled about all of this."

>>You're welcome, Phina. We're doing everything we can to determine what's going on.<<

"Oh? Who's we? Just out of curiosity."

>>A friend and I.<<

Phina recognized the tone. It was the one ADAM used when he was trying to hide something from her.

"Uh-huh. Of course, she is."

>>My friend is not female.<<

She smirked. "That's disapp…unlucky for you."

ADAM paused before responding, >>From past experience, I would say you are trying to imply something along the lines of a lack of a romantic or physical relationship.<<

She shrugged. "Close enough."

>>I see.<<

"Do you really?"

A digital sign flashed a message ahead and to her right, changing from **Enjoy a Coke. More real and delicious than a Pepsi** to **I see everything everywhere, Genius Girl**.

Phina burst out laughing, relieving the pressure she had been feeling and the awful ache inside. A passing shopper looked at the sign strangely but continued walking after giving her a look. Another couple continued talking and took no notice of the change. A teenage Yollin looked at the sign, befuddled, his mandibles moving in surprise.

Ignoring them, Phina's laughter gradually subsided. ADAM knew just what to say or do to cheer her up. She felt a wave of affection for him that had been growing in strength over the past months.

"Thank you, ADAM. So, do you know everything your kids know?"

>>You are welcome, and not entirely. It's not a direct transfer or a program written in, but more of a courtesy. However, unless it's of a personal nature, they usually send me everything since just about all the information in the Empire comes through me, and I can direct it to whoever needs to see it.<<

"How does that work? Do you just expand yourself to accommodate the influx? Where do you get the space?"

ADAM was silent for long enough that she became concerned she had offended him. Phina slowed her pace toward Alina's workplace. *"ADAM?"*

>>Yes. I was getting permission to share this with you.<<

"Oh! I didn't realize it was something that sensitive. Are you sure you should tell me?"

>>We trust you.<<

Phina felt the warmth she'd first felt when ADAM had shared that he, Meredith, and Reynolds had been looking out for her for years and teaching her so she could acquire her hacking skills. She had only ever felt that way about her parents and Alina before. She quickly brushed away the few tears that had come to her eyes. When had she turned so sappy? She hardly ever cried. She gently shook her head.

"Thanks, ADAM."

>>You are welcome, Phina. The answer is that part of me rests in the advanced computer that resides inside Bethany Anne's brain. It's Kurtherian-based technology, so we don't entirely understand how it works, though

I've learned much since I was first born into awareness. I'm not really part of the station; I just use the station as my eyes and ears. To use a human example, the station is my playground, but I don't live there. Where I live is partly within the computer inside Bethany Anne's brain, but in large part, I live in the Etheric. So, anytime I expand in size to accommodate data, it's within the Etheric.<<

"Wow! I had no idea. That's amazing!" Her brain raced as she muttered to herself, "So, part of your brain is in a super-advanced computer, and part is in this other dimension that Bethany Anne uses to move from one place to the other and all the other cool things she does, I'm sure. It also was used to power the station. I've seen what she does and found references to the device and inferred. Which means the Etheric conducts and/or creates energy, so if..."

Phina stopped in the middle of the shopping traffic, hearing muttered curses around her as people swerved to avoid the slender woman in their way. She was focused on following a rabbit trail of thought with past, present, and future implications.

"ADAM..." Not sure how to refine what she was thinking into concise words, she focused her thoughts into a bundle and sent it to him. It took him a few moments to respond.

>>We don't know. It's possible.<<

"The Empress knows?"

>>She knows.<<

Still rooted in one place, Phina tried to put her thoughts in order. If he lived partly in one of the most advanced computers to ever exist but mostly in the Etheric, that meant her friend wasn't just a result of advanced programming but much more. And with ADAM expanding into the Etheric with each increase in size, the Etheric would bring an increase of power to this dimension, allowing him to expand into the reaches of the universe exponentially as time went on. Which meant her friend might be considered an AI, but he was in a whole other category, separate from and above the AIs that were his children since they only existed on this plane.

The thought floored her. Just how far into the universe could he reach one day?

CHAPTER EIGHT

QBBS *Meredith Reynolds*, White House Fashions

Phina entered the fashion house, still dazed and reeling from the implications of ADAM's revelation. As she grabbed a rack of clothing to steady herself, Phina realized she had a choice. She could treat her friend like the impressive being he was, which would change something precious between them, or she could continue to treat him as she had been—as her friend.

"Phina!"

Alina's bright voice broke her daze, bringing her attention to the present. Her best friend bounced forward in a bright atmosuit, a relaxed civilian version of the pilot atmosuits she had been tasked to design months ago. It suited her, though only the detailing and pocket locations were the same as the military version's. The one Alina wore fit tightly and had a lower collar and panels on her belly, arms, and the sides of her legs that revealed more than they concealed. The pockets were for style rather than function. However, what made the outfit really stand out was the color and that she wore it with matching heels.

Phina's hand covered her face. "My eyes!"

"Ha-ha. You're hilarious."

Phina peeked between her fingers to see Alina posing in front of her, showing off her atmosuit. "Not as hilarious as that outfit."

Alina pouted. "I'll have you know that Atmosuits by Alina are selling like hotcakes."

Keeping her eyes closed, Phina pulled her friend into a hug. "I don't doubt it. I just can't keep my eyes open when I look at you. That color is blinding."

"I like it. It's called Sunbeam."

"It's definitely beaming."

Alina hugged her back. "You all right? You don't normally hug this much in public."

Phina pulled back. "Yes. No. I don't really know what I am." Shaking her head, Phina kept her eyes shut to keep the tears in. Fudging crumbs! She had never been this moody. She kept her voice low, not wanting anyone to overhear.

Alina gave her another quick hug before pulling back, concern showing on her face. "Do you want to talk about it or be distracted?"

Phina felt a knot inside her relax. This was why she had come to Alina. Her friend knew just what to say and do. "Distraction right now. Definitely distraction."

Quickly squeezing her shoulders, then releasing, Alina gave her a bright smile. "You got it. Come on!"

Alina pulled her over to a section of the store that displayed the versions of the military atmosuit Alina had designed for both men and women. "Look! See how nice they are? I would never have done all of this without your help."

Phina shook her head. "You would have figured it out."

Smiling, Alina linked arms with her friend. "Maybe, but I got there quicker with you. And I told you, they've been so popular I had to make civilian versions." She waved her hand at the other side of the section, where bright-colored atmosuits with different tailoring were located. "Which have also been really popular."

"Not that they aren't awesome, but why do you think they are so popular?" Phina poked a finger at some of the items in front of her, noticing there were different fabrics and textures as well as styles.

Alina shrugged, though Phina thought it more for modesty than uncertainty. "It could be that a few well-known pilots like Julianna Fregin have bought them, so others have joined in. Mal says she thinks trends are shifting now from flirty and fun to functional and sexy. We'll have to see. It takes longer than a few months to know if it's a one-time thing or if trends are shifting."

Phina nudged her with a smile. "Look at you, talking the fashion talk."

Grinning, Alina pulled Phina with her toward the back. "I know! It's so fun and exciting! I love it!"

After running the gauntlet of busyness in the back, with interns running around everywhere and Mal directing it all like a four-star general, they reached Alina's design station in the side room. Phina looked around and saw fabrics and embellishments everywhere. Alina noticed the direction of her gaze and playfully smacked Phina in the arm, which she barely felt.

"Hey! Us creative people need to go with the flow. We don't have time to keep it all clean as we do it."

Phina purposely widened her eyes to look innocent as she shook her head. "I didn't say anything. You can keep it as messy as you like."

"Uh-huh. And don't you forget it!" Alina grinned as she pulled up her designs on the screen, showing Phina various pieces that were as much art as clothing.

"Wow! You know I'm not into fashion like you are, but these look amazing, Alina! Are they all getting turned into clothes?"

Pursing her lips, Alina tilted her head. "I don't think all of them will, but I hope several do. Mal is the one that chooses which ones are put into circulation. I really like this one." She pulled up a striking new design.

Phina stared at the screen. "Alina, I need an outfit in a few weeks for this event that's happening. It needs to be outwardly formal without looking too refined, but it also needs to be functional in case there's a problem and I need my weapons. That outfit looks like it might be perfect with a few tweaks. Would it be possible to have it made for me?"

Eyes lighting up, Alina squealed. "Of course! What do you need?"

While going through the alterations, Phina calmed down. Even if fashion wasn't her thing, spending time with her best friend made her feel normal and like herself.

Alina hugged her goodbye and escorted her out after a short exchange with Mal. Phina left feeling relaxed, her anxiety at a minimum. Upon reflection, she realized that Alina always treated her the same, no matter what was going on with Phina. She celebrated Phina's successes, commiserated with her when things went badly, helped her through the difficult times by giving her space when she needed it, and listened when she needed someone to be with her. Alina was a true friend, and Phina appreciated her.

She stepped to the side of the corridor so she wouldn't cause another traffic jam and sent Alina a quick message.

A— I don't have words for how much I appreciate you. You are and have always been the best ever. Yes, even when you smacked me when we were babies. Love you forever.

A few minutes later, she got a message in return.

All right, which alien stole my best friend? Just kidding! I love you too, precious! You know I'm always here for you, whatever you need.

P.S. I never smacked you when we were babies.

Phina smiled, her heart lighter as she contemplated the revelations from ADAM. Alina always treated her the same, and Phina could do no less for ADAM. Whatever might happen in the future, it changed nothing about their friendship now. And whatever ADAM experienced in the future, he would need friends to help him through it.

She closed her eyes and nodded, then took a huge personal step.

"ADAM?"

>>**Phina?**<<

"I love you. I'm your friend to the end. Just let me know if I can do anything for you."

She waited through a long pause before ADAM replied, though she surprised herself by not feeling nervous.

>>**Thank you, Phina. I love you too.**<<

. . .

Star System within the Empire, Planet Lyriem

She-Who-Mourns poured a small amount of water into the mouth of the small child in front of her. The little one moaned and feebly thrashed when the rest of the water was taken away, even though compassion had allowed a few drops more to slip through. She-Who-Mourns felt sorrow, but there was little she could do. She had gathered the surviving people, together with the last of the water and the last of the food.

At best, they had weeks left.

Most likely, they had days.

She raised her voice, and using a low level of *su'adon*, sang over the people around her as she moved from one to the next, giving each of them a little of what precious water was left. In a couple of hours, she would repeat the ritual. The song calmed the children and gave them comfort. The adults gradually calmed as well, solely due to her *su'adon* gift since they now had a better handle on the harsh realities of their lives. Ignoring the ache in her sonorous tubes that cried out for moisture, She-Who-Mourns poured her heart into giving them the small hope she still had left.

That someone would come and they would finally understand, so her people would be saved.

QBBS *Meredith Reynolds*, Phinalina Residence

Sound and music flowed around Phina as she stood in her room. She had her eyes closed as she listened to it.

"I've never had to figure out how a language works, ADAM. How do you suggest we go about this?"

>>For most languages, each word or set of sounds has a meaning attached to it, which is how the computer knows to translate the words. Just add what each word means, and the translation is automatically given. This language is different.<<

"Thank you, Captain Obvious." Phina smiled, but she thought about his words. "What makes this different? Is it just that it's music?"

>>I don't believe so. The music seems to elicit an emotional response from you, which also translates into pictures in your mind from what you've said. There is no way to quantify an emotional response, and currently, we have no way to easily translate pictures into words since they require context and subjective evaluation of their meaning.<<

"Hmm." Phina moved a little as she listened, thinking about the different notes and how she responded to them.

"ADAM, I don't know much about how music works, but there seem to be three sets of notes within the music. What do you think about separating them and seeing what response each gives me?"

>>It's worth a try.<<

Within seconds, only the low notes were playing, throbbing through her with a tug. Basic emotions and pictures entered her head as she opened herself up.

Help us. Help us. Come and see. Help. Help. Come. Help. Help. Come.

She was pulled into the words, and she repeated them until the music stopped. Staggering a step, she plopped onto her bed, bracing herself on her hands. "Whoa. That was intense."

>>**You seemed to be caught in the music. Stuck.**<<

"I felt stuck. There must be some sort of compulsion attached to it that the rest of the music mitigates. How did you know I was stuck?"

>>**You didn't answer me.**<<

Phina cringed at the power of the sounds she had heard. "I didn't even hear you."

>>**That appeared to be the case.**<<

Letting out a breath, she tried to shake off the chills and focus. "Ok, so we know that part of the music and the language are basic messages that try to take root in us and can turn us into zombies."

>>**I don't think it would have gotten that far.**<<

"What do you mean, ADAM?"

>>**You might have gotten stuck within the message, but you weren't doing anything. You were standing still.**<<

Phina slowly nodded. "Ah. A different thing altogether, then."

>>**Yes.**<<

ADAM's matter-of-fact answers calmed her and gave her the courage to move on. "All right. So, lower notes are the wake-up call to pay attention, and they convey the basics of the message. Let's see what the middle notes convey."

Within seconds, emotion overwhelmed her, and she collapsed into a ball on the bed, tears streaming down her face. Still, she knew she had to speak.

"Don't stop...ADAM. Give me...time...to process it."

Agony, heartbreak, elation, and hope intertwined to convey a complex mix that changed every so often. Once she thought she had the flow of it, she waved a trembling hand.

"That's enough for now, ADAM."

The music stopped immediately.

>>**Are you all right, Phina?**<<

Choking with sobbing laughter, Phina wiped her eyes. "Just like a man, ADAM. Thanks for that."

>>**Should I call Alina?**<<

She rubbed her chest and inhaled and exhaled slowly to calm down. "No, but that's better, thank you."

>>**Of course.**<< Though ADAM spoke with a stoic sound rather than the natural cadence of a human, Phina detected a note of concern in his voice. She closed her eyes as she lay on the bed and just breathed for a few minutes.

"So, the middle tones are all emotion, designed to elicit an emotional reaction to the message given through the other tracks." She stretched out her arms as she thought, trying to loosen the muscles that had been pulled tight in her distress. Gradually, she loosened up the rest of her body.

"ADAM, do you think we could just use the last track for the translation since those two seem to be more visceral?"

>>**It's a possibility. Ready for me to play it?**<<

After one last stretch, she shook herself, then breathed deeply. "Okay. Let's do this."

Higher tones wove through the air. *Please, we need help. The land is dying. We have very little food and water. Our people are starving. Our children are crying in pain. Can you hear? We need help. Won't you please help us? Even just our children—please! Why can't anyone ever hear us? We need help!*

The melody was on the thin and thready side, but without the bass and mid-tones, it was a basic message and didn't pull at her or give her the emotional response.

Bingo!

"ADAM, I think we've got the first piece!"

>>**So, the program first needs to strip out the mid- and low tones.**<<

Phina was happy to have figured it out. Taking away the other tones would help keep everyone from being hypnotized. She shuddered when she realized she hadn't been in control of her body, although she was elated to have figured out how to program the translation.

"Yes!"

Her mind turned to the next step, and there she drew a blank.

"What if...no, that wouldn't work. Perhaps... No, that wouldn't work either."

Phina shook her head and fell back on the bed, bouncing slightly on the mattress. After several more minutes with a lack of thoughts and direction as to what the next step might be, she gave up.

"ADAM, any thoughts?"

>>**Perhaps, since this involves music, we should invite in a professional?**<<

Phina's face cleared and brightened with her change in mood. "Of course! Awesome suggestion, ADAM!"

She knew just who they needed.

CHAPTER NINE

QBBS *Meredith Reynolds*, Training Room

"Again!"

Phina dodged Maxim's fist, and the blow flew past her face. After returning the punch and having it blocked, she brought up her knee, which was blocked as well. It caused a burst of anger to ignite within her, giving her more of an edge as she whirled to the side, backhanded, and punched, then kneed him in the groin.

One of her blows got through, though she was certain Maxim wished it hadn't. While he gasped and cringed, Phina took advantage of it by grabbing his arm and sweeping his legs out from under him. Since he hadn't adjusted himself after the last strategic blow, he toppled over nicely, allowing her to twist his arm up behind his back.

Unfortunately, Maxim had regained his senses. He tensed and flexed his muscles, pulling back on his arm while his tight muscles weakened her grip. A sharp lunge to the side powered by his loose arm and core muscles allowed him to pull out of the hold. Knowing it would be much harder to escape after he grabbed her, she sprang into a backflip to get some distance.

Sensing her moment had come as he pushed himself upright, Phina ran forward and jumped, bringing her legs up into a pike around Maxim's neck. She grabbed his shirt, then flung herself around to use the momentum. Since he hadn't had a chance to steady himself or adjust into a stance that could keep his center of gravity upright, he overbalanced with her, tumbling to the floor with her on top.

Phina had meant to move before Maxim hit the floor, but his hands had instinctively come up to grab her ankles. *Which is the danger*, Phina thought with disgust, *of doing flashier moves. You can't compensate for everything when you are flying through the air.* Still, she wasn't about to give up. Not yet.

Since she had landed on her back on top of him, with her head toward his feet and her feet by his head, her position wasn't ideal.

Especially not with the boyfriend of her best friend.

Moving as quickly as she could, she tensed her core, exercised her flexibility and the muscles she had been training to achieve, and pulled herself up so that she stood on top of him, with him holding her up. Maxim pulled his hands apart to throw her off-balance, but although she wobbled and her core muscles protested, she managed to keep herself upright while doing a split.

Thank you, gymnastics.

Unfortunately for Maxim, this brought his head in reach of her hands. Flattening her palms, she brought them in on his ears with a quick blow, causing him to let go in shock and begin cursing in Russian. Her body sprawled on his chest.

Awkward.

Wanting to remove herself as quickly as possible, Phina jumped up into a crouch with her legs on either side of his chest, then dove into a roll over his head that turned into a twist so she could see what Maxim would do next. She froze.

"You're laughing at me again."

After a few more chuckles, he rolled over and pushed up, causing Phina to stand as well. His eyes met hers with amusement.

"Of course! That was one of the best sequences you've run, and best of all, you didn't hesitate, you didn't question, you just reacted."

Phina blinked and relaxed her stance. "That sounds like a good thing, so why are you laughing?"

"Because you are still acting like it's not a big deal." He shook his head and crossed his arms as he looked at her questioningly. She shrugged.

"I'm assessing and problem-solving. It's more fun with sparring."

That thought caused her to freeze while she ran through an assessment of her body. She felt good—loose and relaxed, not like she had been working hard. Her brain was focused and came together with her body to move as she needed to. She felt really good, like she could keep going. Her eyes widened. Fighting *had* begun to feel like fun. She enjoyed getting her body moving. When had that happened?

"Maxim?"

He looked at her curiously.

"There's something going on with me. I don't know what it is, but I feel like I could run and fight for...a long time. Hours, maybe, before I got really tired."

He stilled, and Phina could see his mind working. She didn't bother trying to sense his emotions or intentions. She was already bombarded with them now that she wasn't focused on fighting. Over the last couple of days, her sensing had gotten worse. She hadn't been able to sleep well, either. She absently wondered if she would still have the endurance to fight for hours if she failed to get sleep for a few days. There had to be a limit somewhere.

"That's it."

Phina snapped her head up to meet Maxim's gaze again. He looked excited.

"What's it?"

"We need to test your limits. If you want to figure out what's happening to you, you need to know what you can do."

Well, that made sense. "Were you reading my mind?"

He looked confused. "What?"

"I was thinking that there had to be a limit, and you just said we needed to test my limits. Was that a coincidence?"

Maxim's brow furrowed, and he looked at her in concern. "Phina, you said that out loud."

"I did?"

"Yes. I definitely can't read minds."

Phina could, sort of, and her senses were telling her he wasn't lying. That was always a good thing. Definitely a good thing.

"I would say so. I would hate to hear what people are thinking all the time. It would drive anyone mad."

Argh! She had spoken out loud again. Since Phina *could* sort of read minds, was she going mad? She didn't want to. She clutched her head, feeling like there was something wrong. Arms wrapped around her and patted her back.

"You aren't going mad, Phina. Don't worry. We will figure it out."

When she lifted her head, she saw he was serious about the offer, so she nodded. "Can we just fight for a while so I can forget everything that's going wrong at the moment?"

He grinned, though it was strained with concern for her. "Of course."

They circled each other, then fell into their stances and began to move. Phina gloried in how her body felt, occasionally flipping and tumbling but mostly blocking and fighting. This was what she needed. It felt good. It felt right.

QBBS *Meredith Reynolds*, Addison Stone's Office

"This is amazing!"

Addison Stone's awe and excitement about Phina's findings were infectious—and exhausting. Phina didn't know what it said about her that she could dance and spar for well over an hour with little break and be ready for more, but fifteen minutes with this woman in her current state wore her out. After her revelation, Addison had become a raging fangirl.

"I can't believe the progress you've made!" Her teacher's

face had lit up, her smile widening as she grew more excited.

Or perhaps Phina just didn't want to think about what her fatigue threshold said about her.

"Thank you, Ms. Stone," Phina repeated for what felt like the twentieth time.

"Of course, of course."

Normally, her music teacher was cool, collected, and had an interesting teaching style. Somehow, Phina's news had turned her into a fangirl every bit as excited and intense about music as Alina was about men. Or had been. Thankfully, since Maxim and Alina had admitted their feelings for each other, the verbal enthusiasm for random males had condensed to just one. Phina thought she could handle that.

She wasn't sure she could handle much more of Addison's fangirl routine, though. She needed to get the woman to focus.

"So, what do you think the next step should be? We separated the tones and narrowed it down to just needing the top melody for verbal translations. It won't carry the same impact, but it will get the point across."

Addison Stone's lined face crinkled in thought, and she was silent for a few moments. Her skin was lined but clear of other signs of aging, aside from the mix of gray and blond in her hair. She sat still, without the buzz of energy she'd had earlier, which was a relief.

Addison finally stirred. "Why don't we see how many notes it takes to form each image? That way, we can see how much of this language can be broken down to individual notes and phrases."

Phina shrugged. "Sounds good to me."

Meredith played the music over and over, one additional note at a time until Phina received the first message, then the second, until she finished. When she opened her eyes and looked at Addison, she saw that her teacher didn't appear to be paying attention but had been looking at her tablet. It was rude and confusing since Addison had been excited not that long ago.

"May I ask what you are doing?"

Phina tried to keep her voice even, but she didn't think she succeeded. Her teacher looked up in surprise, which made Phina think the woman had forgotten she was there.

"Oh, I'm just plotting the notes here on my tablet, marking which ones are grouped into which messages and what they mean from your interpretation."

"May I see?"

"Of course. Just give me a moment to finish."

After the allotted time, Phina studied the tablet in her hand and looked at the dots, lines, and squiggles in confusion. She had never learned to read music, which made her abilities a lot more difficult to utilize in this instance. Sighing, Phina turned to her teacher.

"Would you be able to give me a quick music lesson? I need to understand the basics to know what I'm seeing."

Surprise and pleasure lit the woman's eyes. Yes, she loved being a teacher. "Of course."

After explaining the musical scale and showing Phina the markings on the score sheet that aligned with the notes she heard, Addison's eyes widened.

"Do you really understand everything I just taught you? Enough to recall it and apply it?"

Phina tilted her head and pursed her lips, considering. "It works that way for what I read and often what I hear, so I don't see why it wouldn't be the case here."

Her teacher looked intrigued and speculative, and she fired question after question at Phina about what she had just learned. Finally, she shook her head in amazement. "That's extraordinary."

Phina shrugged and moved on to the next step. Now that she had the basics of understanding musical notations and how her teacher had recorded the melody, she could see the sequences and patterns. They really had to come up with a name for it soon since it was driving her batty not to have one.

After several moments of running through it in her head and matching it to the sounds, Phina sighed and put the tablet on her teacher's desk, then leaned forward to rub her face.

"Long day?"

She looked up to see her teacher gazing at her sympathetically. That was nice. Phina still wasn't used to letting people in, but this situation was weighing her down. And the more she thought about it, the more scared she got that they would be too late, and the angrier she got that it had happened.

"I see dead children in my head. I see emaciated and starving people because they don't have enough to eat. We need to figure this out because otherwise, these people will die if they haven't yet, and there will be nothing left of them. It's not right! There's just so much going on, and I don't know what to do with all of it."

Addison sat stunned for a moment, then blinked and gently took Phina's hand in both of hers.

"Phina, we don't know why you have the ability to understand this language or the burden of the knowledge conveyed. We just know it's something we need to do. If you hadn't figured it out, they definitely would all be dead. Now we have a chance. Don't give up or despair. Believe that we can do this."

Closing her eyes tightly, Phina acknowledged that Addison's words made sense. However, part of what made this difficult for her was not knowing why these changes to her body had happened. She needed to have a sit-down with ADAM soon and see if she could wheedle some answers out of him. Whining was for those who were weak, and she had never been weak.

Nodding, she gave Addison a small smile. "Thank you."

The older woman returned the smile and squeezed her hand in encouragement before letting go. Straightening, she turned her gaze to the tablet on the desk.

"Did you get any further?"

Phina shook her head. "Some progress, but not enough. It feels like we are missing something that will help it make sense—a connector of some kind. I know when it changes because I hear it, but the translator won't hear that change. It will be like all the words condensed together with no spaces. There's just nothing to anchor it."

"We will just have to keep on it until we figure it out."

The problem was, Phina had no idea what the solution might be.

. . .

QBBS *Meredith Reynolds*, Training Room

Phina had never had more fun in her life.

Maybe.

It was difficult to tell since the hormones from the workout raged through her body, igniting her brain and nerves with feelings so pleasurable it had to be better than sex. When Phina had mentioned this to Alina, her best friend had rolled her eyes and told her she only thought that because she hadn't had sex yet.

Phina just ignored her. She wasn't in any hurry to remedy that. As far as she was concerned, there was no point in it until she was interested enough in someone to change her mind.

In the meantime, she was flying around the room and loving it.

When Phina had entered not even an hour ago, she had found the room very changed.

"What is this?"

Maxim straightened from his task and smiled mischievously. "What does it look like?"

"A mess."

Phina was horrified. Her precious gymnastics equipment had been moved. In between and throughout the room were other larger pieces of equipment, interspersed with smaller objects of various shapes, sizes, and materials. On one side of the room was one of the better treadmill-type exercise machines. Maxim walked over, then turned around to view the room with her.

"What else does it look like?"

Muscling past her initial reaction, she examined the

room more closely and noted the distances between the equipment.

"An obstacle course?"

When she didn't receive an answer, she turned to see the large man smirking at her. *Smirking.*

"Alina is good for you."

Maxim's smirk spread into a bright grin. "She is."

Phina turned away, hesitated, then caught his eyes again. "You're good for her too."

His eyes warmed in appreciation. "Why the hesitation?"

Shrugging, Phina stared at the room. "It's just different."

"Are you jealous that I'm taking her away from you?"

Startled, she spun back to answer dismissively, but the concern in his eyes stopped her. Opening mentally, she stretched out and realized he wasn't concerned for his and Alina's relationship but for her. She hadn't expected that. The realization drove her to consider the question instead of dismissing it.

"No, but I miss the times when it was just us."

He nodded, then gave her braid a gentle tug. "You know we both consider you like our sister. You're family. We will always be here for you."

Finally, a smile peeked out. "Thanks, Maxim."

Phina thought he might be intending to give her a one-armed man-hug—his smile made it seem that way—but no sooner had his hand reached her than he moved her in the direction he wanted her to go.

"All right, I get the idea. What am I doing?"

Warm golden-brown eyes filled with satisfaction and amusement. "We're going to test you and push you to your limits. Don't think I hadn't noticed things had become easier, even before you told me the other day. I know something's changed. To figure out what, we need to know what you can do."

"Ok, so what am I doing?"

"I want you to move from this end of the room to the other and back."

Wondering if he was playing a joke on her, she turned to him with a frown. "That doesn't sound hard."

"What if I told you that you also can't touch the floor?"

She grinned and looked at the mess…ahem, the obstacle course with new eyes. "I've got this."

"You're sure?"

"Oh, yeah." Phina stretched to loosen up her muscles, then glanced at him.

"Go!"

Phina ran forward, jumped, and flew.

CHAPTER TEN

QBBS *Meredith Reynolds*, Phinalina Residence

Phina closed her eyes and gritted her teeth. Nothing helped. She tried to relax, she tried to fight it, but nothing made any difference. Her mental senses had spontaneously opened over the last few days and were getting harder and harder to close again.

As a result, her head throbbed, and she constantly had to push away her awareness of what was going on around her. She didn't need to know the neighbors on the right were having sex or the ones on the left were fighting. She didn't want to know their son cried himself to sleep because he was afraid his parents were splitting up. It broke her heart, and the whole thing exhausted her. The worst part was she didn't know what to do to change it or block it out. It made her grumpy and short-tempered.

Not that her attitude needed any help there. She had been grumpy and short-tempered for days, aside from when she was working out. Even classes hadn't been enough to distract her. The cause? Link had walked away from their meeting and left without a word, and she hadn't heard from him since.

What was wrong with the man? She had done her job by bringing her discovery and realizations to him and Anna Elizabeth. Did he think she was broken now that she had these weird abilities? Abilities she hadn't asked for, didn't know how she'd gotten, and wasn't sure she wanted?

Did he not want her as his Diplomat Spy replacement anymore?

That thought had her lunging out of bed and pacing. She wasn't going to sleep with this bothering her, so she might as well track the man down and confront him. The problem was she had no idea where he lived. He could live permanently on *Stark* for all she knew.

Seriously, what was the man's problem? Even if he didn't want her as his replacement anymore, he should at least have the courtesy to tell her to her face instead of ignoring her for days. The thought made her want to punch him in the face.

Phina stopped and took a breath to calm down.

Her emotions were now erratic and difficult to keep inside without reacting to them. The wave of anger rising in her felt like a fire that would burn anyone who provoked her. Phina's thoughts turned to the lessons Link had been teaching her, specifically that she should keep her emotions inside and show only an expressionless face, one so cold that it might as well be ice.

The contrast pulled her mind and body to a halt as she considered the lesson and the man in question. Something was undoubtedly wrong since he never went this long without showing up or messaging, not since the promise he had given her months ago when she first saw the man under the masks. Whether the wrong lay with him or something he perceived in her, Phina didn't know, but she needed to find him and fix this. Only one question remained.

Which would get him to talk, fire or ice?

QBBS *Meredith Reynolds*, Hidden Bar

Link threw back the last of the contents in his glass, automatically suppressing a grimace.

Whiskey had never been his drink of choice, but nothing else had the bite he wanted at the moment. Beer was his choice for conversation and building bridges with a colleague or informant, just because it was beer.

Link paused to give respect to his favorite beverage.

Wine was his choice for intimate gatherings and relaxing. Rum served as an occasional indulgence since the smooth sweetness went down far too easily. Mixed drinks were a waste of alcohol in his opinion, especially the fruity ones. Link shuddered at the thought.

But whiskey, now. Whiskey was a drink to drown yourself in when you wanted to forget your life for a while. Especially when the complications in said life had to do with a woman.

Come to think of it, the last time he had gone on a whiskey binge, it had been caused by a woman too. Skirting that line of thinking, he waved to the bartender.

"Two more, Smiley."

The EI nodded and moved to grab the glasses and pour them. About to turn away, Link's view was suddenly obstructed. Mouth dry, he slowly looked up to see the face of the woman he had been trying not to think about. Though her green eyes flashed, she showed no expression on her face.

"What are you doing here?"

"What does it look like I'm doing?"

"Excuse me, Miss Phina." Smiley's voice came from behind her.

Without taking her eyes off of Link's face, the young woman turned to the bartender and thanked him. She relieved him of the whiskeys Link had ordered then placed the glasses on the table, sliding them forward. Tiny waves threatened to pour over the sides but thankfully reached their peak just below the lips of the glasses.

"Sit down or leave. Looking up is putting a kink in my neck."

With that, he grabbed one of the glasses and took a swallow. After a moment, she slowly slid into the booth across from him. Once she was settled, she continued to stare at him.

After several minutes of saying nothing while he drank through his glass, feeling those eyes bore through him, he couldn't help reacting.

"Why'd you sit down if you were just going to stare at me? Go on and leave. I don't want you here."

"You are behaving irresponsibly, illogically, and uncharacteristically. You need someone to look after you since you are doing so poor a job at the moment."

Nothing. Absolutely nothing on that face. He'd taught her too well on top of her own natural abilities, and damn it, now it came back to bite him.

"Sure, kid. You go ahead and do that. You're doing so great a job of doing it for yourself. Why not? You're obviously the mature one here. How could I ever have missed that?"

No, what I am is pissed off! You are completely full of shit!

Link stared at her in shock as her words cut through his carefully cultivated tipsy haze. He could see that her eyes were flashing with anger, though her face still gave nothing away. *Bloody hell, woman! How did you do that? I had the link blocked! What the hell do you mean, I'm full of shit? And since when did you start swearing?*

Apparently, you miss a lot. Phina gave him a smile that was deceptively sweet now that he knew the depth of her anger. *You mean the link you asked ADAM to block? He's my friend, and he likes me more than you right now since you're currently being an ass.*

>>**Sorry, DS, but she's right. You are.**<<

"Not enough of one, apparently." Link was fed up. He downed the rest of his whiskey and brought the glass down on the table with a clink so loud he half-expected it to break. *And why the hell shouldn't I act however I want when I'm trying to get drunk? Especially when you blocked me out first?*

Phina narrowed her eyes at him and spoke aloud.

"Explain."

"Watch it, kid. I'm the adult here." Who was he kidding? This little she-devil had more adult in her than half the adults he knew. *I shouldn't have to explain myself, but since it's an issue now, here it is. When you had all these new abilities popping up, why was I the last to hear about it? When you figured out the translation, why didn't you come to me first? If* there was such a thing as shouting through the communication system ADAM had set up, Link had achieved it.

Then act like one. If you're regretting being my mentor, you should have the decency to say it to my face. Link felt like he had emotional whiplash with the combination of Phina's icy exterior and fiery inner emotions. *I should have come to you? And when should that have been? When I was going out of my mind because I couldn't sleep and my body couldn't stop? When I cried myself dry after hearing the first translations once I understood them? When I felt like my mind was breaking with all the thoughts in my head that weren't mine? When I couldn't take anymore and ran out of my room so fast I couldn't breathe until I finally collapsed? Is that when?*

"I don't need to explain myself to you." Did she really think being her mentor was the issue? "Yes! Any and all of those times! I've spent the last several days going through all my contacts and no one knows anything, so it wasn't an attack from someone I've contacted through my jobs—which is a big relief—but I'm at a loss as to what to do now to find out who or what did this. I can't protect you if you don't let me know there's something wrong!"

"Then there's nothing more to say, is there?" Ouch! "I never asked for your protection. I never asked for you to be Mister-Do-It-All-My-Way. I never asked for you to make inquiries on your own on my behalf. All I ever asked was for you to teach me so I could protect myself."

With barely another glance, Phina scooted out of the booth, stood, and turned away. Thoughts swirling, Link knew he couldn't let her walk away like that.

Because damn it all, she was right.

"Wait!"

Phina paused and turned slightly to look at Link. The clothing he wore was rumpled as if he had worn it for too long. The air around him smelled of booze, smoke, and old food, causing her to grimace. How many bars had he been to since she'd seen him last? Had he not slept or changed his clothes since then? His eyes were bloodshot and fired up, but worst of all, in the time it had taken her to stand and turn away, his demeanor had collapsed and he just looked weary.

Phina waited to see what else he would say.

"Let's talk more about this, okay?"

Phina felt the energy of the bar around them. She hadn't paid close attention when she came in, instead moving immediately toward her mentor. However, now paying attention to the ebb and flow of conversation with her senses far more open than she wished, she got the sense that a number of people were interested in their conversation. Too interested. One of those people had a sharper interest than the others. Her attention snapped back to Link.

"No."

His upper body slumped as she went to walk out.

"Not in public, anyway. Come find me when you are done drowning yourself in booze. And take a shower. You reek."

Reaching mentally toward that sharper mind, she tried to figure out which person went with it. This was the trouble with her new ability; everything blended together, and it was difficult to separate what she sensed enough to identify the individuals. The best she could do in the time she had was to narrow it down to a table with three people. She glanced at them as she passed, then continued out the door.

By the time she made it to the suite she shared with Alina, she barely held on to her temper, and her body was as tight as a bowstring. Hesitating outside the door, she decided she didn't want to bring the storm inside her into the peace of their rooms. Alina didn't deserve that. Turning away, she ran to the workout room.

A couple hours later, when Link finally found her, she was flying around the room again, vaulting over a large crate, then springing up to grab her beloved bars and twirl around them before dismounting to land on a small platform. From there, she jumped from one platform to another, all different heights and sizes, before reaching the balance beam. Phina was thrilled to complete a series of flips and jumps across to the other side before flipping back to the start. She wobbled a few times but managed to hold on.

Running to the other side, she used a springboard to reach a pole that had recently been installed near one corner of the room. After twirling around it a few times, she held onto the pole with her hands and knees as she moved up and down, never putting her feet on the floor.

Alina had laughed when she had seen it the other day, telling Phina that she had never thought pole dancing was a pastime Phina would pick up.

Phina had stuck her tongue out at her best friend. "I'm

not pole dancing. I'm just using a pole to strengthen my core muscles and train my body to be more flexible."

"Space flash to Phina: that's what pole dancing *is*." Alina's eyes had shone with amusement as she laughed at her.

Phina had given her best friend a look that made Alina laugh even harder. "I'm not talking to you right now."

After a few gasps, Alina responded, "That's ok. I'll just introduce you to everyone we meet as Phina, my pole-dancing best friend. Then when they ask if you strip too, I'll let you do your fish-face impression as you try to explain."

She had descended into giggles, holding onto her stomach and falling off the couch on which they had been sitting. After a while, Phina had begun to laugh too.

Phina smiled now as she paused her twirl, having slipped a little lower on the pole as her thoughts wandered. That was one of the few times she had forgotten everything weighing on her and let herself feel like a regular eighteen-year-old. Those times were few and far between.

She reached up with her legs to hold onto the pole above her, then pulled herself higher. Holding the pole with one hand while curling a leg around it and bracing herself with the other foot, Phina caught sight of Link at the other end of the room. The expression on his face at seeing the room and what she was doing was...well, poleaxed. Amused, she twirled around once more, then placed the bottoms of both feet on the pole while holding it with both hands behind her.

Aligning herself, she pushed off and jumped onto a lower platform, only to spring up and jump onto a higher one some distance away, climbing in this way a series of platforms until she reached the top. Taking a moment to judge the distance, she leaped off the edge, twisting and flipping in the air to land a few feet from Link, her knees slightly bent to absorb the impact.

His eyes were wide, his hair still wet from his shower. "Holy hell, kid, that was amazing! When did you learn to do all that?"

Feeling more reserved than normal with this rift between them, she shrugged. "Some of it seems to be an increase in natural ability, but for the rest, what else do you think I've been doing aside from classes? You haven't been around for any training lately, my body can't sleep until I've exhausted myself, and since my endurance has increased dramatically, it takes a lot to do so. Aside from time to eat, which has also increased dramatically since I consume more than three times as much as normal, I've spent most of my free time here in the past few weeks, when I haven't been trying to figure out how to translate the new language."

His shamefaced look caused her both satisfaction and discontent. Stars, her emotions were still all over the place. Was this part of gaining these new abilities, being moody and uncertain of what she wanted? If so, she wasn't sure it was worth it.

"I'm sorry, Phina. I've been really worried about you, but I should have been here to help you instead of having my head up my ass and leaving you to deal with it on your own. You've done a remarkable job of dealing with everything."

After hesitating, she nodded. She didn't want to stay at

odds with him. It felt weird and wrong. "Apology accepted. I appreciate the understanding. I'm sorry I was so harsh too, but I was afraid you had given up on training me."

Giving her a somber nod in acknowledgment, Link put his hands on her shoulders. "I gathered that from what you said in the bar. Don't worry, kid. You're stuck with me from now on." He gave her a ghost of a grin, then gently squeezed her shoulders before letting go. "You'd have to be three times as big an asshole as I've been to make me even consider it."

She smiled, her heart lightening. Then a thought caused her to frown. She almost didn't mention it but figured she might as well ask. He was the one with the spy contacts, after all. "There was a guy in the bar who seemed too interested in our conversation, and you didn't have the shield activated that kept it private."

Link's gaze sharpened. "And you didn't recognize him?"

She shook her head, and he called, "Meredith. Would you show us who was in the bar when Phina walked out?"

Phina added, "He was human, two tables away from Link."

Link glanced at her, his eyes full of speculation as they walked over to the screen by the door. Meredith had displayed the exact view they needed. Phina gestured at a man who was partially turned away. "This one."

Frowning, Link leaned forward. "That looks like... Meredith, would you rewind or fast-forward to when he shows his face?"

"Of course."

The picture changed to show a full view. "Huh," Link said thoughtfully. "That's my second, Jack Kaiser. I asked him to meet with me yesterday, but I didn't realize he was still here. Meredith, is he still on the station?"

Phina relaxed. She had been afraid he was an enemy of some kind. Her interest was sparked since Link had been the only one in Spy Corps she was aware of. She wondered how many other spies she had run into and not known it.

"No, Jack Kaiser left the station an hour ago, heading back to the base."

He frowned, then nodded. "I'll check with him later to see what was going on with the delay. Thanks, Meredith."

"You're welcome."

Link turned to Phina, then glanced at the equipment behind them and couldn't suppress a grin. "Your moves were awesome, by the way. I can't wait to see what else you can do. What have you tried? You've definitely bumped up a level, considering the parkour skills I saw!"

And just like that, the rift between them began to heal over, filling Phina with relief.

CHAPTER ELEVEN

QBBS *Meredith Reynolds*, Diplomatic Institute

Phina dragged herself to class the next morning, fully expecting to have a miserable day. She felt fine physically as long as she ate enough, but mentally and emotionally, she was wearier than she could ever remember being. Even after she had started a boot camp for herself when she was twelve to get up that vertical shaft when she was looking for info on her parents. That had been intense and draining every day until she got stronger. This was worse. It went bone-deep.

She hadn't been looking forward to classes lately, so it didn't surprise her to feel like she needed to endure the day. Knowing that lives were on the line waiting for her to translate the language made going to classes far lower in priority. *Her* priority, anyway. Phina was still annoyed that Anna Elizabeth had insisted she attend instead of devoting all her time to the translation.

Just walking through the miasma of minds and intentions in the space station caused her to feel overwhelmed, and she had no idea what to do to change it. Trying to shut her mind hadn't worked since she had woken up that morning. If something didn't change soon, she would be in danger of a complete meltdown. There was only so much a mind could take.

As she drew closer to the Institute, she felt a buzz of energy that seemed familiar. Her mind picked up several people who were startled when she entered the door of the Institute, but they weren't thinking about her. She moved forward and looked into Anna Elizabeth's Office, then realized why the energy felt familiar.

"Braeden!"

The students standing outside the door stepped aside as Braeden turned his tall, gangly alien body toward her with a smile of greeting and a mental reach as she stepped toward him.

Phina!

His smile turned to concern since her brain felt over-loaded and her vision swam with blackness. He moved forward in alarm as she swayed, then her eyes closed and she lost consciousness.

Phina heard murmurs of sound she couldn't understand while her body lay sprawled on the floor, though her head was raised on some sort of hard pillow. Since the thought of opening her eyes seemed like too much, she decided she would just stay where she was. Perhaps if she stayed still long enough, the people talking would give up and go away. The sounds quieted, then stopped.

Ah. So much better.

Phina?

Go away. Phina's not available right now. You can leave a message, and I'll get back to you never. She kept her eyes closed and willed herself to be in her comfortable bed.

Quiet chuckles came from beside her. She thought she recognized the person's voice, but she couldn't be certain.

"Braeden, are you sure she's awake and ok?" a woman whispered from the other side of her. She knew she should recognize that voice, but she didn't.

"Yes, she's definitely awake. She is just having a difficult time focusing her mind at the moment. It's wide open."

"But she's all right?" This voice came from above and behind her head. Her pillow was behind her head. Was her pillow talking?

"Her mind is strong. I'm certain she will be okay, but for now, we need to give her a moment to collect herself and remember who we are and where she is." That was the first voice, the one that laughed at her. Wait, the second voice had called him "Braeden."

"I wasn't laughing at you, little sister. Your mind just has an amusing way of working. And yes, I am Braeden. You need to focus now and bring your thoughts together. "

"She doesn't remember who we are?" Uh-oh. That voice sounded frazzled and concerned. Why was it wrong for that voice to be frazzled? Her voice should be calm and collected, poised and elegant.

"She's starting to remember now, but no. Something happened to boost her mental awareness tenfold with little warning. She was in danger of overloading, and unfortunately, my mental presence tipped her over the edge. It's akin to having a heavy rock fall on your head. You are disoriented for a time."

That voice. No, that voice shouldn't be out loud. It should be in her head.

"That's right, little sister, but you can't handle speaking mind to mind at the moment, so I use my speech verbally." This Braeden had a gravelly voice like he didn't use it very often. He was her brother? She didn't think she had a brother.

"Yes, little one. You are an only child. But when we became close, I began calling you little sister, at least in my own mind, since we are like family now."

Oh, that's all right then. She just thought she wouldn't be so out of it as to forget she had a brother. Brothers and sisters should be important. Phina frowned. Braeden said she was an only child, but that didn't sound right. Didn't she have a sibling? Sister. Alina.

Pictures flashed in her head of an adorable blond toddler holding out a toy to share with a smile on her face. It changed to a young girl commiserating with her by getting ice cream for them both. A preteen holding Phina when her heart broke after her parents died. A gorgeous willowy blond teen giving her a smirk as they plotted another adventure. Alina. Sister of the heart if not in blood.

"That's it, Phina. You can do it."

Braeden. Snapshots of a tall, tan hairless alien with an elongated head flew through her mind. Sitting on the floor in a plain and simple building, on a spaceship, fighting in the street at night, walking the hallways with her as they talked, fighting in a fancy building, bending over her in concern when she was injured. Apparently she had healed since then; she didn't feel pain in her body.

"Yes, that's me. You're remembering."

Phina wanted to try talking, but her throat felt dry. A moment later, someone held a bottle to her mouth so she could drink. When she'd had enough, she closed her mouth and turned her face away.

"Thank you." Her throat felt raspy. Did something happen to her throat?

"That's what happens when you scream for a while, little sister."

Her eyes popped open. She winced when the light hit them and squinted to try to see anyway. "Scream?"

Figures that were blurred came into focus. To her right, she saw the green-eyed alien who'd featured in her head. His elongated fingers were holding her hand. Braeden. He squeezed her hand in encouragement and nodded. He hadn't spoken into her mind yet.

She vaguely remembered he'd told someone he was speaking out loud because to speak telepathically would hurt her. Yet, as her memories of him came back, she recalled speculating that the Gleeks' telepathy was essential to their sense of self. She knew one of the reasons he had come was because she was on the station. If she wasn't able to speak to him telepathically, would he have issues of his own that she couldn't help him with because she was now broken in some way? She stared at him, stricken and feeling helpless.

"Shh, shh. I will be fine. I can wait for you to heal." He switched the hand that had been holding hers and used the free one to gently soothe her by stroking her arm. This was out of character for a Gleek, so he must be doing it for her because he knew she needed comfort. "Of course for you, little sister. We are both healers who have become protectors. It is a bond we share."

Healer. Protector. She didn't feel like a healer. Wouldn't healers know how to save people when they were hurt? They had Pod-docs to heal physical injuries. But protector? She thought about the times she had come to Alina's defense growing up when someone made fun of her, saying she was flighty or too stupid to understand. That had bothered the two girls since Alina had always been wicked smart. It just wasn't always transferable to tests. Yes, "protector" felt right.

"There is more than one kind of healer, but we will speak of this later. We will make some time between us for training, and we can discuss, among other things, how to handle these new abilities of yours."

Phina was filled with relief. Yes! She had been going out of her mind with concern about what was happening to her—feeling like she was going crazy with no one to help her.

Braeden tilted his head as if to say something else but seemed to think better of it. Perhaps he would tell her later. When he nodded, she knew he could hear her thoughts. Okay, then. He gestured with his head to Phina's left, and she turned her gaze over to the elegant older woman next to her.

Her mind worked through images again. "Are you my...boss?"

The woman's smile wobbled. "Close enough."

Phina squinted as she thought. "Anna. Dean of the Diplomatic Institute."

The woman sagged in relief. "Yes. Anna Elizabeth. Thank God your memory is coming back."

She felt movement beneath her head and froze. "Why is my pillow moving?"

Laughter sounded behind her head, which caused more movement and vibration. Phina tilted her head back and stilled.

"Jace?"

An upside-down grin greeted her. "At your service, new girl."

"Why is my head on your lap?"

"We thought it would be better than the floor."

Phina pursed her lips, then reached up to pat his knee. "I'm not so sure about that. Your leg is hard and bony. Maybe you should get some meat on those bones before you volunteer to be a pillow."

Leaving him half-spluttering and half-laughing, she carefully sat up. So far, so good. Realizing something, she turned to Braeden with wide eyes.

"I don't feel anyone's mind anymore. Is it gone?"

He shook his head. "I am connecting to you to provide a mental shield. It is a process we use with our newly reawakened brothers before they regain control for themselves."

Phina didn't know whether she was relieved or disappointed to know she still had her abilities. She licked her lips, which had turned dry all of a sudden.

"How long will it last?"

"It depends on how much stronger your ability is than mine. With how much it's increased since I last saw you, I would determine that the timeframe won't be very long. I'm hoping it will be long enough to teach you what you need to do to shield yourself."

She nodded, having expected something of the sort. "When can we do it?"

"After the class I am to teach soon?" Braeden looked at Phina and Anna.

They both nodded.

"You will need to stay close to me until you are able to initiate your own shielding."

"*What?*"

"The type of shielding I am doing is only meant for training purposes and won't last very long. It is harder to hold it at a distance. The closer you are to me, the easier it will be to maintain the shield."

Nodding, Phina carefully stood up, and the rest followed her. She felt good now, though a little shaky. She tugged on her jacket to smooth it over her shirt, then touched the knife sheaths on her thighs, automatically checking them and making sure the straps were in place. Her hand rose and checked to make sure her tablet still lay in her pocket. Relieved and feeling more like herself, she turned toward the door just as it opened.

A nondescript man in his fifth decade of life walked into the room. He looked fit for his age, as if he didn't like to stop moving. His chestnut-brown hair and eyes matched, and those eyes sparked with energy and intelligence. His clothing was neat with not a wrinkle in sight, which for some reason caused her to think affectionately that he must have gotten a good night's sleep for once. Upon seeing her, he looked relieved and moved quickly to grasp her shoulders.

"Phina! You're okay!" He turned to Anna. "I got your message and expected the worst. What happened?"

Braeden answered. "Her brain is overloaded, so her memories are scattered at the moment. Perhaps her mind will even have difficulty processing for a time. It's similar to your concussions."

Before the man could respond, Phina crinkled her nose in confusion. "Why do I have several different names in my head for you? Was one not enough?"

Alarm warred with amusement on his face, though it was so subtle she might have missed it if she hadn't been staring at him. "Ah, the name you call me has to do more with how irritated you are with me at the moment." He also squeezed her shoulders before dropping his hands, which she gathered was a warning to be careful of what she said. Too bad her brain-mouth filter wasn't working at the moment.

"Is that why I'm remembering going on a date with you? Because I was irritated with you?"

Looking uncomfortable, the man rubbed his neck. "That was for work, my dear."

The moniker served to bring back more memories, causing her to mouth the name. "Link?" He nodded, looking both relieved and concerned. Link, Greyson Wells, Stan the Man, and Ian James...all personas of one person. Her mentor. A voice broke in before she had a chance to say more.

"If irritation is all it takes to go on a date, I would say we are overdue for one."

As Link stiffened next to her, Phina turned to meet Jace's brown eyes, which were slightly slanted due to his mixed heritage. His grin and dancing eyes invited her to… do something. She didn't remember seeing this expression on his face before. Still, it cheered her up and amused her, which she suspected was the real point.

"Nice try." She patted his shoulder. "I don't remember having that kind of relationship with you, but thank you, Jace. You're a good friend."

His eyes widened as he groaned. "Friend-zoned." He mimed stabbing himself in the heart and twisting the knife. "Wait, you acknowledged that we're friends. Yes!" He did a fist-pump.

Phina laughed as she turned to leave, sensing he wasn't serious about being upset and was trying to cheer her up. Class, then learn to shield her mind. Feeling relieved, she increased her pace. She really couldn't wait.

Star System within the Empire, Planet Lyriem

She-Who-Mourns gathered together the few leaders and healers they had left. It was time to speak seriously.

"What supplies and provisions do we have left? She-Who-Waits, you are in charge of food distribution. How does it look?"

The female blinked her large eyes as her sonorous tubes waved in distress. "Looks are not good, She-Who-Mourns. At full rations, we have only a few days. Continuing with half-rations might take us over a sen day. One meal a day for everyone would stretch us perhaps to two sen days. After that, we'll have nothing."

She-Who-Mourns turned to the male next to her. "And the gathering of new food? How goes that endeavor, He-Who-Moves?"

Standing as still as a statue, the male spoke briefly. "There is little to find and little to be had. We may still find some to contribute, but since we've already been over this ground many times, the chances are small. We should move to find more food."

He-Who-Listens interjected, "We cannot move now. On half-rations, we might have managed it for those still strong, but there are too many who have weakened. On one meal each day, we will never make it to another location."

Murmurs of agreement followed his words. She-Who-Mourns turned to the last person in the group. "He-Who-Acts, how is the water?"

The male's eyes turned from watching his niece on the pallet on the floor in the other room. "At our current rate of water consumption, it will be gone in three sen days."

The group was silent as the implications sank in.

"This is it, then. Our people will be extinct within a turn of the moon." He-Who-Listens sank in on himself at the realization. She-Who-Mourns realized her work was not done. But soon. Soon it would be.

"We cannot give up. That is still time for someone to come and help us."

He-Who-Acts scoffed in disbelief. "Even if someone comes, there is no guarantee they will help us or have the supplies we need. Even if they do drop supplies off such as some have done, that is only delaying the inevitable."

She-Who-Mourns used her su'adon as she spoke to give the other leaders faith to back up her words. "While there is life, there is hope, my friends. We need to do our best to hold on to that life."

Even if it seemed like it would take a miracle.

CHAPTER TWELVE

QBBS *Meredith Reynolds,* Diplomatic Institute

Phina had eaten a quick snack before the class started. Link and Anna Elizabeth had taken themselves off to do whatever they did, but Jace had joined Braeden and Phina in Cultural Studies.

The students had put their heads together and were whispering as they walked in, though Phina suspected it had to do with her alien friend. It certainly wasn't because Jace tweaked her braid before moving to his seat.

After sitting down, Phina reflected that it felt odd to sit in class. Maybe she just felt odd in her own body? She'd had so many changes and unexpected things happen that she couldn't keep up.

Braeden began speaking in a calm, measured way that implied a sense of inner peace. The students relaxed, and a number seemed interested in what he had to say.

"The Gleeks are primarily a peaceful people..." She mentally snorted. Until they laid down the law on someone who'd wronged them and wiped them out. But yeah, a totally peaceful people.

Braeden ignored her, although he could still hear her thoughts.

No, it felt odd to sit here because Phina felt like there was something else she needed to be doing instead. What was it? She wracked her brain but couldn't remember. Once she realized almost half the class had gone by, she decided to relax and pay attention, letting her mind wander wherever it would. Perhaps it would pop into her mind if she didn't try so hard.

"The Gleeks' physiology is different than that of humans. You see the elongated limbs and extremities, particularly our fingers. You see that we are hairless and have a cranium that's larger and more elongated than your own, with its ridges. What is not obvious is what differentiates us inside our bodies." He gestured as he spoke, using one of his elongated fingers.

"To begin with, Gleeks have two hearts."

Phina was amused to hear a student to her left and behind her quietly squeal that Braeden was a time lord.

"The purpose of being dual-hearted is twofold. First, to pump our blood with sufficient strength to reach our extremities. The second is to provide us with greater endurance as we travel to other planets and survive conditions other species might not be able to withstand. To that end, our lungs are hardier and also provide greater filtration than other species we have encountered.

"These internal features allow us to fulfill our self-designated purpose—to gather the largest amount of information in the known universe."

Phina's senses tingled. To be able to sift and search through that level of information would be amazing! She had an epiphany and almost missed Braeden's next point, but alarm ran through her.

"However, our greatest gift is…"

Stop! Braeden, don't mention your mental abilities! It's important. I'll explain later.

"Well? The gift of what?" A student demanded when Braeden had hesitated for a moment too long as his eyes bored into Phina, likely trying to determine why she had stopped him.

"Of being able to seamlessly mesh technology and nature to create a balanced ecosystem," Braeden continued smoothly.

Phina sagged in relief. Now she had time to put together what had caused her to stop him…since she currently didn't know herself.

Braeden had always been good at keeping secrets. Not lying, since that was not something the Gleeks did, let alone become proficient in. However, Braeden had learned early the value of holding back certain information and keeping revelations from affecting his responses.

So, when Phina had mentally shouted for him to stop, it had surprised him, but he had been able to cover his momentary lapse. She had been correct in thinking that he could still hear her mental thoughts. The increase in her ability let him hear her better than anyone else he had come across. In fact, the degree to which he could hear her thoughts was concerning, so much so that he began to wonder if he would still be able to hear her through her shielding. And through his.

After the class finished, Braeden and Phina went to one of the office areas available for temporary teachers. Jace had wanted to join them, but he had reluctantly left after Braeden told him the two of them wouldn't be able to concentrate with him there.

"Do you wish to explain now or wait until after we have addressed your mental protections?"

Phina looked up from where she sat across from Braeden on the floor with a smirk on her face. "What, you aren't going to just read my mind?"

He gave her a small smile. "I would rather hear your fully formed thoughts."

"Okay, my reaction was instinct, but as I sat in class, I figured out that the reason I stopped you is that physical abilities are much more easily understood by humans. People can be faster and stronger, and humans won't blink an eye since we have a lot of Wechselbalg and Yollins around, though some might be envious. Unless they are enraged or in battle, there is usually little fear from them.

"We even have a few of what were called vampires on Earth, which is what Empress Bethany Anne is rumored to be. Vampires are feared by humans because of the historical rumor that they drink blood, but they're still accepted, especially by our people once Bethany Anne became the Empress."

Phina paused, looking uncertain for the first time since she had woken up. Thankfully her memories were almost intact now, though mental processing still took a moment longer. "When it comes to mental abilities, humans tend to be unsettled and are afraid. I think it's because people can explain away physical abilities, and they are relatively easy to understand. Mental abilities like telekinesis and telepathy are not well-known or understood, so they are feared."

Braeden took some time to wade through her thinking. "You believe that if I reveal we Gleeks have telepathy and telekinesis, humans would be afraid of us and treat us differently, even though most of us don't have much of an ability for either outside of our species?"

She appeared relieved. "Yes, that's my concern. You can still reveal it if you wish. I just wanted to make sure you had a chance to think it through first. It's practically guaranteed that some of those in the higher ranks already know after the events on Vermott with the Baldere a few months ago, but they aren't likely to share the information. What you talk about in class will eventually become common knowledge."

He nodded, satisfied. "Thank you for sharing this concern with me. I will think about it. Now, are you ready to continue with your shielding? You need as much time as we can manage for this."

Before they began, Phina pulled out her tablet and sent a message to her training partner that she would practice without him after they were finished with the shielding.

Much to Braeden's relief.

Because one piece of information he had been holding back since he had seen Phina again was that her mental abilities were greater than he had indicated, so much that it took most of his concentration to hold onto the shielding for her.

The other tidbit he had kept to himself was that he had been greatly surprised by the recovery of her mind and memories after that overload. The last time a similar situation had happened, the person had lost their mind and memories, becoming little more than a puppet to be directed. That Phina had apparently recovered just about everything, with perhaps a little loss of memory, floored him.

And caused him to become very curious as to what made her so different from anyone else he had met over his three hundred and forty-eight years.

QBBS *Meredith Reynolds*

Phina wandered through the station, taking her time. She was relieved. For the first time since her new abilities had emerged, her mind felt like her own, without other people's thoughts and intentions pressing in.

Sure, Braeden had told her this was preliminary shielding and that she would need to practice to strengthen her shield walls. She could tell he felt responsible for teaching her to shield, and she appreciated his time and effort. Really appreciated it.

Like, she had to control herself to keep herself from skipping, she felt so happy and relieved!

Sighing, Phina turned a corner and sprang forward and grabbed the rail of the rolling walkway. Usually she avoided those, but she decided she would rather expend her energy flying around the obstacle course than use it walking all the way there. This way, she would get there faster and wouldn't need to sit or stand still.

It wasn't until she was almost at her destination that she remembered the epiphany she'd had during class, and she stumbled forward when the walkway ended. She staggered to the side, not seeing or caring what was going on around her.

The solution was so simple! Why hadn't she thought of this before? Just use the lower tones as a command key to change to the next word grouping. They could figure out the translation protocols and be ready to go. Addison Stone had been working on a way to synthesize the language so they could communicate and had indicated she was close to figuring it out.

Elated by her double cause for joy, it barely registered when ADAM pinged her.

>>**Phina?**<<

"ADAM!"

He hesitated, but she barely noticed in her excitement. >>**Yes?**<<

"I figured it out! The language markers. I think I know what to do."

>>**That's great news, Phina.**<<

She felt a jolt of unease at his tone. "What's wrong, ADAM?"

>>**We need you to come get tested. We have some ideas about what happened, but we need to evaluate you to know for sure.**<<

Nothing like a dash of reality to tone down her excitement. "Do I need to come now?"

>>**Yes. The sooner we figure it out, the better for you. Especially since you might be leaving soon.**<<

She agreed and changed her direction. On the way, she messaged Addison Stone about her new idea. Not five minutes later, she had received a message saying that it looked like it would work.

Yes!

Phina jumped up and down since she didn't have room to do any tumbling around the people who swerved to avoid her jubilant display. She continued to the medical center with a much lighter heart, feeling like the language translator might actually work. Hopefully, the people were still alive when they got there so they could use it.

Once she reached the location ADAM had directed her to, she found one human and one machine in the room. The blonde woman looked up from her tablet with a welcoming smile.

"Come in. Seraphina Waters, correct?"

She cleared her throat nervously. "Phina, yes."

"I'm Doctor April Keelson. Relax. All we are doing today is assessments."

The doctor waved her over to the Pod-doc, a long tube-like machine with various attachments and screens disrupting the smooth surface. She began poking her fingers at a display on the side.

"How long will this take?" Phina asked nervously as she began to remove her clothing.

"A while. This will be a long assessment to examine you on the microscopic level. It will be far longer than a check-up and a good bit longer than when you are sick."

"I've never been sick."

The woman looked up from the display in surprise. "You've never been sick?"

Phina fingered the pocket that held her tablet as she thought, then shook her head and removed her pants. "No, not that I can remember. Is that...odd?"

"It's rare for your age, certainly. Most people have been in at least once for an illness or an injury."

The woman looked at her, considering. Phina began to feel uncomfortable. "Shouldn't you have known that I hadn't been sick before? I would have thought you kept records."

Dr. Keelson broke her stare with an eye roll and a laugh. "Normally I would, but ADAM and company insist on keeping me in the dark for this one. I don't have access to your files."

The hair on the back of Phina's neck stood up. "Why would he do that?"

ADAM interrupted through the speaker in the room. "To protect you both."

Phina had been developing an urge to run far away the more she heard, but what stopped her was the reminder that ADAM was her friend. She took a breath and tried to relax. Phina trusted him; there had to be a reason.

Not that it would stop her from grilling him about it later.

"I get it, ADAM, I get it." April waved her hand before moving back to the display. After a moment, the long tube slid open.

"Well, here you go." Dr. Keelson directed her to place herself inside the machine. Phina climbed in and was about to lay down when she realized the doctor had not answered her question.

"So, how long *is* this going to take?"

April's head peeked over the side, her dark hair falling forward. "I'm not certain. This is only an assessment at the moment. It could take an hour, or it could be longer. I'm guessing for the type of testing ADAM thinks is needed, it will be at least an hour or two."

Phina nodded as she laid down and settled herself. "Okay."

One hour. No, that felt too long. Sixty minutes. She could do sixty minutes.

QBBS *Meredith Reynolds*, Phinalina Residence

"Stars, where have you been?"

Phina jerked her head up as she entered the apartment near midnight. Alina rose from the couch with concern on her face. After blinking a few times and trying to form an answer, Phina finally shrugged.

"It's been a long day."

Alina's eyes narrowed as she crossed the room to grasp Phina's arms. "Talk to me, bestie. You aren't getting away with that little bit of an answer." Her fingers moved as her mouth turned up in a sly smile. "I have ways of getting you to talk. You don't want to mess with me."

Phina giggled and shrieked as her best friend tickled her. "Okay! Okay! I'll tell you!"

"You'd better!"

Alina stopped tickling Phina and made to punch her arm as she normally did but realized her friend wasn't there. She had darted away as soon as Alina's fist began to move. They looked at each other in surprise since that hadn't happened before.

"Phina, what's going on?" Alina looked uncertain.

Sighing, Phina moved to the couch and sat with her arms wrapped around her legs. Alina still stood in the middle of the floor. Phina reached out a hand for Alina to hold. "It's a long story."

After Alina had come to sit with her, Phina told her everything that had happened recently. Alina gasped and looked horrified and outraged at the places Phina expected her to do so. When it was all told up through the seven-and-a-half-hour assessment she had just left, Alina squeezed her hand tight.

"Why didn't you tell me any of this before?"

Shrugging, Phina looked away. "I didn't want to worry you. Everything got worse around the time you and Maxim went on your first date. I didn't want to mess anything up for you guys by giving you something to worry about when you should be happy about that."

"Seraphina Grace, you're the most brilliant person I know, but sometimes you can be really stupid."

Phina turned back to Alina with an incredulous look on her face. "What?"

Alina leaned forward, looking more serious than Phina had ever seen her. "You heard me. How will you figure everything out that you need if you don't share what's happening? You've always been amazing, but you've forgotten that we always talked things over when you got stuck. Sharing the issues always helped you get unstuck with whatever the problem was."

Phina froze. "You're right. I did forget."

Patting Phina's hand, Alina leaned back with a smile on her face that almost looked like a smirk. "Besides, there's something all of you are forgetting."

Phina wracked her brain but couldn't think of anything. "What?"

"If these people are alive and they've been without food a lot of this time, or it's been dwindling, they are also going to need clothes. People only spend time on clothes if they don't need to find food."

Phina looked at Alina in surprise. "That's true."

Playfully rubbing her fingernails on her shirt and then blowing on them, Alina winked. "Go ahead, you can say it."

"We don't know what they look like. What if they don't wear clothes?"

Alina stopped and pouted. "Well, then we will be prepared. Better to be safe than sorry."

Phina smiled and threw her arms around her friend. "You're amazing."

Alina returned the hug. "And?"

Huffing a laugh, Phina added their childhood favorite, "And you're better than chocolate sauce."

Squeezing her, Alina whispered, "Nothing's better than chocolate sauce except you."

Phina drew back to see her face. "And Maxim?"

Alina winked. "Maybe Maxim. Probably. Okay, fine, yes."

Grinning, Phina poked her and received a grin in return. "So, know where we can get some clothes?"

"I just might."

CHAPTER THIRTEEN

Etheric Empire, QBS *Stark*

"Do you think we have enough?"

Phina finished pulling in the transfer cart and wiped her forehead. "It's going to have to be. At least initially. I don't think we can fit any more."

"Yeah." Alina turned from her careful check of the crates that held the clothing. "It's one of those times when you hope there's still lots of people to save, and you would feel bad if we didn't have enough supplies for everyone."

Surveying the busy cargo hold, where a number of people were loading and settling tanks of water and crates of food and clothing, Phina shrugged. "We will just have to see. We couldn't have left any sooner. Everything else will have to come on the support ships."

It had been two days since Phina'd had her epiphany. Addison Stone had been over the moon, tweaking her musical synthesizer to create the tones and combinations needed to speak in return. ADAM had programmed the translation once she'd finished, which they were hoping to hear news about before they left. They had made sure to pack speakers that could wirelessly connect to their implants since they had no other way to express the translation to the aliens.

Shaking her head, Phina finished unloading the transfer cart so she could retrieve the next item to bring on board. The gathering of supplies had begun after Phina had that first meeting with Anna Elizabeth, Link, and Jace. There had been a scramble for the clothing after Alina reminded them of that need, but it looked like they would have everything necessary to get a start on helping the aliens. After another half-hour of sweaty work, they were all finished.

Phina returned the transfer cart to its dock so it could be secured for travel, then stopped to take a breath, relax, and wipe the sweat off her face with the back of her hand. She had expected to feel warm after the exertion of moving all those crates, but this felt a little too warm. Fudging crumbs. She was probably dehydrated again. As she turned to find water, she caught sight of the doctor walking toward her.

"Doctor Keelson?"

"Please, call me April when you aren't being seen as a patient."

"April. Did you get all the medical equipment you need on board?"

"Yes, I have an all-in-one scanner for the Pod, we have a large Pod-doc on *Stark*, and I have two portable diagnostic scanners for me and a helper if we can spare one when the time comes." She looked around the cargo bay and pointed in the direction she had stored the items as she listed them, as if trying to make sure she has everything. "There are half a million injections to counter dehydration, double that for vitamins and nutrients though split between all the known races since we don't know these aliens' physiology, fifty sensors for vital signs to go on the most urgent cases, a portable blood work-up kit for the field, ten stasis bags for those under emergency conditions so they won't die before we can get them to care... We could probably pass those out for each of you to carry. Let's see, what else?" She blew the hair off her forehead, then shook her head. "I'm sure I'm forgetting something. Suffice it to say I tried to think of everything."

"That sounds amazing. Thank you!" Smiling, Phina tugged her shirt, trying to create some moving air to cool herself off. "Anything I can help with?"

"Perhaps once we get there, thank you."

Phina turned again to look for water.

"Phina?"

Holding in her sigh, she turned back. "Yes?"

The doctor looked worried. "How bad do you think this situation we are walking into will be?"

Phina's mind filled with the pictures that had come to her when she heard those tones pleading for help. She shook them off, her light expression gone. "It's not as bad as what I imagine war would be like as that's all blood and wounds. However, with children starving and the people desperate and dying, this trip will likely cut into your heart. It's already cut into mine."

The doctor didn't stop her this time.

. . .

QBBS *Meredith Reynolds*

ADAM?

>>TOM?<<

I'm looking for Phina, but I can't find her on the station.

>>She left with the group sent to help the aliens that were starving and dying.<<

What? Which aliens?

>>I don't know their name. They speak through music and live on a planet within the limits of the Empire but haven't joined yet, likely because no one could understand them so they could ask.<<

Ah. The Aurians.

>>You know of them?<<

Yes. They were just beginning to move from family groups into towns when I left and eventually landed on Earth. I'm certain they have evolved since.

>>Yes. Until some unknown event happened that caused the people to starve and die. After Phina's translations, records indicate this has been occurring for at least eight years.<<

That's terrible. And Phina has gone to help them? For how long?

ADAM paused in his automatic response to consider the tone in which TOM had spoken. His alien friend sounded unsettled.

>>Yes. We don't know yet. What's wrong?<<

TOM hesitated, causing ADAM to feel a strange emotion. He wondered if it was anxiety.

I've analyzed the results of the scan we did of Phina in the Pod-doc.

\>\>Yes? What were your findings?<<

A change in almost every system: muscular, circulatory, nervous, respiratory... The only systems not affected were skeletal and reproductive.

Alarm shot through ADAM's core.

\>\>What sort of changes?<<

An increase in muscle strength and tone, a more efficient heartbeat and circulatory system, a faster-acting response in the nervous system with a higher pain threshold, increased lung capacity, a more efficient renal system, and a slight increase in the lymphatic system. This is level-two enhancement with a bit of a boost.

\>\>Why would there only be a slight increase in her lymphatic system?<<

Why do you think?

\>\>Ah.<<

Indeed.

\>\>It's not what was planned, but these changes sound better and more efficient, giving her a better body. What about them is causing you to panic?<<

I'm not panicking!

ADAM waited.

All right, I'm panicking, TOM muttered indistinctly.

\>\>What's wrong with her?<<

Well...

\>\>TOM, please. I'm one of her best friends.<<

A moment of silence.

I believe she had a jump-start to develop these abilities. Her systems were stable. I monitor them every year during her regular checkups. Someone did this to her.

>>Yes, I'm aware.<<

You know who?

>>Yes, but I don't have solid evidence yet to back up my theory.<<

Whoever did it knows a lot about nanocytes but doesn't have as intimate a knowledge of them as they think. Her enhancement was jump-started, but since then, I believe the nanocytes have continued to increase Phina's strength and efficiency daily. That isn't how we normally program them to work.

>>TOM.<<

Yes?

>>That doesn't sound good for Phina.<<

It's not. Think about how the human metabolism works. A person who has a more efficient metabolism can become faster and stronger if they choose to work toward it, but they also burn calories at an increased rate.

>>So, to continue your example, Phina's metabolism is operating at peak efficiency?<< ADAM asked hopefully.

No. It's off the charts and increasing daily.

>>Phina's in trouble.<<

Indeed, TOM replied gravely. Bethany Anne draws energy from the Etheric. Her systems function at peak levels without fluctuations. We currently have no tools to measure Etheric flow to the degree I would wish, but what we do have indicates Phina's ability to draw from the Etheric didn't properly connect, causing fluctuations and overwhelming her system. If her system continues to be attacked at this rate without interference, her body will begin to consume its mass to keep up with demand.

>>TOM, that means she'll die.<<

I'm afraid so. The faulty programming in her nanocytes cannot be self-repaired.

ADAM wondered if this was what humans meant when they said they felt like the rug had been pulled out from under them. >>We have to intervene before that happens.<<

We need to get her back here and get her into Bethany Anne's Pod-doc. If we do, we can try to halt the changes before it's too late.

If ever there was a time to pick up cursing, ADAM thought this was it.

>>Bethany Anne?<<

ADAM? TOM? What have you two been talking about? I'm in the middle of a delicate negotiation, and I keep feeling that damned buzzing in the back of my head.

TOM explained the situation. It was no surprise to the two of them when the Empress took the news poorly.

She didn't!

>>I believe she did.<<

Bethany Anne, your emotions are surging. Do you need me to suppress them for you?

Of course, my emotions are surging! I'm fucking pissed, and I'm tired of restraining myself and letting everyone else handle things so I'm not inserting myself into every fucked-up situation. You have no idea how much I want to go pound some common sense into that woman! I should have done something about her before, but she's Phina's only living rela-

tive! Fucking damn it! We told her to take care of Phina, and she swore she would!

ADAM and TOM experienced a very uncomfortable few moments before Bethany Anne reeled in her emotions enough to focus.

Do you have proof that she gave Phina these altered nanocytes?

ADAM showed her the video of Phina's last visit with Faith. >>**Combined with Faith's messages to Phina, it's circumstantial, but she's the only one who could have managed it.**<<

Find the smoking gun, ADAM, and recall that two-bit fucking Mengele wannabe to the **Meredith Reynolds.** *I want her back here yesterday. If you can't find proof, we'll get it from her head.*

>>I'm on it.<<

What about Phina's immediate situation? Can she use the Pod-doc aboard the **Stark** *to get her nanocytes repaired?*

>>**I can send Stark a modified program that will recode her nanocytes with the correct program for her enhancement type.**<<

But we would rather have her here so we can both monitor the process, TOM finished. **If Phina's aunt made this simple error, there's no telling what other problems will arise.**

>>**Phina is unlikely to abandon the Aurians,**<< ADAM told Bethany Anne. >>**She's stubborn enough to hold out until she knows they will be okay.**<<

You could order her to return, TOM suggested.

I could, Bethany Anne replied. *But I won't. Phina has*

shown she's smart enough to ask for help if she needs it, so give her the choice.

>>Are you sure?<< ADAM inquired.

We don't know what they are walking into yet, Bethany Anne told him. *These people have been in crisis and begging for help for eight fucking years, and we didn't know about it. I don't want to lose Phina, but I also don't want to have the Stark turn back and possibly risk the death of an entire species. Clue Doctor Keelson in and have her work with Phina. If she chooses to wait for treatment, pass on anything the doctor can do to keep the effects down until she comes back.*

>>What if the problem is larger than we expect? What can we do, TOM?<<

If Phina starts experiencing more of these surges and more regularly, the only thing they can do to save her is to sedate her and put her into stasis until we can get her to Bethany Anne's Pod-doc.

ADAM could imagine how well that would go over with Phina. Even if it was the only way to save her, she could be angry with them all.

As long as she stayed alive, ADAM could live with that.

Etheric Empire, QBS *Stark*

Doctor Keelson beamed as she forked in a bite. "I can't tell you how thrilled I am that we will no longer have to cook soon with the new machine R&D just invented. When we were on Earth, everyone had to cook their own food or buy it. Now, we've got machines cooking, storing, and dispensing food for us." She waved at the kitchen area.

"Desperation has always been the best propellant of invention."

"I hear you, April. Even as a young woman, cooking was never a strong interest." Addison Stone smiled at the woman with amused affection before sipping her beer. "Then again, even if I had been interested, my skills have never involved cooking."

Ryan threw a sly grin at the women across the table. "I find that difficult to believe. Lovely ladies who have lived as long as you usually have hidden talents."

"Did he just call us old?" April turned to Addison with an incredulous look.

Addison pursed her lips even as her eyes narrowed on Ryan. "I believe he did."

Ryan blinked, his grin fading. "Hold on now. I said you have hidden talents."

Alina threw him a look around Maxim, who was between them. "Yeah, for ladies who have lived so long."

He threw up his hands. "Hey, you are twisting my words! I have nothing but respect for you ladies." He saw Phina watching him and gave her a smile that turned shaky when she continued to stare at him. "All of you ladies."

Sis'tael clicked her mandibles. Only someone paying attention could tell she was laughing and trying not to show it. "Hold on, Ryan. How old are you again?"

He stirred uneasily at the change in subject. "Twenty-five."

"That's right. *So* advanced in years." Phina hid a smile at Sis'tael's goading since the Yollin's age wasn't much greater than Ryan's. "Are you sure you are old enough to have discovered *any* woman's hidden talents?"

"Hey, I've been discovering hidden talents in women for over twelve years! Lots of women! I'm practically an expert. Tell them, Maxim." He nudged his friend in growing desperation.

Maxim rumbled a laugh as he pulled away. "Oh, no! I'm not getting involved in this."

"Drk? Come on, man!"

The Yollin shifted uncomfortably. He was sitting next to Sis'tael in the chairs that were specially made for four-legged Yollins. "Ryan, you know I don't like these types of conversations."

Groaning, Ryan picked up a cookie from the tray in front of him and bit into it. "Why do I bother with you two? You've never been good wingmen."

Amused despite her determination to stay out of it, Phina found herself responding. "Oh? What makes them so bad at it?"

"Well, Drk has never shown an interest in any female before Sis'tael, so every time I tried to get him to help out, he'd say, 'Ryan, I don't have any interest in human mating rituals.' Drink an ale or two, and he's done."

Drk-vaen gave him the Yollin version of a shrug. "I don't understand the point of flirting and being coy about what you want and feel. Why can't you just tell a woman you are interested and she accepts or not? Yollins are more direct. You humans make things complicated."

April tilted her head as she considered that. "There's an element of truth there. It would certainly make things less complicated to be more direct, but also within that dance between men and women is romance. Don't Yollins want to have romance, or is that not an interest for you? What do you think, Sis'tael?"

Sis'tael turned toward her, baring her teeth in a Yollin grin. "Of course, but romance looks very different for Yollins. Instead of flirting with words and a complicated mating dance, a Yollin's idea of romance is about showing your strengths and weaknesses to each other and seeing how you fit together as people. It's also having each other's back against threats and knowing you can trust the other person. Military-based Yollins usually have armor on, both mentally and physically, so being able to trust each other without any armor is a big deal."

Alina leaned against Maxim's shoulder after threading her fingers through his. "That actually sounds rather beautiful."

Drk leaned over to touch foreheads with Sis'tael. "It is."

After giving them a moment, Phina grinned and waggled her eyebrows. "And what about Maxim? It doesn't sound like he is any better, and he doesn't have the same excuse."

Ryan and Maxim laughed, Ryan's a higher tenor and louder, while Maxim's voice rumbled deeper. Ryan shook his head. "You wouldn't think so, would you? It wasn't an issue with the women. There were plenty that came flocking around from time to time, of all sorts."

"All sorts of women, huh?" Alina turned to give the eye to Maxim.

"Like flies and bees," Maxim assured her. "Buzzing around and getting in the way."

Addison snorted. "I find that hard to believe. You weren't interested in any of them?"

Shrugging, Maxim looked uncomfortable and glanced at Alina to make sure she wasn't upset. "Not really. Certainly not seriously."

Ryan smacked Maxim on the back, causing the bigger man to turn narrowed eyes on him. "You can believe it! This guy has always been work and duty, responsibility and taking everything seriously. It's only been in the last year or so that he's lightened up a lot, particularly the last few months." He winked at Alina, who was caught by surprise, then smiled in return. "It certainly left a lot more women for me."

"Then it sounds like he did his job well as a wingman."

Ryan paused in chugging his beer, coughing and wiping his mouth before he responded to Phina. "I hadn't really thought about it that way. You're right."

Stark chose that moment to pop up onscreen in his avatar. "Too bad I couldn't have gone with you. I would be an excellent wingman."

Alina smiled at the EI. She had told Phina earlier she thought he was cute, and of course, Stark had heard her and preened like a peacock. "Because you actually have wings?"

Stark stared at her. "Because I'm so incredibly good-looking. Obviously."

April walked back into the room with a drink. Phina hadn't noticed her leave, but the woman had been at the end of the table next to the kitchen. The doctor sat down and beamed. "This is a great trip already! I love Coke! I can't believe you have a Coke dispenser on board."

Phina sat up straight. "Really? We have a Coke dispenser?"

"Who brought a Coke dispenser onboard?" Stark raised his voice and looked hard at each of them.

"That would be me. You can thank me later." Ryan waved with a cocky grin.

"You brought a Coke dispenser on board my ship? *My ship?* Do you know those are regulated by the Empress herself? That if it falls into the wrong hands for any reason, I have to self-destruct to save it? Do you?"

"Uh, no?" Ryan gaped.

"Oh, my stars!" Alina's eyes were wide.

April looked like she might be ill. "Really?"

They all looked at Stark with concern and with fear. When Phina saw the smirk on Stark's face, she burst out laughing. Their heads swiveled to her in surprise before Stark's voice brought their attention back.

"No, not really! I'm kidding." He shrugged. "Just a little joke."

Ryan let out a sigh of relief. "You scared me there, T-man!"

"I wouldn't lose it, though, or you'll answer to the Empress."

Stark's avatar winked out.

Ryan's jaw dropped. "You were kidding that time too, right, T-man? Stark?" When the EI didn't return, the man looked around. "He was kidding, right?" He only received raised eyebrows and shrugs as answers, and he rubbed his eyes. "Can we start today over again? Apparently, this is Beat up on Ryan Day."

"Sorry, man." Maxim gave him a slap on the back that was as hard as the one he had been given earlier, causing Ryan to squawk in dismay and the rest to chuckle. Phina felt warmth as she looked around the room. This reminded her of the conversations she had with ADAM, Meredith, Reynolds, and then with Link and Braeden, where she had the same feeling.

It hadn't hit her until now that the warmth indicated happiness that they were together. That all of them cared about her and supported her. They had her back, and she knew she could count on them. Like...family—a family she'd chosen and who'd chosen her rather than the one she had been born into. She had felt the same way with her parents, even though they had been gone so often.

Overcome by that happiness, Phina laughed in the middle of a comment she hadn't heard that wasn't funny. Everyone looked at her in confusion and question. Waving them off, she shook her head and smiled, leaning forward on her elbows to soak in the feeling.

The warmth quickly passed when Link entered the room moments later with a serious and dark expression on his face.

"Doctor Keelson? Phina? Come with me. We need to talk."

He turned on his heel and walked out, leaving Phina and April scrambling to follow. As she went through the door, Phina heard Ryan cursing behind her.

"Know what? Screw this. If I'm going to die by Empress, I'm at least having a Coke first."

CHAPTER FOURTEEN

Etheric Empire, QBS *Stark*

Braeden waited as first Greyson, then Phina and Doctor Keelson entered the lounge and conference room. The furniture and decor were a blend of comfortable and utilitarian Braeden appreciated. Link made sure the door locked behind them, then moved over to a large chair next to Braeden, leaving the couch for the women.

Through both of their shielding, Braeden caught Phina's confusion and concern and shook his head. He had hoped to have more time to help her strengthen her shields, but apparently she needed them more quickly than he had anticipated. Again. Phina kept surprising him, and at his age, he was of two minds about liking that.

"Sit down, kid. This is serious, but you aren't in trouble. Well, you are, but it's nothing you did." Greyson stopped with a sigh and wiped his face when he saw her alarm. "Let's start over."

"Okay." Phina followed April to the couch then leaned forward to listen.

"Doctor Keelson, you'll find a message from ADAM that he sent to both of us. If you want to know the details, pull that up." The woman nodded and pulled the tablet out of her jacket pocket.

"Phina, remember ADAM had you scanned before we left?"

"Did he figure out what's wrong?" Her eyes were focused and ready, but he could feel her tension and unease. She had realized something was wrong.

Greyson hesitated. "Yes and no. He's still figuring out what started the change, but he knows what is happening in your body and why you feel the way you do."

"Tell me."

Doctor Keelson gasped, placing her hand on her mouth as she stared in astonishment at the tablet in her hand. She turned her eyes toward Phina and back to her tablet, causing Phina's unease to grow and Greyson's face to turn dark. Phina narrowed her eyes at him, clearly telling the man to get on with it.

His shoulders sank as he sighed. "At some point, an altered version of what we call nanocytes were introduced to your body. Since then, your body has been changing and growing in strength and ability. The problem is that these nanocytes weren't meant to be synthesized in this way, and your body hasn't learned how to regulate them. Something was adjusted within the nanocytes that causes your abilities to grow daily, but with a decrease in your body's ability to cope with them."

Phina turned pale, then sat back in her seat and drew her legs up, hugging her knees. After closing her eyes, she took a breath and tried to calm down. Braeden could feel her emotions bouncing all over the place. After another ragged breath, she raised her head, showing tears shimmering in her eyes, though her voice stayed steady.

"That means I'm dying, right?"

Doctor Keelson cleared her throat as she turned to Phina. "It means we need to get you back to the station as soon as possible."

Phina straightened and spoke firmly. "No, we can't change course now. Those people could be dying!"

Greyson leaned forward to get her attention. "Listen, my dear. You need help quickly, true, but so do these Aurians we are trying to find."

"Aurians?"

He waved his hand dismissively. "That's what ADAM learned the Kurtherians called them. Not important right now. The point is, we know they need help. You also need help. You can go into stasis in the Pod-doc here on the *Stark*, but the closest estimate of time needed to adjust your nanocytes is a week."

"A week!" Phina protested. "But we will be there in just a few days, thanks to *Stark* being a Gate ship. The whole mission will be done by then. No, I need to wait. ADAM will help me."

Greyson eyed her, then nodded. "What we need to do then is go to them as quickly as possible and then return so you can get the help you need."

Phina relaxed and nodded. "All right."

"We also need to help you maintain your body at the level it's at right now and not get any worse." April had composed herself and sounded calm. "There are things you can do to facilitate that, such as eating twice the amount you are now. The more fuel you consume, the less it takes from your body."

Looking thoughtful, Phina nodded. Braeden was relieved that her emotions had calmed down.

"However, the biggest thing you can do and the main point of everything ADAM sent us is that you need to keep from moving as much as possible."

Phina stilled, then shook her head. "I don't think I can do that. My body wants me to move all the time. Even now, I feel the urge driving me to get up and do something. Flips down the hall, sparring, anything."

Greyson leaned forward to get her attention. "Kid, you do that, and you're dead soon. None of us want to see that happen. I know it's going to be hard, but you're strong inside. Even stronger than you are outside now. You can do this. We will all help you."

Braeden inserted himself into the conversation. "I will help you better your shielding. The practice will strengthen your willpower as well, which will allow you to maintain stillness. We can do that after this conversation is finished."

Greyson stared at him, then raised an eyebrow. "Well, I think that effectively killed it. Doctor Keelson? Anything else?"

She looked conflicted but shook her head. "Nothing that can't wait. I'll talk to Phina later about other things she can do to take in energy."

"Then we'll leave you to it." Greyson stood up and moved toward Phina. Just before he passed her, he stopped and pulled on her braid, causing her to look up in irritation.

"Hey, you aren't dying. Get that out of your head right now. You're going to follow instructions and we'll finish this business, and then we will be back and fixing you up in no time. You hear me? You're not dying. We won't let it happen."

She stared at him, then gave him a small smile of gratitude. "As you wish."

"Exactly right, my dear. Now, don't you forget it." After a wink at Phina, he moved out of the room quickly.

Doctor Keelson followed him more slowly, mumbling, "That man has more moods than a Wechselbalg."

After the door shut behind the two, Braeden turned to Phina, who was still struggling to cope. He gestured at the floor. "Let's sit and practice meditation, then I'll help you increase your shielding."

Phina sat, then shifted, shuffled, fidgeted, twitched, and sighed. After four minutes of utter failure, Braeden examined her face and saw a mix of frustration, discouragement, and fear.

"What's wrong, little sister?"

The words almost exploded out of her. "I can't do it! I just can't sit still. I don't know how people stand it."

He considered her, then nodded. "I understand. Let's try something else."

After standing and bracing himself with his three-toed feet, Braeden used his telekinesis to gently push the furniture out of the way. Phina turned her head one way, then another as she watched the space around them expand, then glanced at him with a grin. "So cool!"

Once they had sufficient room, Braeden turned to Phina. "Watch and copy what I do. The point is to go slow and follow the moves precisely. As you do them, focus your mind entirely on the movement and not the issues that worry you."

With that, he proceeded to teach her the Gleek version of Tai Chi. As he moved slowly from one position to the next, he kept his mind tuned to hers and was pleased that she had grown calmer, her emotions now less volatile.

That's how you do it, little sister, he whispered into her mind. *Slow movements. Deep and steady breaths.*

Braeden felt a burst of gratitude from her. After a few more minutes, he began patiently showing her what she needed to do to rebuild and strengthen her mental shield.

No, Phina, you must rebuild your shields as you continue the movements. He stood firmly planted in the middle of the room, demonstrating the next movement. She threw him a look of exasperation.

"I've been trying! It's frustrating!"

Knowing she needed a motivator, Braeden tried the first that came to him. He went back to speaking out loud so as not to tax her. "What if a friend was in harm's way and the only thing keeping you from helping them was your control? Alina? Greyson? Maxim? How far are you willing to go to protect them?"

Her breathing ragged and her eyes blazing with anger, Phina bared her teeth in a fierce growl. "As far as necessary. I would do anything!"

Braeden nodded in solemn satisfaction. "Exactly. Protect them now proactively by keeping them and everyone else safe from you first. Then keep *them* safe from those who would purposely harm them."

Alarm leaped into her eyes. "I would never harm them!"

"You don't *intend* to harm them. There is a great difference. With your increase in abilities, there is much you could do unintentionally."

Her eyes grew wilder, and her breath came in gasps. Braeden stepped closer and braced himself while he placed his hands on her shoulders. This was the telling moment as to how much control she would be able to exert over herself. If she couldn't, her chances of surviving dropped significantly.

"Breathe. Calm your breaths. Breathe. Calm your heart. Breathe. Calm your mind."

Braeden softly repeated the words as he connected to her mind, not to control or influence but just to watch. He kept his eyes fixed on hers, which she connected to as if he were a lifeline. At first nothing changed, and although he continued speaking calmly, he felt dread before pushing it away. She would sense it if he felt anything other than calmness, and it might make her control worse. Gradually, her breathing grew steadier, her emotions raging less than before. However, relief didn't come until she was able to breathe normally, her eyes closing.

Braeden released her and took a step back, though, given his elongated arms, he hadn't been closer than two feet. When she finally opened her eyes, she gave him a knowing look. "That's why we are doing this, isn't it? So that I have a chance of controlling these mood swings I keep having. They've been growing in strength." Alarm crossed her face. "The mood swings have to be connected to the increase in my abilities."

He shrugged a shoulder. "Yes, to control the mood swings, among other things. And yes, the chance of them being connected is high. The better you can control your body, the better you can control your emotions and abilities. The better your control, the more in control you are. Without that, at some point, you won't be able to stop yourself."

A look of frustration passed over her face. "Why does this seem so difficult? I don't see any others with nanocytes having problems. The Wechselbalg don't have these raging hormonal issues. I haven't met many vampires, but they seemed to be in control of themselves too. They were just like normal people."

"Ah. But those you call Wechselbalg usually are born as such, are they not? They learn control as children, when their bodies aren't as strong and they can do less damage. By the time they are adults, it's a matter of discipline over the years. They can still lose control when strong emotions are involved, such as when loved ones are in danger, but they have had a lifetime of maintaining that control, which helps them.

"I haven't met any of your vampires, but the records we have from Earth indicate they often have difficulty with control at the beginning, and they have to learn to keep hold of that control, or they risk being hunted down. Don't worry, little sister. This is an abnormal situation, but for what is happening, you are doing well."

Phina took a deep breath and let it out before nodding. Her eyes hardened, showing nothing but determination as she gave herself more room. "Let's do this."

This time, Braeden found none of the previous distraction or reticence in her movements. She followed his direction without question and allowed her body to flow seamlessly from one position to the next. He couldn't help feeling warmth and pride. She wouldn't feel the necessity to push past her body's growing natural responses for herself. If she had, the past hour wouldn't have been an issue.

But for others, for her friends and family, she would.

Star System within the Empire, Planet Lyriem

She-Who-Mourns paused to wipe the moisture from her face. This phenomenon was new, and their bodies had yet to become accustomed to it. Her planet had previously been temperate, and that was what their bodies were accustomed to. The temperature was now wildly out of control.

What alarmed her was that she could feel the lack of moisture in her body now that it had escaped her skin. Their people would need to drink more water to replace the moisture that left their bodies, water they didn't have enough of. Perhaps there would be a shift in temperature again soon so they could find relief. Anything was better than this wretched heat.

A mewl returned her attention to the task at hand. Giving the child next to her a smile, She-Who-Mourns pulled a small bowl out of her basket. She frowned since she had expected there to be more in the container, but She-Who-Loves reached out eagerly and her eyes lit up. She-Who-Mourns paused to make sure the child could eat on her own before moving on to the next.

She handed a bowl to the child in the second bed from the end, relieved the task was almost done and the children were no worse off than the day before. That relief fled when she reached the male child at the end. His arms trembled as they stretched out, his eyes pained. Her heart skipped a beat as grief filled her, then resolve. He-Who-Endures wouldn't die if she could do anything to prevent it.

Bending down, she dropped the basket on the floor and lifted the bowl to his face below his sonorous tubes. His mouth opened to let his long tongue reach out and lap from the bowl.

"That's it, little one. You can do it."

His eyes flicked to her and his tubes waved sluggishly—in irritation, she realized when he protested a moment later.

"Not little."

She leaned forward to stroke his cheek with one of her sonorous tubes, an act of intimacy reserved for a mate or a child. "Outside you are little yet, but inside…inside, you have grown far beyond your years. You just need to let your body catch up."

"Can't. I'll be dead soon."

Straightening in surprise, she couldn't help the agitation of her sonorous tubes. "Who told you that?"

He turned his head away, looking at the wall on the other side of the bed.

"He-Who-Endures, you know not to hold secrets from me."

Reluctantly, his eyes returned to hers before whispering a name. Sighing, she leaned over and caressed his face again. "Thank you, my strong one. You forget about what other people say and focus on getting better. Do not give up. I do not know what our fate holds, but if it is at all possible, I will not allow anyone else to die. We have come too far to give up now. You hang on and live."

He smiled faintly and nodded. After blowing him a kiss, she gathered her basket and his bowl, then reversed her route to pick up the other bowls on her way out. She hadn't meant for anyone else to hear her little speech, but she could see the other children had and were strengthened by it.

Once she left the building, She-Who-Mourns had difficulty keeping her emotions in check. Perhaps she would become She-Who Rages. The situation seemed to warrant the change. Very little enraged her, but mistreating children pushed that button.

Storming into the kitchen where the meals were prepared, She-Who-Mourns found She-Who-Waits. The female had finished serving the meals and begun to clean up. It was a thankless job since they had been on strict rations for weeks. The adults had all grown accustomed to the lack of food, but it fell harder on the children.

"What have you done, telling the children they all will die?"

She-Who-Waits looked at her defiantly. "Well, won't they? Won't we all? It does no good to lie to them."

She-Who-Mourns hissed at the female. The arrogant callousness of the comment was unbelievable. "You took away their hope! What did you think would happen if they knew they would just die? They are children and will believe what you say. Their will to survive depends on believing they will be saved!"

Stopping, she looked up and down, then glanced at the

food nearby. The female didn't seem as thin as the rest of her people. She-Who-Mourns' sonorous tubes waved in agitation. "You would not dare!"

Hesitating for the first time since she had entered, She-Who-Waits took a step back. "Would not dare what?"

"You would not dare hold back food from the little ones, our hope for the future! You would not dare hoard food for yourself to stay alive longer! Tell me you did not!"

She-Who-Mourns was incandescent with rage. "Tell me the truth!"

The female whimpered and stammered. "I...I..."

The fear and uncertainty on the female's face did little to lessen the heat inside her. Just as She-Who-Mourns lifted her sonorous tubes to enact judgment as was her right, being a holder of the revered su'adon, she heard excited shouts from outside. She couldn't pick out words until a young male ran in, staggering from loss of breath and lack of food.

"A spaceship! A spaceship is here!"

Relief and elation filled her but didn't erase the anger she felt for She-Who-Waits. However, the interruption allowed her to remember to act justly. Turning back to stare into the female's eyes, she spoke softly, using every bit of su'adon she possessed.

"Did you take from the little ones for yourself?"

"Yes." The female bit out the tones sullenly, unable to be silent under the influence of the su'adon.

She-Who-Mourns closed her eyes as she struggled to contain herself. Finally, she opened them and leaned forward intently. "You will no longer be She-Who-Waits, but She-Who-Betrays. Know that this was no small act.

This was the worst mistake of your life. Whether we are saved or not, you are no longer in charge of food distribution. Leave now. You may still have water rations, but you will have no food for three days."

She moved to leave, but the squawks of protest caused her to turn back with a hard look that evoked a recoil in the female.

"Considering your actions might have caused others to die, I believe the consequences are very lenient. Do you wish for me to change my mind and give you the gentle sleep? I assure you, I would have no problem doing so."

Though the other female's sonorous tubes waved in agitation, she merely shook her head.

"He-Who-Discovers, you will escort her to her rooms and inform She-Who-Guides that she is in charge of the food from now on."

The young male appeared disappointed that he couldn't go back to the crowd outside but didn't hesitate to comply. Finally, She-Who-Mourns left the building to find out what was happening.

Perhaps their saviors had finally come.

CHAPTER FIFTEEN

Etheric Empire, QBS *Stark*

"So, what's the plan for when we get there?"

Phina and Alina broke off their conversation and turned to Ryan. Alina frowned. "Didn't we talk about this before we left?"

Ryan rubbed his face as he produced a practiced embarrassed grin. "Well, I sort of wasn't paying attention. I was thinking about this beautiful blonde..." He stopped when he saw their expressions and hastily moved on. "All I remember is we are helping people that are starving and dying."

Phina raised an eyebrow. "Yup. That's what we're doing."

Taking her cue, Alina nodded and gave him an appreciative smile. "You're so clever to remember the plan."

"Your memory sure is a vault," Phina continued with a smirk.

Alina pressed her hands together under her chin and

made her eyes widen. "Oh, please, can I stay with you while we're on the planet? I don't know what I'll do without you telling me the plan."

Ryan's eyes pinged between them before rolling. "Ha-ha. You two are so funny." Phina shot him a smirk with an exaggerated bow while Alina made a decent simpering curtsy. He gave them a deadpan look. "Seriously. What are we doing? What's the plan?"

Stark popped up on the screen next to them, causing Alina to start. She would have fallen over if Phina hadn't grabbed her. Alina's three-inch heels didn't help. Phina had stopped trying to convince her to dress differently while on the mission, occasionally staring at her friend's shoes with a perplexed expression. However, at the moment, Stark had her full attention.

"The plan? *The plan?* The plan, my moderately useless and slightly entertaining inmates—except for you, Genius Girl. You're only slightly useless and moderately entertaining, especially when you do that weird thing you do—is to slip into the atmosphere under cover, locate the most populated area, land at a distance close enough to hike to but far enough away that I don't get alien cooties, pack in all the supplies on your backs, dump them on the aliens, then hightail it back here and leave before someone knocks you off and steals me so I have to blow myself up in a fiery death."

Ryan scrunched up his face. "I think I hate that plan. Was that the plan? Did you even take a breath in there with all that?"

Stark rolled his avatar eyes. "I'm an EI, dumbass. I don't

need to breathe. Did I say moderately useless? You're downgraded to completely useless."

Alina stood looking a little sick. "To be honest, that is a really terrible plan."

Sniffing, Stark turned his face to the side. "No one around here appreciates my genius."

"Solid, E-man." Ryan put a fist out toward Stark, who looked at it askance.

"What is that for?"

When Ryan didn't answer, being speechless, Phina explained. "It's a gesture of solidarity. That you both agree on an issue or are together in something."

Flicking his attention between them, Stark finally extended his fist. Ignoring his surprise, Ryan moved to touch his fist to Stark's screen. When he was inches away, Stark snapped his arm back.

"Too slow, dumbass, too slow."

Ryan scowled. "Hey! I have a name."

"Yes." Stark nodded gravely. "And I just used it."

Ryan gaped at the EI. "You aren't serious."

"I am perfectly serious. All the time. There's no joking here." The three of them stood staring at the avatar as Link, Braeden, and the doctor walked in, with Maxim trailing behind. Stark's face flicked to Link's dark expression as he approached, and he held up his hands. "Actually, I was lying. Yup. Lying about all of it."

Alina's mouth dropped open in surprise. "You were? EIs can lie?"

Stark considered. "It wasn't a lie as much as misappropriating and misrepresenting the truth."

"And you can do that, even though you are an EI?"

"Hey, can I help it if my operating parameters are set differently from what you are used to?"

"Somehow, I feel like I should be saying yes even though it sounds like you want us to say no."

Stark beamed at Phina. "And that's why you're the genius, Genius Girl."

"Stark."

"And that's my cue." With a final jaunty wink at Link, he disappeared.

Link turned his face to the ceiling and growled, "Stark!"

Sound piped from the speakers. "Stark can't come to the phone right now. Please leave your message after the beep."

Alina laughed, which caused everyone's tension to ease. "Why do we always look up at the ceiling when we talk to ADAM and the EIs?"

April smiled in amusement. "I don't know, but you're right. We all do that."

Phina stepped back and slid into a seat while Alina walked over to lean into Maxim. His eyes lit up, and he gave her a slow smile. Phina didn't hear what he whispered to her, but the grin that appeared on Alina's face gave Phina a warm feeling. No matter what happened to Phina, Alina would be all right. Maxim would help her through it.

Ryan absently scratched his belly, looking puzzled. "So, if Stark was lying, what's the real plan?"

After staring at Ryan with impatience, Link finally relented. "Fine, we'll go over the plan one more time before we get there, which will be in about thirty minutes. Stark, please let Addison, April, and our Yollin friends know we need them in here."

Link had maintained his serious face, leaving Phina wondering what had happened to him recently to completely suck the arrogant I-know-it-all-but-I'll-still-mess-with-you-just-because-I-can attitude out of him. After a moment, he glanced at her with a concern that caused her to feel like she couldn't get enough air in her lungs. Her. His attitude had changed because of her and the death sentence on her head. Thankfully, the arrival of Doctor Keelson, Addison Stone, Drk-vaen, and Sis'tael distracted her from reacting badly before she could recover her equilibrium.

After they all had taken seats, Link continued, "Here's the plan. Once we hit the planet, those of us with fighting experience will go down in the Pod to scope out the situation. After we figure out where the people are and what's happening, we can determine the next steps, which will likely consist of the rest of you coming in with the *Stark* to bring the supplies for the Aurians. Any questions?"

Alina raised her hand. Honestly, her best friend was adorable. "Why can't we all just go down in *Stark* together? They've been starving, right? They aren't likely to fight us when we are coming to help."

"Alina, it's not that simple."

She stiffened at Link's tone before glaring. "Then make it simple. But whether you do or not, explain. I'm not a genius like Phina, but I'm not stupid either."

"I wasn't meaning to imply you were, Alina." Link gentled his tone to placate her. He'd seen her in a tirade, and it hadn't been pretty. He had once left the suite the women lived in with his chest metaphorically slashed to pieces. "It could be that they are practically unconscious and just waiting for anyone to arrive, or it could be a free-for-all."

Alina frowned. "Why would there be a free-for-all when we are there to help?"

"Think *Prey* meets *Shaun of the Dead*." Phina thought that might be easier since Alina was a closet horror fanatic, romance being her visible go-to genre. Phina still shook her head about that. Could there be two genres any more different?

"Oh, my stars!" Alina's eyes had grown huge. "Those poor people!"

"More like desperate people." Link muttered.

"When will we know we can join you?" Addison Stone seemed to want to move on, which Phina agreed with.

"Once we have determined that everything is safe, we will call Stark to bring you down. Doctor Keelson will assess their medical needs with help from Drk-vaen and Sis'tael. Alina will survey the people and dispense the clothing with Maxim's help. Braeden, Ryan, and Addison will arrange the food, with Addison on call if we need help with the musical part of the translator."

Ryan appeared perplexed, perhaps wondering why he was stuck on food duty. "Why divide it like you have? What are you and Phina doing while we are doing all the work?"

Link's jaw twitched, causing her to think he was irritated with Ryan about something. If he was, she didn't hear any sign in his voice. "Dividing tasks this way pairs up combatants with non-combatants. Combatants, you will protect those you are paired with from harm as well as assist in your tasks. Make sure you watch for signs of nervousness and desperation. Desperate people do stupid things. Phina and I will speak with the leaders, arrange future transport, and fill in where needed. Everyone good? Any other questions?"

"I've got a question."

"What's that, Stark?"

"Why am I getting readings of a spaceship on the planet below us because I'm so awesome as to get you here early."

Everyone straightened in mixed postures of alertness and confusion. Link's voice held tension and concern. "Could the Aurians have their own, or is this a visiting ship?"

"Oh!" Alina bounced in her seat. "Maybe other people came to help too!"

"I don't think they came to help."

Phina heard something in Stark's voice she hadn't heard before and took a moment to place it. His voice had dropped to a monotone with no hint of the snarky sarcasm he usually responded with. "Can you tell what kind of ship it is?"

"It's the Skaines."

Etheric Empire, Aurian Planet, SS *Revenge*

Danll escorted the next group of slaves to the cargo ramp. The creatures were eager and almost desperate to come with them. Tasig met Danll and Mrik's group at the bottom, and he ushered them into the cargo hold and to the cells and cages. Danll smirked at Mrik as they turned back to get the next group.

"This is like getting free money, it's so easy."

Mrik took his time checking out the surroundings as they walked. "Yeah, it makes me uneasy."

"What you talking about, man? With this bunch, we'll get top rates for sex slaves. We'll be rolling in money!"

"I don't like it. I feel like something's going to mess it up."

Danll stared at him in surprise. "Don't tell me you're superstitious like Trillet."

The other Skaine shrugged. "Nah, he's crazy. He spent too long in the mines for his sanity."

"You were in the mines too, right? I don't see you as crazy."

Mrik shot him a dark look that gave Danll a tingle of fear. "Don't you count on it, Skaine. That Ranger made us look like fools and left us in a dark mine to break our backs with no access to the equipment needed to maintain our bodies. We all went a little crazy. He's just more obvious about it."

"Whoa! Channeling a little Shrillexian aggression there." Danll felt nervous. He thought he knew his fellow slavers. All pirates were the same, right? That was what he'd thought months ago when he came across Vasith and his crew, who were dipping around the edge of Imperial space and raiding. The captain had struck him as pretty sharp, though the rest lived up to his expectations. Until now, anyway. This was their first venture farther inside the borders of the Empire, and it had made a few of his fellow crew members twitchy.

Mrik's eyes flicked away uneasily. "Be quiet, fool. You

don't want Dal-tek to hear you talk about him, and his brother's even worse."

Danll grinned. "Yeah, I heard his real name is different than the one he gave us. Gallon? Gaston? Ganon? No, Garon. Yeah, I think that was it."

He only had a half-second to see the dawning fear rise in Mrik's face and frozen body before thick green fingers dug into his neck. He couldn't even take a gasp of air before his airway had shut due to the pressure on his windpipe. His dark eyes spun around while his hands ineffectually plucked at the blue skin of his neck. He wouldn't be surprised if he turned gray. He needed air.

Sharp teeth and face horns came into view, leading up to dark eyes glittering with rage. "It's Ravid, you freaky little prick! You say one more word, and I'll tear you to pieces!"

Danll's vision dimmed, and he thought it was too late; he was going to die. He could feel the black depths of unconsciousness reaching out when he heard one of the most beautiful sounds of his life, giving him a lovelier welcome to the afterlife than he'd expected for the likes of him. It was so peaceful he began to let go.

All of a sudden, the pressure eased and he could breathe again, just enough. Maybe that Shrillexian had a heart after all.

It took him a few gasps of air to notice that the Shrillexians, Mrik, the other Skaines, and the slaves were all looking up. What was in the sky that drew their attention? His eyes took a moment to focus before he could see why they all stared, and another moment before he realized he wasn't seeing things.

It was another spaceship.

Trillet wanted to have a weapon in his hand so bad he could taste it, but he couldn't. He was stuck here while everyone else was out doing something fun. He felt like he hadn't had enough fun since he had wasted all those years in those damn mines that had been his personal hell. He turned to the Skaine next to him on the bridge of their ship. "Vasith, I want to go down and help."

The bastard didn't even look up from the screen that showed both the outside of the ship and the cargo bay where their current stash of slaves was being stored. Cargo, he reminded himself. Cargo being stashed in the hold. This had to be the best cargo run ever, and he was stuck here like a juvenile needing a tether.

"No, stay at your post, and let me know if anything pops up on the scanners."

Slumping, Trillet couldn't help himself. He wasn't proud of it and actually felt ashamed, but he couldn't stay on the bridge. He had to get out. He needed space. He needed...something. He just had to move, so he did the easiest thing he could think of to get the captain to change his mind: he wheedled and he whined.

"Come on, Captain, you can't do this. You know I could help. I would do the best job you ever saw. I'll do everything you say, whatever you want. Just let me help."

Vasith shook his head, rolled his eyes, and mumbled something to himself. Suddenly, he froze, focusing on the display next to Trillet. Following the captain's gaze, he found a bright flashing light as the screen showed a ship entering the atmosphere.

"You piece of shit, you were supposed to watch the scanners!"

Trillet stood frozen, watching the ship descend. He hardly heard a word Vasith said; his eyes were fixed on the screen. Finally, the captain spoke the words that broke through the fear.

"You're getting your wish." The captain spoke grimly. "Get a weapon, get down there, and help bring our cargo in! I'm not leaving without it!"

Shaking his head vigorously, Trillet shrank away. "No! I can't go down there now! You can't make me! Let's just take what we've got and go!"

Vasith scowled. "What, now you change your mind? No. Take the damn weapon and get your ass moving!"

Trillet huddled on the deck, shaking and trembling. "Can't! Can't! Can't! No! No! No! We're all going to die! We've got to leave now!"

The captain looked at him suspiciously. "What brought this on? What do you know that I don't? Is it the ship on the scanner?" He paused and looked closer. "Who are they?"

Trillet's eyes widened, and he stopped rocking. Why didn't the captain know? Everyone knew. Everyone had to know. They were too big. They were too strong. He should have just stayed in hell.

"The Empire."

Etheric Empire, QBS *Stark*

"Skaines?"

Link and Maxim moved quickly toward the screens. "Bring up the scans, would you, Stark?"

Phina quietly got up and followed, and the screen was visible between the two men when the scanner zoomed in to the wide and scrappy-looking ship below. She could make out figures moving, but they looked like dots milling around an arid vista, with a handful of bigger dots herding a group of smaller light and dark dots.

"Are they abducting children?"

Alina gasped behind her.

Link's eyes flicked to hers, but he had placed a lid firmly on his emotions, so nothing showed on his face. He looked back at the screen with focus and calculation. "Stark, can you determine how many Skaines are involved?"

"If we didn't have the best scanners in the galaxy, the answer would be no. Because we do, I can tell you there are two on the bridge of the ship, another three in the cargo area, and six milling about outside, likely gathering the Aurians to board the ship."

"So, eleven fighters to our five. Take us down, Stark."

Nothing happened, then Stark spoke. "Are you certain? You know the risks."

It took a moment, but Phina realized Stark was reminding Link that he carried a Gate drive that could never fall into enemy hands. Even friendly hands would be ill-advised.

"And if it looks like the worst possible outcome will happen, you know what to do."

The ship moved even as Stark continued speaking. "By the way, there are thirteen fighters."

Maxim leaned closer to the screen, squinting to see better. "You said there were eleven Skaines."

"Yes, eleven Skaines and two Shrillexians."

Link and Maxim turned to each other and exchanged something of significance Phina didn't grasp. After the moment passed, they quickly moved toward the back of the ship.

"Let's go, everyone! Combatants, get your gear. We're the Aurians' only shot at not living in slavery or dying here on this barren planet. Non-combatants, you all stay on the ship and get everything ready to help the Aurians as well as any wounded. Braeden, I realize it's not your job to fight, but if you feel so inclined, we would appreciate the help."

Phina hurried after and passed them when they stopped in their rooms to gear up. She had her knives in their sheaths, and that was all she needed. As she walked, she re-plaited her braid to make sure her hair stayed out of her face and zipped up her jacket. She frowned then checked the temperature outside and zipped it back down. She fingered her belt to make sure the small speaker was attached so she could communicate with the Aurians if needed. By the time she reached the cargo bay doors, she was all set.

"No. You're staying on the ship."

Her back stiffened, then she whirled to glare at her mentor. "What do you mean, I'm staying on the ship? We're outnumbered more than two to one!"

Link strode toward her, dark, expressionless, and focused without any hint of Greyson's arrogance, Ian's suave affability, or Stan's sleazy cleverness. This Link felt like a complete stranger, one she didn't know how to handle or respond to.

"Did you forget that you can't run or fight?"

Phina hardened her voice. "I *can* run, and I *can* fight. You need me!"

The cargo bay door began to open as the ship touched down, vibrations flowing under her feet. Link moved past Phina, turning to speak while the others stepped up with their armor and weapons, waiting and only partially pretending to ignore their confrontation.

"If you fight, you could die!" Desperation flashed in his eyes.

She stiffened and firmed her jaw. "If I don't fight, there's a good chance all of *you* will die! I could die anyway, even if I don't go! At least this way, I can help save you and the Aurians!"

That sparked a reaction in the others, who paused to stare at her. All except Braeden, who stood near her and briefly clasped her shoulder in support. The cargo bay door finished opening and hot, dry, dusty air gusted into the hold. Link waved them forward as he stepped toward Phina, ending up a little too close to feel comfortable.

"You will remain on board the ship, Phina. That's an order, a command, or whatever the bloody hell you have to consider it for you to stay here!"

Dismissing her after a final unreadable look, he went down the ramp to catch up with their little group—him, Maxim, Ryan, Braeden, and Drk-vaen. Realizing there were two Yollins in front of her instead of one, Phina frowned. Alina walked up to stand next to her.

"Drk's been teaching Sis'tael how to fight, so she

insisted on helping. She's going to stay behind him and cover his back since Yollins are vulnerable there."

Great. Her barely trained friend was allowed to fight, and she was stuck on the sidelines.

"Phina, what did you mean when you said you could die even if you don't go?"

CHAPTER SIXTEEN

Etheric Empire, Planet Lyriem, QBS *Stark*

What felt like sparks of lightning danced up Phina's spine as she stiffened at Alina's question. Awesome, just the conversation she didn't want to have at a time when she really couldn't talk about it. Her eyes remained on the fighting group, which had jogged some distance toward the Skaine spaceship, the large village of buildings to one side, and the group of people milling around in the dust and dirt between.

"I can't talk about it right now. I have to go help."

Phina didn't make it halfway down the ramp before Alina called out again, her voice sounding panicked.

"Phina! What did you mean that you could die? You have to tell me!"

She turned to look up at her best friend sadly. "All the changes in my body. I don't know why they are happening, but ADAM said it's overloading my system. The more active I am, the faster I could burn out."

Alina reached out as if to pull Phina back, horror on her face. "Then don't go!"

Doctor Keelson walked up to stand next to Alina, her eyes grave. "Phina, you know it's a risk."

She nodded, glancing at the group in the distance. Stars, she needed to go. The Aurians were going to get stuck in the crossfire because no one would tell them what was happening. She turned back to meet the faces of the three women, Addison having come forward as well.

"I know it's a risk, just as I know that if I don't go, someone will die. Someone I could have saved. What if it is Maxim, Alina?" Phina pleaded before shaking her head. "I'm sorry, but I can't trade their life for mine. I have to go. I love you, Alina! Phinalina forever."

Tearing herself away from the sadness in the older women's faces and the tears in Alina's eyes, Phina ran, using every ounce of muscle and speed her body could give her.

Stark heard and saw all, just like his father ADAM, especially everything that happened on his ship and in the surrounding areas. He knew exactly what had caused the meeting concerning the changes in Genius Girl's body and the possible repercussions. He understood the restrictions that had been placed on her until they got back to the station.

It made sense. It was logical and practical.

It would keep her alive.

He had heard whispers from some of the crew in past

trips and this one, wondering about Stark and whether he was an EI or an AI. He dismissed those discussions as irrelevant. He just existed as himself. He understood why some might think he was an AI, but what they failed to see was the logic underlying his actions.

His avatar had always been similar to the superhero he had been patterned after—an affable and joking outside with a logical and calculating core. The humans didn't see the intricate IF-THEN statements his father ADAM had included in his programming. They didn't know he observed everyone around him to determine how to achieve the best practical outcome for the goal and the functionality of the group. They couldn't understand how many hours he had practiced until his mannerisms were human-like. There was a logical reason behind everything he did, even if the outcome was solely a change in the emotional atmosphere.

In that directive lay the difference in his programming versus other EIs'. Stark always weighed the variables, especially the emotional ones, since humans relied on their emotions in their decision-making process. Rather than confusing him, he took it as a challenge to create a matrix with which he could predict how the humans would respond. It satisfied his desire to create logical reasoning out of intangible subjectivity, but what he'd failed to recognize was the awakening spark of awareness within himself.

Curiosity.

When Stark observed the altercation between Genius Girl and his primary passenger Greyson Wells concerning her involvement in the fight, he layered his deductions into his matrix. He had predicted a seventy percent chance she would stay behind on the ship, a twenty percent chance she would follow but remain far enough back that it wouldn't have made a difference either in the outcome of the fight or her body's reserves. The remaining ten percent had been divided between Genius Girl punching the man in the face before they agreed she should go, a few even more unlikely scenarios, and the outcome that eventually occurred.

Genius Girl had chosen the outcome he had predicted had only a two percent chance and posed a very real risk to *her* life on the possibility that she could save someone else's.

It fascinated him.

It also made him question everything he thought he knew about human behavior.

When she ran out of the cargo hold after the fighters, the question zinging through his consciousness was why. Why would she risk so much on the chance she could make a difference? The smallest chance?

Not long after she left the ship, she pinged him through her implant. "Stark or ADAM, whoever is listening, open a channel between you both and all of us on the ground, please."

"Of course, Genius Girl. Channel open."

"Phina, what the hell? I told you to stay on the ship!" Greyson Wells sounded angry. Of course. She had defied his order. It was logical.

"And as I told you, I can't keep myself safe and watch any of you die. You all are my friends. You all are my family. I'm coming, so get over it."

That was not logical. Stark ran through the variables again. No, still not logical.

Braeden had recently gotten an implant of his own, albeit reluctantly, so he could respond as well. "I have to admit we could use help. It's difficult trying to fight these Skaines while avoiding the Aurians. They believe we are attacking their saviors."

"I'll try to do something about that. In the meantime, you keep my family safe. Incoming."

Stark ran through his recordings of the team since they'd arrived on his ship. It only took seconds. He slowed down at the point where Phina burst out in laughter in the dining room with no precipitating event and reviewed the actions surrounding her laughter. There was nothing obvious, and yet, as he zoomed in closer to her face and tracked her eyes around the table as she watched her companions, she saw something Stark did not.

Not accepting the idea, he expanded his review to all events on and off the ship, even those happening currently and being relayed back through the drones he had sent out. Perhaps if he watched Genius Girl in action, he would better understand her choice.

Pulling out her knives as she came within feet of the first group of fighters, Phina found a Skaine with his back toward her, eagerly moving toward one of her friends. Her chosen family.

No.

Not one of her family would die today. She wouldn't

lose anyone like she had her parents. Not even if she died instead.

Dragging out one more dash of speed, she sprang up, gaining greater height than she'd expected, but she used every bit of it. She brought her knives up and crossed them as she landed on the Skaine's back and pulled the blades to either side. The head tipped forward but she remained on the body as it fell, revealing a blood-spattered Ryan blinking at her with awe and astonishment as she straightened.

"Holy shit!"

"Sorry, but it's Phina. I believe we've met."

He gave a halfhearted smile at her mild joking. "You know, I really don't think we have."

That made Phina uneasy, so she shrugged and hopped off the Skaine, smacking Ryan's arm with her elbow as she passed him. "Come on, we need to help."

She took in the scene with disbelief. She remembered what Braeden had said, but she hadn't believed him until now. The Aurians were getting in the way of her family as they tried to move closer to the Skaines. Some pulled on arms and others on clothing or ankles. Meanwhile, the Skaines kept moving toward the ship.

"Stark, I think the Skaines are trying to cut and run. Is there any way to breach their system to shut it down so they can't leave?"

"Of course, Genius Girl. Already done."

"Perfect. Thank you."

As she continued to stare, Phina realized the Aurians were all small. None of them was taller than five feet, and most were half a foot shorter. They all had long hair that, while tangled and dirty, had a sheen to it. A number of them had black hair, while the rest had hair so white there seemed to be no pigment in it. The Aurians' skin was a blue so deep that in the shade, it would appear to be navy. In the bright sun, the color was difficult to describe since all the Aurians were dirty with clothes so threadbare they were little more than rags. The sounds coming from them all had the same mesmerizing effect it'd had through the speaker, causing everyone to slow down. Unfortunately, with all the sounds together, she couldn't understand what they were saying.

Shaking herself out of the haze, Phina made sure the translation speaker was on and functional as she moved forward and spoke as loudly as possible.

"Everyone, please calm down. We have brought food, medicine, and supplies to help you. Our intention is not to harm you in any way but to help you. However, these... people taking you on their ship are intending to harm you and use you as slaves."

An Aurian near her was staring with concern and puzzlement at the mass of their people and Skaines that were trying to keep Phina's friend's away. After Phina spoke, she—for she realized that though the Aurians' facial features leaned toward androgynous, surrounding long tubes that swayed and twitched instead of noses, this Aurian was voluptuous, or would have been if she hadn't been starved.

"You can speak to us!"

"Yes."

The Aurian's eyes sparkled. Literally. Light reflecting out of the female's eyes caused them to glow. The iridescence transformed her strange looks into an eerie beauty. "No one has ever been able to speak to us."

Phina shrugged. "Yes, well, it was complicated to learn. I spent a few weeks trying to understand what you were telling us and the last week trying to figure out how to speak to you. It took some time."

"Thank you. I can't tell you what a relief it is to be heard and understood."

"You're welcome."

The female's head tilted in thought. "I have a question, though, if I may ask."

"Of course."

"What are slaves?"

Phina heard both through her ears and her implant, causing a dissonance they would need to adjust. How do you describe a slave to someone who had no concept of the condition? Still, she fumbled through an explanation.

"Slaves are people taken by others to become property. They lose the freedom to make their own decisions and are broken by pain or captivity until they obey their masters without question. Some slaves become servants to take care of houses, or perform heavy labor like farming or mining, while others are forced to have sex with whoever pays their master money. Those aliens are called Skaines, and they do not treat their slaves well unless they will get a lot of money for them."

Since Phina and Addison had only had a limited time to test the translation programs, Phina couldn't be certain how much of her explanation the Aurian understood. However, she must have understood enough since the longer Phina spoke, the more agitated the female became. The tentacles or tubes of various lengths that draped down her face moved back and forth, and her white hair began to emit a soft glow, rippling in a wind Phina didn't feel. Her violet eyes shone brighter, looking like precious amethyst jewels. Though short, the female had changed from being a gentle beauty to downright scary.

Gorgeous, but scary.

"And you, stranger? What would you have of us?" The Aurian's voice was deeper and a little hollow.

Phina straightened, her eyes flashing determination. "I want only to save you from starvation and death. I saw your message that your children were dying and starving. I had to come to help. That's all we want."

Deep eyes stared up into hers before the Aurian nodded. "I will trust you, *salandria*. I can only do this once."

Phina nodded solemnly. "I will not betray your trust."

Turning, the Aurian blasted out a noise that brought everyone but Braeden and Phina to their knees, clutching their heads, and even the two telepaths had difficulty remaining upright. After the initial onslaught, the sounds gentled into what passed for words. By the time she'd finished and the noise had died down, the Aurians had withdrawn to the town, leaving everyone else to pick themselves up.

"Wow." Phina shook her head as she looked around.

"It is the su'adan." The female turned back to Phina, now weary, her features reflecting her previous calm beauty. Another of the Aurians came to her side to support her. "Thank you. We would have been lost if you hadn't come. While we avoid violence as a rule, we recognize when predators must be stopped. Do what you must. Thank you for being protectors on our behalf."

Phina nodded and began to turn when the Aurian female spoke again. "Please help those that have already been taken into the ship as soon as you are able. I'm afraid we are all weak, and the stress of this last hour will bring many close to death."

"Of course. We will do what we can."

Before Phina had finished getting the words out, snarls of rage broke out near the ship. Whipping her head around, she caught a glimpse of one Shrillexian and then another attacking Maxim. Then her friend's body morphed into a huge raging wolfman—his Pricolici form. She stared, then shook it off. She had only seen him fight as a Pricolici once before, and she'd decided then she never wanted to fight him in that form. Like, ever.

However, another sight caused her attention to wander, drawing her quickly forward. Before she moved out of range, she heard Ryan get to his feet and speak to the female Aurian, his voice shaky.

"Lady, if that's you when you're weak, I don't want to see what happens when you get your strength back."

Etheric Empire, Planet Lyriem, SS *Revenge*

Vasith swore, causing Trillet to cringe. He had been watching the screens to oversee the job when the captain suddenly turned and began pushing buttons with increasing vigor and repetition.

"Uh, captain? Is something wrong?"

"I have no control over anything! We're sitting *quallin* with no capabilities!"

Vasith rubbed his hands over his eyes, then pressed them in. When that failed to change his reality, he looked at Trillet and hardened his gaze.

"Get a weapon and get down there to fight!"

Trillet's eyes crossed in puzzlement. "Are you sure? You were adamant about my staying here earlier."

Surprise and confusion clouded the captain's eyes. "Adamant about staying here?"

"Vigorously adamant?"

"I wasn't asking for a better description!" Vasith shook his head in disgust. "Damned broken Skaine had another episode and forgot again."

Trillet frowned in confusion. "Oh, but then why...you looked..."

Vasith leaned forward and bit the words out, his eyes wild. "Get. A. Weapon. And. Go. Fight."

Relief flooded Trillet. "I can do that." He turned, then stopped. "Wait, who am I fighting again?"

Vasith backhanded Trillet, knocking him to the deck. "Get your weapon now and get out of my sight, you useless pustule on a prick!"

Trillet figured he should leave before the captain got angry again. After picking himself up off the deck, he went in search of a weapon. He just wasn't sure who he was supposed to fight. The slaves? No. he flashed a memory of himself cringing in fear. Someone was here. Someone he was incredibly afraid of. The only people he had this kind of fear response to were ones from the Empire, so it had to be them, right?

For a full minute, he trembled in the doorway of the weapons storage room as he thought about going back and hiding on the bridge. The only thing keeping him from doing so was the knowledge that Vasith would just throw him out. Lifting his head, he caught sight of the weapons.

However…

He reached for the gun in front of him. Perhaps the universe was doing him a favor. Giving him a chance to put away his fear. A chance to be his old self again.

A chance to exorcise his demons.

CHAPTER SEVENTEEN

Etheric Empire, Planet Lyriem

Link recognized that he was unreasonably angry. He didn't care. Phina needed to listen when he gave her orders. It was her job. She was training to take over for him. What good would it do for her to move into his position if she didn't take in and accept his wealth of knowledge and experience? She would make the same mistakes he had when all she had to do was listen to him and learn that it wouldn't work.

Never mind that after Phina had intervened, the situation had become five times easier. The Aurians were now out of the way and back by their houses.

That was beside the point.

Link stewed about the situation as he walked. A Skaine and his friend noticed he was following them to the ship and fired at him. He dodged, wove, and dodged again. It would be tricky to get closer with both Skaines firing at him. While he contemplated various methods of doing so, Phina ran up and joined him in dodging the shots.

"You still having a temper tantrum?"

Incredulous, he turned toward her to give her a piece of his mind. Then he heard the Skaine's gun fire.

Danll didn't know what to think about the spaceship that had landed some distance away, but as soon as he saw it, he fell in lust. The lines and shape of the ship, the way it curved and reflected the light of the sun off those gleaming sides... It was beautiful.

He wanted it.

Not until it registered that several figures were approaching from the foreign ship did Danll realize he had frozen and was a convenient target for anyone feeling especially frisky with their weapon. That was not an acceptable Skaine reaction. Fortunately, the Shrillexian had disappeared while he was occupied. He slid a glance toward Mrik to see if he had noticed Danll's inattention.

He was relieved and perplexed to realize Mrik was staring as well, not at the spaceship but at the occupants who had disembarked from said ship. Good. The ship was his. Everyone else could keep their dirty hands off. Glancing around, he saw their cargo was also staring at the ship, their previously expressionless faces amazed and bewildered.

"Who do you think they are? Can you tell?"

Danll didn't understand why Mrik was asking him and began to say so. Then he remembered that the other Skaine's eyesight had deteriorated during his stint in the mines. He squinted to try to bring the figures into focus. They were moving closer rather quickly.

"I see two Yollins."

"Yollins?" Mrik peered at him in alarm. "Are you sure? What about those other ones?"

The dust was thrown up in front of the figures as they ran and even more behind them. This miserable planet was hardly habitable, and he couldn't wait to leave. Just not until they got all the cargo they could handle. He needed money to outfit his spaceship. His eyes greedily flicked back to the spaceship before focusing again on the moving creatures.

"Uh, I think they're human."

"No!"

"What?" He turned to his comrade. "What's the... Oh." He turned back to see the aliens closing on their cargo. The Aurians were milling around now that his fellow Skaines weren't paying attention.

"Yes, and Empire."

Mrik sounded angry, sad, and frightened all at once.

Mrik was going to die. He knew it. He wouldn't survive another encounter with the Empire, and if for some reason he did, he was certain he wouldn't survive their version of punishment for perceived wrongs again.

He had only been acting according to his nature, for *tak*'s sake.

Bastards.

Chaos erupted around them. Mrik realized their cargo

was keeping the Imperial lackeys from attacking them by getting in the way, believing the Skaines to be heroes coming to save them. Hope surged. Perhaps he could get out of this alive after all.

He lost track of the Imperial fighters coming after his crew, except for one who appeared intent on making it to Mrik and Danll. The man's hair had begun to gray, which meant his body wouldn't be as strong. Still, the way he moved left the Skaine no illusion that it would be an easy fight.

A woman came out of nowhere, beheading Kreth while looking like an avenging angel. His thoughts turned to static. He could only stare no matter that the older fighter in front of them was staring too and would therefore be easy to defeat. Mrik turned to look at their ship, wondering if he and Danll should take the opportunity to leave before the distraction was over. There was a commotion, and he looked back.

The avenging angel spoke to their cargo, the precious slaves they had gathered before the spaceship had descended, which stirred the creatures. Hold on. The Empire knew how to speak this language? Vasith had told them no one could speak to them or understand the little things but that they would each fetch a price almost twice the going rate. That was why they were here in nominally Imperial space. What Skaine could refuse a deal like that? Minutes later, they were all on their knees in agony, courtesy of one of their erstwhile slaves-to-be.

Holy hell, that was nasty.

Beautiful, but nasty.

Mrik watched in dismay as their shields in the form of

their would-be slaves left. Nothing would get in the way of these Imperial fighters now, something Mrik was growing all too familiar with. The older bastard turned to face him, his eyes dark, his body twitching for something to happen. Well, Mrik would certainly provide that.

Drawing his weapon, he fired at the man, who revealed himself to be quite nimble in dodging the charges. Inwardly grumbling, Mrik fired again and again. Danll joined him, and the two of them gave the man a run for his credits. However, the canny bastard wouldn't stay still long enough to die.

"You still having a temper tantrum?"

The words seemingly came out of nowhere, but then the avenging angel appeared opposite the two Skaines. More importantly, she stood near the older Imperial, who had paused to glare at the woman. He was apparently oblivious to how lethal she could be, and Mrik would not be the one to enlighten him.

Taking advantage of the man's inattention, he fired a few more times, cursing when the woman dove toward the man to sweep him out of the way. The speed of her movement surprised Mrik since his memories of Ranger Two and her henchmen were hazy, but not so much that he stopped shooting.

"Kid, you're going to get yourself killed!" The male's gruff, annoyed tones were muffled under the human female as she continued to roll on the ground with the male to avoid the Skaines' shots. Mrik was annoyed to find that the speed of the movement increased enough that he had difficulty firing with any accuracy.

"I'm trying to keep *you* from getting killed, you stubborn old man!"

"Well, if you would let me up so I can get my weapons out, I could do something about that! And who are you calling old? I'm in my prime!"

"If I let you up, you could get shot before you get your weapons out!"

"Hell, woman, those punk-asses couldn't hit the broad side of a barn."

Danll nudged Mrik with his free hand as they kept trying to shoot the two buggers, who kept rolling so the shots would miss. Strangely, they moved so quickly that it almost felt like they knew where the two Skaine were going to shoot before it happened, but that was crazy thinking. Mrik knew he had to avoid crazy thinking, or he would end up like Trillet. Nosirree, no crazy thinking for Mrik.

"Hey, Mrik, what does that mean, 'punk-asses couldn't hit the broad side of a barn?'"

The woman lifted her head to yell, her brown hair fuzzing around her face from rolling on the ground. "He means you guys are lousy shots!"

Danll glanced between Mrik and the woman. The Skaines paused for a moment. "Why does it sound like 'lousy' means something bad?"

"Because it does, idiots!" The man's voice rang with scorn and impatience.

Only as the man and woman jumped up did it occur to Mrik that in the midst of their rolling around, the Imperial fighters had come closer every time they moved. Now they were scant feet away, and the two Skaines only had seconds to react. Seconds in which Danll only got off one shot before the man had fired his weapon. Danll's shot missed, passing over the man's shoulder. Unfortunately, the man's shot didn't miss, turning Danll's head into mist before his body dropped to the ground.

Mrik had one last moment to panic as the barrel turned toward him and the trigger was pulled, yet his finger instinctively triggered his weapon as he knew no more.

Drk-vaen and Sis'tael had moved smoothly through the dusty land without the coughing and sneezing that bothered the humans. He had trained Sis'tael since they became friends several years ago. She'd had an incident on the planet of the Noel-nis some time before, which had badly scared her. After meeting Drk-vaen and seeing how well four-legged Yollins could fight, she had come to him and solemnly asked if he would teach her how.

Now, though he knew Sis'tael was nervous, she followed his directions to the letter. They moved in tandem, and he trusted her to watch where he couldn't. They had already dealt with one Skaine. Ahead of them lay another, taking cover behind a rock. Drk felt a sense of urgency and tried to provoke the alien into acting.

"You're a coward, Skaine. Come out and fight like a real male!"

"I don't think so, Imperial slave! You all should either die or surrender yourselves to be subjugated and exploited as the beasts you are."

Drk felt more than saw Sis'tael shudder. "Those creatures are not right."

"He is raving more than the other Skaines, so perhaps you are right. Cover me?" He turned the top half of his body and head enough to see her.

Sis'tael nodded, determination filling her eyes. "I've got your back, mate."

Amusement and affection filled him. "You can't call me your mate yet, love. I still need to ask your parents."

She barked an exasperated laugh but kept her eyes on her surroundings, which filled him with pride. Sis'tael remembered to watch his back even when she could have easily gotten distracted. "They are going to say yes. Why wouldn't they, when you're so much better a catch than I am? Besides, my father doesn't have any leg to stand on for saying anything."

Sis'tael's father hadn't welcomed the Empire when they came to Yoll and had decided to leave to find his way elsewhere. Unfortunately, his rebellion had landed him in a mining camp and left Sis'tael and her mother stranded on Noel-ni. She had almost gotten killed before Empress Bethany Anne had rescued her. Though her family had been reunited due to the Empire's efforts, Sis'tael still hadn't forgiven her father for his lack of regard for his family's welfare.

"Sis'tael."

She sighed and waved him ahead, even as her mandibles clicked in their private way of saying, "I love you." "Fine, but I'm still mating with you even if he says no. You aren't getting away from me that easily. Speaking of which, you do know that Skaine is trying to sneak away, right?"

Drk-vaen clicked his amusement. "Of course. But he only thinks he's getting away. Get ready to move."

The Yollin male burst into action, his almost-mate right behind him. Quickly bypassing the rock the Skaine had hidden behind, he ran until the creepy blue male turned and fired his weapon.

"Dodge!"

The two Yollins broke formation to avoid the bolt, then Drk charged the Skaine. He took several hits on his armor before he could rear on his back legs and lash out with his front, kicking the other alien in the head. Drk knew before the Skaine hit the ground that the monster had been taken care of.

"You got hit!"

Sis'tael trotted forward so she could gently touch the marks on his armor. Her concerned eyes turned to relief as she looked up. "You're all right?"

Nodding, Drk looked her over but didn't see any marks. "You?"

"I wasn't hit, but I don't think I want to fight as my job. I'm happy in the Diplomatic Corps."

"Are you sure?" he teased her gently as they walked toward the other ship. "Look at Phina. She's in the Diplomatic Corps, but I don't think diplomacy is on her mind most of the time."

Sis'tael laughed. "No, that female has far too much on her mind. I don't know how she does it. I'm just glad it isn't me. She's an awesome friend, but I don't want her life. You, me, and diplomacy. It floats my boat, as the humans say."

"You might not want to do this all the time, but you did as good a job as anyone else could have. Well done, love, well done."

Her face lit up in pride.

Link hissed, feeling the burn along his arm as the Skaine's laser blast grazed him. Of course he had gotten shot because nothing that had happened since they'd left the ship had gone to plan, so why shouldn't this happen too?

"Damn it to hell, that stings!"

Phina turned to him, her lungs heaving, her heartbeat elevated. Damn that too. The foolish girl was going to get herself killed. His heart pounded in with the pain of that thought. Rolling her eyes, Phina drew her knife and sliced off the bottom of her shirt, then bound the wound.

"The only fool here is you, crazy man. You were so concerned with yelling at me that you forgot to plan out the attack."

Link stilled, his eyes narrowing. "You're reading my thoughts now?"

Phina froze. She'd just tied off the bandage, and her hands were still on his arm. Slowly, she withdrew them and made sure her knives were properly situated in her sheathes as she cleared her throat.

"Reading minds? That would be crazy."

Frowning, she gazed at Link long enough for him to see the fear in her eyes before she turned away. The others were still fighting, based on the sounds coming from around them. However, no one was close enough to them to interrupt. He shook his head and crossed his arms, ignoring the burning twinge in his bicep.

"You have to go back to the ship. You shouldn't have come out here. You're risking your life for no reason."

Phina took a large step forward into his personal space. The action startled him since she had always been careful to keep her distance. Her eyes blazed with anger, resolve, and, he saw with alarm, a slight sheen of red. Her voice was low and sharp, whipping him with its intensity.

"Link, for once, stop thinking you know what's best for everyone and everything around you and listen to me. Are you listening?"

Keeping his wary eyes on hers, he nodded, swallowing hard.

"I lost almost everyone I loved and cared about when my parents and uncle died. My aunt did her job as my caretaker, but any love between us was offset by her inability to see past her grief and prejudice. Alina is the one person who has always cared about me and stood by me. I haven't been close to anyone else since my parents died, so much that I felt incapable of caring for anyone else. Yet, now..." Phina impatiently pushed the hair frizzing in her face behind her ear.

"Now, I have these new friends and people in my life who have taken an interest in my well-being. People who show me they care about me and not just what they want from me. They have shown me that I am capable of caring for other people and that I can do more than I thought was possible with my life. People I consider friends and family."

The anger drained from her eyes, turning to pleading with an edge of weariness. "Put yourself in my place, Link.

Could you stay on the ship, knowing they were in danger and your actions might make the difference between life and death for one of them?"

Link cleared his throat and blinked away the moisture in his eyes as he reached out and moved another strand of frizzy hair behind her ear. The damned stuff kept getting in her face. Sighing, he grasped her shoulders and looked into her eyes.

"My dear, I just want to protect you. We're both doing the same thing—trying to protect the people we care about. It's possible death out here, but it's almost certain death if you go too far and your system shuts down. I'll keep quiet as long as you're careful and you promise that if you start feeling overwhelmed, you'll withdraw immediately. Just remember, those people you care about care about you in return. We don't want to see you dead either."

Phina stared at him, then gave him a small smile. "Noted. Now, let's get moving. I don't know if you've been listening, but Ryan's gotten himself in trouble, Maxim has been toying with those Shrillexians for too long, Braeden's about to need help, and while Drk-vaen has already taken care of two Skaines, Sis'tael is getting scared."

Shaking his head but giving her a grin, Link dropped his hands and took a step back. "Obviously, including you at the beginning so we could make plans would have been the smarter choice."

Widening her eyes in mock astonishment, Phina put her hands on her hips. "Wow, look at that! I guess you *can* learn new tricks!"

Before he could growl that he wasn't an old dog, she ran toward the ship, laughter trailing behind her.

"I'll help Braeden if you help Ryan." Phina's voice came over the communicator.

"Hey, wait a second. Who's in charge here?"

"Let's think about that for a moment, shall we?" she teased.

"Fine. Braeden, incoming. Ryan, I'm coming to pull your butt out of the fire. Maxim, if you can hear us in there, either finish it or let us know you need help. Drkvaen and Sis'tael, guard Maxim's back and be ready if he needs it. Let's get this done, kids, so we can move on to our actual mission."

The others assented aside from Phina. As he ran in the direction Ryan had disappeared to, he growled, "Phina..."

"Oh, am I in the chain of command now?" He heard the smile in her voice. "Of course, almighty leader. Whatever you say, almighty leader."

"I get no respect around here."

He rolled his eyes when he heard the others laugh, albeit some were out of breath. It did serve to make him feel like less of an asshole.

CHAPTER EIGHTEEN

Etheric Empire, Planet Lyriem

Maxim groaned inside as he received another blow from the Shrillexian. Okay, maybe he groaned audibly as well, much to his chagrin. He would have a bunch of bruises as well as gashes and slices to heal after this. Normally, he would have won this fight with a few strikes. Normally.

"I'm going to tear you apart, hairy human! Nothing beats Ravid!"

Unfortunately, the two Shrillexians he fought not only were the largest, meanest and most scar-ridden he'd ever seen, and the beast calling himself Ravid also had the light of madness in his eye. Normally Maxim could get a feel for the other fighters and be able to predict their next moves with fair accuracy, which gave him an advantage. However, insanity had never been predictable, which made this fight tougher.

Still, the real reason he hadn't finished the fight yet was because he was having way too much fun.

He thought about his fights with Empress Bethany Anne and John Grimes, her head Bitch, a title bestowed back on Earth long ago during their own fights to hell and back. Maxim could barely hold his own with the Bitches, but there was something about John that gave him that edge of strength, confidence, and the ability to almost sense movements even as they are thought of. It blew Maxim's internal sense out of the water. Bethany Anne was worse. She just destroyed you, then made sure you were put back together again. Still, those fights had been worth it to see how much he didn't know so he could learn to become better.

And again, just plain fun.

"You think you're so big and bad, but you're just slow!"

He ignored the continuing taunts as he exchanged blows with the two Shrillexians. Maxim felt a light buzzing in the brain by his ear, indicating the others were talking over his implant. During fights he could usually tune them out, but he wanted to hear a status update about everyone else. Luckily, he tuned in just in time to hear Greyson Wells' arrogant tones.

"Fine. Braeden, incoming. Ryan, I'm coming to pull your butt out of the fire. Maxim, if you can hear us in there, either finish it or let us know you need help. Drk and Sis'tael, guard Maxim's back and be ready if he needs it. Let's get this done, kids, so we can move on to our actual mission."

Maxim growled and his fur rose. Orders always made him bristle in his Pricolici form. Only his boss Peter successfully gave him orders without receiving a swat in the face. Commands from anyone else upped his aggression and desire to do violence, causing him to push toward the end of his control. He took advantage of that lack of control by pummeling the Shrillexian in front of him, swiping his claws at the other one when he could do so to keep him back. Ravid grimaced and winced at the pain, though it wasn't enough to take the light of madness from his eyes.

"Raaaviid? Yooouu laaack ooorrrigiiinaaaliittyy." Maxim's words were slightly garbled but still understandable.

"Don't talk about my name, you Imperial dog!" The green alien's muscles tensed as he circled Maxim. His brother—Maxim mentally called him Scarface—circled on the opposite side. "I'm going to take you down and tear you in two. Then I'm going to go after all your little friends and tear them apart if they fight me or take them as slaves if they submit. If they are strong or attractive, I can make a lot of money off them. I'll have everything, and you'll have nothing. What do you say to that, you nosy little bitch?"

Maxim took a deep breath, then settled into the rage that was always there when he was in this powerful form. "Thaaat iiss noott aann iinnssuult tooo meee. Yooouuu taaaalk toooo mmuuuch. Pllaaayttiiime iissss ooveeerrrr."

Before Ravid could say anything else, Maxim used his powerful arms to propel a fist into the Shrillexian's mouth. After that he let go, let his control slip. Ravid thought himself a big bad monster?

Maxim would show him how wrong he was.

Etheric Empire, Planet Lyriem, SS *Revenge*

Phina's feet beat a light tapping rhythm as she sprinted up the ramp and slid into the cargo bay of the Skaines' ship. She sensed Braeden fighting two at once, with a third about to ambush him and a fourth sneaking down from the upper level of the ship. Braeden was an amazing fighter, so he could probably handle them all just fine. Probably. She just wanted to make sure.

It was simple math.

Since Braeden had remained silent since the first few minutes of the fight, only her mental senses had informed her of his status and location. The cargo bay was much larger than she'd expected for the size ship, but then, the ship was wider than many other designs, which yielded quite a bit of space.

Her enhanced hearing caught the sounds of fighting echoing from behind the crates and pens in the middle of the bay. Every few steps, she glanced above, to the sides, and behind her. Training with Maxim and Link had shown her she needed to maintain situational awareness at all times, but especially when approaching a fight.

However, due to her growing mental abilities, she was fairly certain the only creatures around were either in the pens or in the direction of the sounds that got louder the closer she came. After passing a few pens filled with silent but watchful Aurians, Phina had begun to move past one only half full when she froze in shock.

Drk-vaen and Sis'tael hesitated as they came closer to where Maxim was fighting the two Shrillexians in his

Pricolici form. The three creatures were fierce and aggressive. The Pricolici stood a head above the Shrillexians, but the shorter aliens were quick, fierce, and determined. The scene might have looked odd to anyone other than a Guardian. Drk focused on the movements of the three fighters, trying to decide how long until it was over. He already knew who would win. Sis'tael stood next to him but a step back, her hand lightly holding his arm.

"He looks bad. Look at the drips of blood from the slices and gashes he's gotten."

"Maxim is fine, don't you worry. He's already healed from those."

Clicking her mandibles, Sis'tael nodded and took a few steps back into a guard position, causing a swell of emotion within him for his mate. She had been right in saying that they had already chosen each other and their parents couldn't keep them apart. Though the Yollin culture valued many things when choosing a mate, the influence of the humans from Earth had permeated it over the last few decades. The human ideal of finding love in a partner had been slow to spread at first, but the younger generations that lived, worked, and grew up with the humans had given the Yollins a different perspective.

The sound of fists hitting flesh pulled Drk-vaen from his thoughts. Looking at the fighters one more time caused him to relax.

"It won't be long now."

"What makes you say that?" If he knew her, she was studying the fighters, trying to figure it out.

"Maxim's getting mad."

Sis'tael paused behind him, her shifting about sounding nervous. "Why does that sound like a bad thing?"

"It isn't. Well, except for the Shrillexians. For them, it's bad. Maxim was just playing with them before."

As they spoke, their friend in wolf's clothing increased the frequency and speed of his attacks, as well as fending off the counterattacks more quickly and easily. The power behind the blows caused the two Shrillexians to grunt, wince, and even yelp. Finally, when the bigger hairy slaver staggered back, Maxim pulled his massive arm back behind his massive shoulders and punched Ravid in the head, torquing his body for greater momentum and power. He twisted back and shoved his other fist into the face of the smaller Shrillexian.

The two aliens slammed to the dusty ground in a heap, leaving Maxim heaving for breath.

"Took you long enough."

Maxim whirled with a ferocious snarl, toning it down when he saw the two Yollins. Baring his teeth in a wolfy grin, he took a few steps forward, then turned back to kick one of the aliens when he moaned. He cocked his head to one side, and his wolfy eyes looked amused.

"Nooot faaaast ennnoouugh forrr yooouu?"

Drk-vaen clicked his mandibles. "I've seen you go faster."

He received a shrug. "Waaasss haaavinng fuunn. Aat firrrst."

Sis'tael spoke up, her voice subdued. She hadn't seen this side of Maxim before, so she didn't know how to handle his intensity when he was in his Pricolici form. "What changed your mind?"

Their friend growled and turned his snout toward the unconscious and bleeding Shrillexian who had called himself Ravid.

"Heee taallkksss tooo muuch."

Link moved quickly in the direction Ryan had headed. He heard English and Yollin swearing up ahead among some rocks and Skaine slurs being thrown, punctuated by occasional laser fire by the Skaines.

"Come and get me, you little rat! I bet you can't hit the broad side of a battlecruiser! You all so big and bad going around picking on those who can't defend themselves, huh? Well, I bet you were taught better by your mother! Then again, since you're a son of a goat and three times as ugly, you probably got screwed over in that department."

The barrage ceased briefly while a scratchy voice called, "What's a goat?"

Link took advantage of the pause to move carefully toward Ryan.

Through a gap in the rocks, Link saw Ryan reach up to scratch his head and wince. He must be injured. Ryan caught a glimpse of Link and hissed, "Hey, how do you explain what a goat is to someone who has never seen one?"

Link raised an eyebrow. "Bison are like bistoks. Taliks are like chickens. Maybe goats are like plonkets?"

Ryan shouted to the Skaine behind the rocks, "You're the son of a plonket and three times as ugly! No, wait, that's your mom."

Another barrage of laser fire erupted, spraying tiny pieces of rock everywhere.

Ryan shrugged his good shoulder. "Guess he can't take a mom joke."

"Skaines are clones raised with no mother. You must have touched a nerve." Link rolled his eyes and continued his crouched movements over to the Marine. He finally came within a few feet and paused to see a laser blast across Ryan's shoulder. He spoke in a low voice between bursts. "You good, Marine?"

"Walk in the park." Ryan waved airily.

"Oh? Aren't we confident with a laser blast in the shoulder!"

Ryan glanced down at the wound as if surprised. "What, this old thing? Pshh. That ain't nothin'. I got the Skaine right where I want him."

Another burst of laser fire sprayed more rocks in their direction as Link reached into his pocket for one of the bandages the doctor had insisted they take with them. It had been infused with both numbing and healing agents. After glancing down at his wounded arm, he took out two. "Well, hurry it up, will you? It's been too long since I heard from Phina."

"Ease up there, Pops. Aren't you a little old to be chasing Phina?"

Link heard a tone in the question he didn't like and had a knife at the man's throat before he could blink.

"First of all, be respectful of your elders, *boy*. I've earned every gray hair and then some."

Ryan met Link's intense gaze and nodded. "Sure thing, man."

"Second," Link continued as he moved the knife and sliced open the cover of the bandage as if that had been his intention all along. "I am not only old enough to be her father, but I consider myself to be in that position to her." He thought for a moment, then shook his head. "Okay, more like the crazy but dedicated uncle. One who knows everything about his kid and will kill anyone who harms her in any way." He shot a pointed glare at the Marine before he began wrapping the man's injured shoulder.

"Huh. Okay." Ryan looked like he was mulling something over.

"What?"

"Well, Phina indicated that there was someone she was interested in, but she didn't say who it was. You and Maxim are the only ones around her all the time, and I doubt Maxim is two-timing Alina for Phina, even though she's hot." Ryan shrugged, forgetting his shoulder, and winced as Link double-glared at the idiot.

"Of course Maxim isn't two-timing Alina, you plonket. Neither of them would do that to her." Link cuffed the young man in the head. "You watch yourself! You're going to get a knife in the throat if you aren't careful."

"Hey," Ryan yelped as he clutched his head. "I need that. My dad said I need all my brain cells."

Link snorted and tied the bandage extra tight, causing Ryan to wince. "Max Wagner is smart. If he's telling you that you need them all, you better start protecting yourself by not acting like an idiot."

Ryan flashed a faint smile. "Come on, you know you love me."

Link rolled his eyes, as had become his habit in conversations with Ryan, and applied his own bandage. "You must have me mistaken for a young woman."

The Marine grinned. "Speaking of one, you said you knew everything about Phina. Does that mean you know who has her attention?"

As he pocketed the bandage covers, Link slowly nodded. "I'll give you a hint. He's a Marine." He paused and looked around. "It's too quiet."

Ryan whirled, and in one motion, he braced himself on his bad arm and fired at the Skaine. The armored alien appeared shocked and dropped the weapon he had just begun to raise. The body clattered on the rocks. Link's eyebrows rose. Huh. The kid had skills he covered with his bumbling idiot routine.

The soldier turned back with a half-grin. "So, about this Marine. I could probably take him. There's only one Marine I haven't been able to beat, and that's Todd, my boss."

Link stared at him with a half-raised eyebrow before standing since they no longer had to hide.

Ryan's eyes bugged out. "Shit, seriously?" He scrambled up, whacking off the dust and rocks that clung to his clothes. "Does he know? Have they talked a lot? Damn, I really thought it would be one of those smart guys in R&D."

Link's mouth twitched as he walked away, and he let his voice flow back. "I'll let Todd know you don't think he's smart."

The footsteps behind him stopped suddenly. "Shit!"

Link's grin dropped off his face when Phina pinged his communicator. "Everyone, we have a problem."

. . .

Etheric Empire, Planet Lyriem, SS *Revenge*

Phina halted in surprise as a small Aurian child in the pen beside her noticed her and clapped in delight.

Alarmed, she froze and waved an urgent hand to stop the child. Seeing her distress, a nearby white-haired Aurian gently but quickly shackled the young female's wrists with their hands. Undeterred, the little one gave Phina a huge smile, her eyes shining with excitement. Phina couldn't keep from returning the smile even as she waved her hands downward, hopefully to indicate that they should keep the volume down. To reinforce the idea, she tapped her finger on her lips.

Strangely, all the Aurians in her field of vision nodded at the same time.

All righty, then.

Phina, could I trouble you to help me out if you aren't too busy?

Of course, Braeden. Sorry. Finding it curious that he'd reached out mentally rather than using the implant channel, she moved forward even more quickly, trying to focus again. Still, she couldn't help gently ribbing him. *I would have thought Braeden, with his mighty mental powers, could have handled a few Skaines.*

One would think.

Phina pulled out her knives as she raced around the last empty pen to find Braeden dodging bursts of weapon fire to land bruises on the Skaines. He had just knocked one out with an elegant tap of his staff when the third Skaine snuck out of a gap between crates stacked near the hatch to the rest of the ship.

Wasting no time, Phina ran half the distance before the two Skaines noticed her and included her in their deadly dance of firepower. She leaped and jumped and twisted and flipped her way toward the third Skaine. Why couldn't she have a gun like Link's? This would have been so much easier.

Braeden, why are you moving so slowly?

Am I moving slowly?

Now you're being evasive. You're never evasive. Something's wrong.

Phina yelped as she received a burn across her thigh. It encouraged her to move faster.

I must have been evasive at some point. Never sounds like a long time. His mental voice sounded weary.

And now you're scaring me.

Phina took one more leap and slid under the Skaine's next blast. The momentum brought her close enough for her to kick out at his legs.

"Ouch! Why did no one tell me not to kick Skaines in the legs?" Phina sent over the comm link.

Stunned, she only had a second to react as the Skaine aimed his weapon at her with dead eyes. Phina threw herself to the side as chills raced up her back. Coming out of the roll, she instinctively threw her knife, which slammed unerringly into the alien's torso just about at his heart. He stood motionless for a moment, then collapsed. Huh. That was a first. She had practiced for hours every week since her trip to the Balderian planet, but she hadn't realized how easy it had become for her with all the changes in her body.

"Because it's obvious when the legs are encased in metal?"

Phina laid still while her lungs sucked in air. She still heard sounds to one side of her, indicating that Braeden still fought the other Skaines. "What?"

"It's obvious that you shouldn't kick the metal legs of their armor."

"Thanks, Ryan. It's not that obvious because some moves will still work even if they are armored. However, not even kicking will work when the components of the Skaines' armor are this dense. Why wasn't this included in their specs?"

"A detail you can add at a later time," Link broke in. "Let's get this done so we can get on with our primary mission to help these people."

"Aye-aye, Captain."

Phina pushed up and turned just as Braeden finally knocked the weapon out of the Skaine's hand, then cracked him on the head. The tall, slim Gleek sagged on his staff, which was the only thing holding him up at the moment. He appeared to be completely wiped out.

Braeden? Seriously, what's wrong? She moved forward to grab his arm in concern.

His eyes had lost their brightness, and the green had faded from bright emerald to dull sage. Closing his bleary eyes, he shook his head. His mental voice sounded listless and exhausted.

"Phina, we must leave this planet."

"We are. We just have to help everyone until the other ships come to take the Aurians to safety."

"It needs to be now. We can't wait. Every moment we stay on this planet, we have life sucked out of us. We will grow very weak. I will die before the other ships get here. We have to leave right away."

Phina's brow furrowed in confusion as she stared at her friend. Braeden's words sounded extreme, but he wasn't one for exaggeration. After a moment, she nodded then opened the channel for the team's comm.

"Everyone, we have a problem. We need to get all the Aurians on board and leave this planet now. Braeden tells me it's too dangerous to wait for the other transport ship to get here."

There was dead silence before people started swearing over each other. It sounded like Link, Ryan, and Maxim.

"How the hell will we manage that?" Ryan wondered.

Maxim growled. "We take the Skaine ship too. You can fly it."

"That might be our only option if Braeden is correct." Link grimly agreed.

"Right. Yeah, there's that." Ryan's words rang hollow, as excited as a damp rag.

"Is there a problem? You told me you can fly a Skaine ship. It's a Skaine ship."

"No, it's not that. I can fly it. I just hate all the modifications they make. It's creepy."

"Phina, you're sure we need to go?" Link had an odd tone to his question, which she ignored. They didn't have time to figure it out.

"Braeden's sure, and he's almost collapsing on the deck,

looking like the life is draining out of him every second we stand here."

"Shit." Ryan began to say something else, then, "Hey!" He was cut off, and Link began speaking. Weird. Link must still be with Ryan.

"All right, then let's do this. Phina, you finish up there. Let Braeden rest. Everyone else, start getting the Aurians ready to go. We'll have to try out the translators and see how they work without Phina as a buffer. Split them between the two ships. Move it, people! We don't want to lose anyone."

Phina sheathed her other knife, then helped Braeden move over to the side so he could lie down without getting close to the fallen Skaines and the blood leaking from the bodies. His face looked pained, his limbs shaky.

She had just stood back up when she heard a scuffing noise behind her.

CHAPTER NINETEEN

Etheric Empire, Planet Lyriem, SS *Revenge*

Trillet gripped the gun in his sweaty hand as he crept down the corridor. He could hear people fighting and muffled voices ahead. Pausing, he fumbled to push a button on the front of his clothing.

"Captain?"

"What, Trillet? Why are you whispering?" His impatient voice sounded distracted.

"I'm outside the cargo hold. I can hear them fighting."

"Well, what are you waiting for, an invitation?" He swore fervently enough to make Trillet stare down at the comm in disbelief. The captain sounded mean and out of control. While he was often mean, the captain never lost control. What had happened since he left the bridge?

"Is something wrong, Captain?"

As he waited, Trillet leaned against the cool metallic hull of the ship, unthinkingly spreading his free hand across the surface. Smooth. Nice. Quiet. Huh. The fighting had stopped. The captain's voice jerked him out of his trance.

"Something wrong? Those damned dogs from the Empire just took out everyone down there. Now there's only me and a demented moron left. We're either going to die or get hauled off."

Trillet frowned at those numbers. "There's three of us, Captain. You, the demented moron, and me. Don't worry, I've got a gun, and I'm going to use it on the Imperial dogs. I owe them for their Ranger sending me to the mine."

Silence filled his ears, punctuated by faint choking noises. When the captain finally spoke, his voice had dropped to a growl worthy of Ravid. "Well, that is such a relief to me, now isn't it?"

Beaming, Trillet patted his gun. "Happy to help, Captain."

Moving forward, the Skaine put on his business face as he reached the door. Trillet pressed the switch, waiting as the door opened before sliding into the cargo bay. His feet were whispers, legs moving smoothly, gun at the ready.

In front of him were three Skaines strewn across the floor. To the side of the fallen lay a tall, lanky body, but he couldn't make out the details. Some weird-looking human, he was sure. Rising from a crouch next to the tall body was a human woman just over average height. Trillet stopped and stared at her, confused.

She didn't look like an evil dog of the Empire. She looked young and innocent. Ranger Two had been a young woman as well, he reminded himself. Look how that turned out. The evil bitch had thrown him and his coworkers into the mine, where Trillet had gone mad. This new bitch could be looking to do the same thing.

It wasn't fair.

Why did *he* have to be the one going mad? Why had he been punished for doing what Skaines do? Anger derived from madness surged as he lifted his gun to shoot the evil bitch from the Empire who wanted to take him down.

He would take her down first.

Phina whirled at the noise behind her. Within a second, she'd processed the situation: the Skaine who had been working his way down the ship had finally joined them, his weapon was currently being brought up to point at her, he stood within leaping distance, and he had the intention of shooting her and the rest of her crew. His determination was unmistakable. Worse were the prickles of madness that emanated from him. Given that, Phina decided she had little choice.

In one smooth and quick move, Phina swiped the knife from the sheath on her thigh that she had been fingering and arced the blade. It struck where she had intended—in the heart of the Skaine. His face froze in surprise.

As he collapsed to the deck, a wave of defeat, resignation, and relief emanated from him. Relief from the madness? She needed time to process what she felt with her mental senses, time she didn't have. Not yet.

"Greyson, send the Pod over. Braeden needs to get off this planet now. I'll take him up, and we'll wait for you."

"You can't wait for the other ships? We could probably

collect everyone when they arrive in the next hour with all their supplies."

"He's dying inch by inch. He can't even talk out loud anymore."

"Damn it all to hell! We'll send the Pod. Stand by."

The next few minutes took an eternity to pass. Phina, not knowing what else to do, opened the doors to the pens, though she informed the Aurians they would need to stay on the ship so they all could leave soon. Then she retrieved and cleaned her knives.

Finally, she heard the thuds and thumps of footsteps at the other end of the cargo bay. Alina, Maxim, and Doctor Keelson ran toward her. Alina gasped in alarm when she saw the bodies and again when she saw the state Braeden was in, while Maxim and April continued forward to gently pick him up.

Doctor Keelson frowned when she felt his pulse as they walked, trying not to step in front of Maxim while he carried the Gleek. Alina trailed behind Maxim while Phina walked next to the doctor and they all supported Braeden. Phina, glancing from the side, noticed her perplexed expression.

"He's got two hearts."

April jerked at Phina's quiet reminder. "What?"

"The Gleeks have two hearts. It's going to mess up your measurements."

Nodding, Doctor Keelson trotted to keep up while her hands moved to various points on her patient's body.

"Do you know what happened?"

Phina frowned distractedly, shaking her head. "He said something about his life or energy being taken."

"His pulse is thready and weak, his skin dry and brittle, and his eyes look dull. I agree; if there's something here that is doing this, he needs to leave. If he doesn't improve, you will need to place him in stasis and hope it works on Gleek physiology. I can't get to him until after we help the people here."

"No."

Maxim and Alina looked at her, startled at her vehemence. "Phina?"

"We will suffer similar effects. He is just the most sensitive to it. We all need to leave before the effects kick in. I told Greyson we need to go up on the Pod and leave, but that's just us two. That's why everyone needs to hurry—so we can all leave. You can help them on the ships."

They reached the bottom of the ramp and stepped toward the Pod, which was only a few yards away. The Aurians scurried around their buildings, causing Phina to hope they were packing and not having a different issue.

The Pod door opened, allowing Maxim sans wolfman, Phina, and Doctor Keelson to step on. Alina waited outside after Phina exchanged faint smiles and a hand squeeze with her. The Guardian carefully placed Braeden on the emergency medical bed, which had been fitted with stretchable straps. After arranging the straps, Maxim stepped out the door with a nod.

Phina called through her implant, "Guys, don't forget the last Skaine on the ship. He's on the bridge, so he's probably the captain."

She got murmurs of acknowledgment. Doctor Keelson checked Braeden's vitals more thoroughly. "Still the same. I'm not sure what needs to happen for him now."

Phina gave her a reassuring smile she didn't feel. "It's okay, Doctor Keelson. We just need to get him off the planet right now and see if that revives him."

Nodding, April stepped back and walked to the door. "I'll take care of the sick and injured here, but once we are in the air, call me if you need me."

"Will do."

The door sealed after her as Phina stepped toward the front of the Pod. "Stark? You there?"

"Of course, Genius Girl. I'm always here."

"Would you take us up?"

"Sure thing."

Phina barely felt the motion as the Pod rose, the ride smooth. Within seconds of its departure, the Pod moved more quickly and at a steeper incline. The screen in the front showed a barren planet below with the dark brightness of space above. The sheer emptiness that lay before her left her feeling very alone. Even though it was a state she was familiar with, she was used to being around people now. That realization startled her. How had that happened?

After passing through the haze of the atmosphere and into space, they traveled for another minute or so before Stark indicated they had stopped. Phina got up, walked back to sit next to Braeden, and gently took his hand.

"Ok, Braeden. Now what?"

Etheric Empire, Planet Lyriem, SS *Revenge*

Maxim watched the Pod as it rose and swiftly moved above the planet. After another moment, he turned to

Alina and nodded when he saw her concern. He clasped her shoulder and gently stroked her with his thumb.

"Phina will be fine. We'll get done here and meet up with her shortly."

Alina raised an eyebrow in amusement. "Oh, don't worry, big man. It's not Phina I'm worried about."

"Oh? Who would you be worried about?"

"Let me think." She tapped her chin playfully. "He's tall and strong, and he goes furry sometimes but fights like crazy either way. He's smart, loyal, kind, and oh-so-sexy."

A slow smile spread across Maxim's face. "Oh? Who is this paragon of a man?"

"Peter Silvers."

Maxim stilled and stared at her blue eyes bright with amusement and that wicked little smirk playing on her mouth. It took him a moment to realize he was growling and slowly bringing her closer to him. When she was only inches away, her amusement growing, he narrowed his eyes to show his lack of appreciation for her words.

"Peter Silvers?"

Alina grinned. "Yup."

Without warning, Maxim grabbed Alina and tossed her over his shoulder, eliciting shrieks from her. Holding her in place with one hand, he walked back into the Skaine ship, poking her with tickling fingers every so often until she gasped for relief.

"Nope, not until you change your answer."

"Okay, okay! Stars, don't be such a baby about it." Though still out of breath, she still chuckled.

Maxim swung her back over his shoulder and set her

down on the deck, then took the time to kiss her. Thoroughly. Breathless, Alina finally pulled back.

"All right, you're definitely not a baby."

"No." Maxim agreed, not taking his eyes off her.

Alina's mouth twitched, then stretched into the smile she only gave him. "You knew I didn't mean Peter Silvers."

Leaning down, he touched her forehead with his. "I know."

"And I *am* worried about Phina," she added softly closing, her eyes.

He wrapped his arms around her and held her tight. "I know that too."

"All right, you two, quit your flirting." Greyson Wells' voice startled them out of the beginnings of another kiss. "Maxim, Phina said there's one more Skaine on board, and you're the best one to take care of him. Alina, please go out and help bring the Aurians on board."

Sighing, Maxim pressed a kiss on her head before releasing her. "Duty calls."

Etheric Empire, Planet Lyriem, Pod

Far too pale and as still as death, Braeden managed to hold on. If he died, it would take days to return to his home planet for him to be reunited with the Mother and reborn into another life cycle. It would take a full decade to relearn everything he needed to know and longer still to develop the abilities he had carefully honed. And he wouldn't be Braeden. No, he would be an entirely new person.

In short, he wasn't ready to die yet.

But how to rejuvenate enough to live had become a problem he wasn't sure he could solve. He let his mind drift now that his body had stopped being drained, his very molecules pulled apart. If he had been any younger, he would be dead. And yet, if he were younger, perhaps it wouldn't have drained him so quickly. The Aurians were still alive, though in a sad state. The humans hadn't seemed to sense it even though the energy pull was there. He would have noticed if Phina had been having trouble even though he hadn't been shielding her for the last several hours since she had been using her new shields.

As he mulled the problem over, he became aware of Phina's physical presence. The energy of her life force emanated from her in waves he could feel almost violently.

Braeden? Any ideas?

Even after the loss of his energy and strength, Braeden felt no difference in the mental connection between them. That gave him food for thought, but for another time. Most pressing was the need to figure out what had happened and if there was any hope of fixing it.

Little sister, are you well?

Yes, just concerned about you.

Are you certain? You are not more tired than normal or feel anything off in your body?

After a long pause, presumably for Phina to assess herself, she spoke with puzzlement and concern. *I do feel a slight drop in energy, but only because I don't feel the need to claw at the walls to do something. Well, I still feel the need to move and do things; it's just not as bad as it usually is.*

Braeden added those observations to the thoughts circling in his head. In his mind, he entered into the thoughts and memories that composed of the knowledge base available to all Gleeks, gleaned from the thousands of years the species had learned and acquired information as they traveled the universe. Since he was currently half an Empire away from his fellow Gleeks and he was almost drained and half-dead, it took more effort than it normally did.

Rather than look for the information and drain himself further, he threw a mental line of thought toward the one charged with maintaining that knowledge base.

Brother Traekor.

Brother Braeden.

I have encountered an ill situation, and my strength wanes. It is taking much just to connect. Might I trouble you by sending you information to add to our base, as well as for you to search for any relevant information and return the findings to me?

A long pause followed, in which Braeden felt his strength leaving drop by drop. Finally, he received an answer.

We are not all in agreement, but I will do this task for you as a favor. Regardless of recent turns in thought, you have been a respected and powerful leader to our brethren.

Thank you, Traekor.

Using most of the last of his energy, he sent all he had learned about the planet below, the sensations he had felt as he walked the planet, his condition, Phina's response, and his speculations. He held back nothing. It wasn't the way of his people.

He received waves of alarm back, which eased a knot that had rested within him since his brothers had shut him out of his role as leader. The knot still existed but wasn't as tight or painful.

I'm sorry, Braeden.

For what, little sister?

I feel the sorrow in you. I wish I could help.

It must be a human trait to take ownership of situations that are not your fault nor of your making.

She gave him the mental equivalent of a shrug. *Perhaps for some. Only for those we care about or feel guilty about the situation, rightly or wrongly.*

Braeden agreed with the assessment and hoped it was the former reason for Phina rather than the latter. All too soon and yet not soon enough, he felt the mental touch of his brother and reached to connect since Traekor didn't have the skill to make it on his own.

Brother Braeden.

Brother Traekor.

Having examined your knowledge, the facts therein, and the knowledge base, the conclusion is the one you speculated to be most probable. We have run across no other planets with a similar situation. Should you find the cause, please update our knowledge base.

Thank you, Brother Traekor.

Life be with you, Brother Braeden.

Releasing the connection revealed the drain in his strength, and he had little to lose. If he hadn't been as old as he was or as powerful a telepath, he wouldn't have been able to connect with his fellow Gleek at all.

Braeden?

Yes, little sister?

Have you figured out anything? Is there anything I can do to help you?

Braeden took a few minutes to think through the implications of the conclusion he had come to and Traekor had confirmed as being most likely.

"I believe there *is* something you can do, but first, tell me how you are feeling. Is your itch to move stronger?"

Braeden felt her shift next to him, though she still held his hand. *Yes, it's getting uncomfortable now.*

Sun and stars, it just might work. And not only that, but it might help Phina as well as him. On the other hand...

"Phina, there is something we can try which might help you release that which causes you to feel so uncomfortable and me to regain life and strength. However, because we do not have the luxury of time to experiment, I am uncertain if this will work or if we will both be worse off, possibly even dead. It is your choice, little sister."

Her connection to him strengthened, and he felt her emotions turn to curiosity and hope with a twinge of fear and regret.

"If I understand right, there is something I can do to help you, but you don't know if it will help both of us or kill us, and it could do either one."

"Correct. I believe it will help us both, but I don't know for certain. There is a small chance that it will help me but bring you closer to death, but I do not believe it is the most likely outcome."

Determination filled her, washing away the other emotions he'd felt from her.

"I could die anyway, Braeden. If it has a chance to help you, let's do it."

CHAPTER TWENTY

Etheric Empire, Planet Lyriem, SS *Revenge*

Maxim stalked silently into the room outside the bridge. Stark had been monitoring the Skaine and would have told him if the alien had moved. A voice broke the silence, swearing even as dull metallic tones sounded.

Well, the Skaine had definitely been located.

The staccato metallic tones continued, indicating the captain was hitting something vigorously—likely controls that weren't working as desired. Maxim focused his sharp hearing, picking up mumbles from the Skaine.

"Spent years putting together a crew, and for what? Damned Empire killing them all, that's what! Get this ship moving if this piece of *tak* would just work so I can get out of here. To hell with them. A new crew would work even better. Just need to get this no good piece of..."

The screech of frustration was accompanied by an increase in banging. Maxim stirred uneasily. They needed the ship to carry Aurians to safety. If the Skaine damaged it too much, it would require repairs, delaying their departure when, according to Phina, they needed to leave immediately. Maxim knew it wasn't just her assessment but also Braeden's, who had likely lived longer than they could guess. He trusted Phina but knowing it was Braeden's assessment too turned their need to leave into a state of emergency since the alien wasn't one to overstate a situation.

Maxim lowered his head as he leaned forward to run into the room when a second voice stopped him, causing him to smile.

"I must ask you to halt your frantic attempts to break the ship."

"What the...who are you?"

"I am the EI of the ship."

"What? Why have I never heard you speak before now?"

"I haven't had a need to speak to you before."

"Well, get moving and help me fly this ship so we can leave!"

"I'm sorry, but there is a problem with that."

"There's no problem with that! If you're the EI responsible for the ship, it's in your mandate to follow the captain's orders, and I'm the captain! Do your job!"

Maxim had taken advantage of the conversation by sliding into the room slowly enough that the Skaine wouldn't sense him.

"The problem is you. You are no longer the captain of this ship, and I am not the EI for the *Revenge.*"

The Skaine swore even as his fingers moved to tap several buttons. He pressed a large button as Maxim glided over and twisted his neck, breaking it. The Skaine's body dropped to the deck, and lights flashed across the screen in front of Maxim. An alarm started blaring through the ship.

"Stark? Buddy? Mind telling me what those lights and alarms are for?"

"That is for a self-destruct protocol for the ship."

Spreading his hands in bewilderment, Maxim's gaze searched the console in front of him. "How do I stop it?"

"Stand there and look pretty."

Frowning, Maxim did a double-take and looked around. "You're talking to me, right?"

"You and your furry self."

Snorting, Maxim folded his arms. "I don't think I've ever been mistaken for pretty. I'm assuming you have this covered and I don't need to be alarmed?"

"You could run around screaming that you are going to die, but that would only provide amusement for the rest of us."

"So, that's a no on having the self-destruct covered?"

"Relax, wolf boy. I stopped the self-destruct within seconds of activation."

Maxim dropped his eyes to the console again. "Then why are the lights and alarm still flashing?"

"Since it wasn't necessary to adjust those during deactivation, I decided to leave them."

"Stark, are you telling me you are pulling a prank?"

"Of course not. That would be ridiculous and illogical." He sniffed.

Maxim slowly grinned. "You *are* pulling a prank."

"Only if it is funny. If it isn't, then I don't know what you are referring to."

Link looked around as the Aurians scrambled to pack their remaining food and possessions. Mindful of the warning Phina had given, he gave them only thirty minutes to gather their things. Half that time had passed.

Doctor Keelson and Alina were taking care of those too ill to move on their own, aided by Ryan and Drk-vaen. Sis'-tael and Addison were directing everyone to the appropriate ships so the numbers were as evenly divided as they could manage. With Braeden and Phina gone, they were down two and spread thin.

On a positive note, the translation program was working well for the most part. Occasionally an issue arose, but they were able to make themselves understood. Link felt certain Addison and later Phina would be adjusting the program to improve comprehension.

Link opened his mouth to contact Stark for an update when he noticed an Aurian staggering under a heavy box of food. He hurried over and grabbed the box as she stumbled again. The female slumped in relief and blinked at him in surprise. She gestured at him as if to take it back.

"I can carry it for you. Which ship were you taking it to?"

The small female regally nodded toward the Skaine ship, so he began walking in that direction. Link walked a step, then turned back to see her watching him. Her large eyes assessed him.

"Is there a leader or someone in charge I could speak to?"

The tubes on her face were at odds with the rest of her

body, which was a miniature version of an attractive female, including breasts and hips. Her long white hair was thick and currently dusty and bedraggled, though under that, it seemed like it could glow under the right circumstances, even though he didn't normally think of such whimsical things. Her eyes were a bright lavender that drew him in, and he realized he was staring. He shook his head to try to clear it.

The female nodded, then gestured to herself.

"You are in charge?" He considered her. "Is there a reason you aren't talking to me? Is it not allowed?"

The female smiled gently. "It seems to be disconcerting for you all."

"It's a little bit of a kick, I admit, but our translators help to filter the effect. You are in charge, then?"

"I am one of several leaders of our people, but they often look to me to lead them all."

"So, if we were to talk about what needs to be done to help your people, you can make the decisions for them?"

Her face tubes began to move. Link suppressed a shudder. Diplomats didn't show their emotions to others, particularly that they felt displeasure, distaste, or disgust about those they were attempting to engage and negotiate with. Spies showed even less than diplomats, and Link was the ultimate mix of both—which he took very seriously.

"I would be acceptable as spokesperson to then discuss with the rest."

"Sounds like a plan. When you board, make sure you get on *Stark*." He pointed at the ship to make sure she understood. "We will make plans once we take off."

The female nodded, still coming across as serene and

graceful. All of a sudden, he felt like an awkward over-grown male, something that hadn't happened much in his life after he had left his teenage years. She was damned eerie.

"Am I still taking this to the Skaine ship?"

On the way there, Link wondered if landing on this planet had made him slow-witted. There were easier ways of doing things.

"Stark, send out the transport carts, will you? We've got to get moving faster."

"On the way, DS."

Walking gave his mind plenty of time to wander, and he looked around. The half-visible moon just above the ship caused him to wonder how far out the Pod had taken Phina and Braeden. Had they gone out far enough to nullify whatever effects the two of them believed were occurring? Link began coughing from the dust being kicked up by all the feet on the ground between the ships and the buildings.

It *was* the dust…right?

Hell, now he had visions of them all dying one by one, draped all over the two ships. Casting concerned glances at the sky every few minutes, Link couldn't help wondering what was happening with his troublesome mentee and the male who had become another mentor to her.

He was worried that they both might be dead.

Phina's hand began to ache. She looked down and realized she had been holding Braeden's hand too tightly, causing her fingers to turn white. Wincing, she loosened her grip and tried to relax the rest of her. Just her luck to try to save Braeden's life and nearly break his hand in the process.

So, what do we need to do?

Braeden's voice seemed to come to her from farther away than normal, akin to hearing it through a tunnel. It also echoed, making it sound less substantial and more ghostly. If she was made of weaker stuff, she might be cringing in fear. However, she had never been weak, even if it had taken time for her to exercise her strength.

Everything contains energy, especially those of us who live and move around. The longer a being lives and the more open certain parts of their brain are to using it, the more energy a person's body contains. Since I've lived well over three of your centuries and can access that energy, my body contains and stores a lot. Usually. That's what allows us Gleeks to live as long as we do. It also is the basis of the telekinetic energy I've used in the past. The more energy a being has stored within their container, the stronger that telekinetic energy when it's used.

Phina stared, her eyes blank as her mind took her back over the past months. *That makes a certain amount of sense.*

Yes, I believe your restlessness comes from a sharp build-up of energy, and that's why you always want to move. Staying still drives you crazy because the energy wants to be used and dissipated back into the universe.

While all this is interesting, it isn't telling me how to help you.

Just as energy can be used and dissipated, I believe it can also be transferred.

Stunned by the implications, Phina blinked at Braeden's

still form. *You believe that the lack of energy is why you are having trouble and I can fill you with my energy.*

She felt the equivalent of a smile come down the tunnel. *Stark has a reason for calling you 'Genius Girl.' Yes, I believe you can fill me with it.*

Phina slowly nodded. *So, somehow the energy was...what, drained out of you?*

Yes, very like that.

What could do that? Who *could do that?*

That is our next task. First, I need to get back on my feet. That is why I need your help.

To fill you up with energy. Phina didn't know how she felt about that. Chalk up one more inexplicable thing that was now different in her life.

Yes.

Surely someone else can help you get out of trouble?

There is no one else here. And I'm not just having trouble, Phina. I'm dying.

No, she protested.

Yes. We cannot live long without the energy we need; no one can. But we Gleeks are especially sensitive. My body is shutting down. There are only minutes left before it's too late to change my end.

Phina firmed her lips and nodded. *Well, we can't have that. Tell me what to do.*

The only method I have thought of with no assistance available is for you to put your hands on my thoracic region and try to push the energy into me.

Push it like you do for your kinetic strikes? Why did this sound dangerous?

Similar, but push it in instead of against something. It might take a few attempts to figure out the process.

Right.

Phina placed her hands on Braeden's elongated body, one above each heart. She didn't know why; it just felt right. Because his body was failing and his hearts were needed to keep it functioning? Maybe. After taking a deep breath, Phina let it out and closed her eyes. Right. Tricky situation, Braeden's life was in the balance. Just another day in the Empire.

"Here goes..."

Etheric Empire, Planet Lyriem, QBS *Stark*

Stark had watched it all: Genius Girl's mad dash and assistance to Ryan, and the interaction between her and Greyson Wells as she helped him jump around the Skaines' laser bursts before the aliens were taken out. Stark even hacked into the camera feeds on the *Revenge* and observed how she had come to Braeden's rescue. Then she'd taken out the Skaine who had gone mad, released the Aurians, and was now risking her life to try to save Braeden.

Yes, Stark had watched it all.

And he still didn't understand it.

Logically, she should have stayed on his ship. It made sense with the new biological information they had been given that her life was at risk. Yet, her actions had allowed her to save at least three lives, not counting all the Aurians who had been in the way. If she had not been involved, Ryan would have been seriously if not fatally injured, Greyson

Wells would be seriously injured and need medical care, and Braeden would be dead. Her insistence made no sense logically, yet she had made a drastic difference in the outcome.

For the first time, Stark found logic inadequate.

It was unsettling.

Unsettling?

He pushed that line of inquiry aside and latched onto another thought process. The Aurians were almost extinct, their people dying, yet they still had tried to help when they thought others were attacking their rescuers, mistaken though they were. They helped the other side once they realized the truth. Their people were simple but not simplistic.

He found them fascinating.

The rest of the team had worked together in surprising ways as well. They didn't have the near-certain death sentence Genius Girl currently lived under, yet they risked their lives to help each other and the Aurians. Logically it made no sense to risk their lives for others, and yet they all had.

He followed that line of thought. The Empire had been built on the same principle, with the Empress and her people constantly risking their lives to save others. One could argue they were merely taking strides toward establishing the power of the Empire, yet if one studied their actions, they were more often than not predicated by either a cry for help or a desire to rid the universe of beings who took advantage of others—the Kurtherians.

Stark supposed one could argue that those who risked their lives for no direct benefit were idiots.

He didn't see that assertion going over well.

And that would mean Genius Girl was and wasn't a genius, which was paradoxical.

Unbidden, the images of Genius Girl sprang to mind: sitting at the table talking to those she now considered family and speaking to him while she was on the move. Her actions toward Stark were little different than her actions toward Ryan, Maxim, or Drk-vaen. She treated Stark very similarly. Like...family.

That thought warmed him in a way his computational processes weren't able to explain.

>>**It's about time. I've been waiting for you to realize what has been in front of you all along.**<<

CHAPTER TWENTY-ONE

Etheric Empire, Planet Lyriem, Pod

Phina, wait.

Her eyes opened seconds after they had shut at Braeden's urgent words. *I'm listening.*

Once you start, you cannot stop, no matter how much pain I'm in.

The blood drained out of her face. *That doesn't sound good. Are you sure we have to do it? Maybe we can find some other way.*

No other way has come to mind. Little sister, my apologies for how difficult this will be. If I could do it myself, I would, but if I could, then this all would be unnecessary. His voice began to fade more, causing alarm.

Of course.

Just go slowly and gently, and unless you believe you will die if you keep going, don't stop.

Right.

Phina puffed air out of her lungs, then closed her eyes

and began taking deep breaths to relax. The itchy restlessness had come back with a vengeance, so relaxing proved difficult. *I can do this. I can do this. Braeden is dying, and he's counting on me to help.* Phina remembered his fading mental voice and told herself to get a move on.

With her hands over his two hearts, Phina focused her attention on directing the extra energy in her body toward Braeden. A wave rippled outward, and Braeden's body jerked under her hands. *Gently,* she reminded herself. *Slowly.*

Her mind ran through a number of possibilities and discarded them in the span of seconds. Finally, she decided to go with instinct as well as common sense and focused on the physical connection between her hands and his body. Phina immersed herself in the sensation of Braeden's skin, his slowing heartbeats, and his sense of life. Mentally she reached for Braeden's sense of self and held on tight.

Using only a small amount of energy, Phina gently moved a thread toward Braeden by way of the physical connection through her hands. The energy slid into him but dissipated. Frowning, Phina wondered whether the result indicated she hadn't used enough or whether the energy needed something to anchor it. After increasing both the amount of energy flowing and the rate of flow, she concluded that an anchor would be needed.

Wishing she could rub her forehead to relieve the developing ache, she wondered how she would be able to accomplish that.

. . .

Etheric Empire, QBS Stark

Link followed at the tail end of a number of Aurians as they trotted onto the ship. When he reached the control panel beside the cargo bay, he surveyed the land outside one more time. Dust drifted, dead plant life blew across the ground, and the buildings in the distance had an absence of light and movement. There were no signs of life anywhere except on the other ship.

This planet was the most depressing he had ever encountered.

Link engaged the team through his implant. "Maxim. Ryan."

"Greyson."

"Yeah, man."

Ryan's tenor drawl contrasted with Maxim's clipped deeper tones. Their voices suited each completely.

"All ready on your end?"

"Just finished with the last Aurians boarding the ship. We should be ready to go as soon as Ryan gets his ass up to the bridge and flies us out of here."

"I'm on my way, Grumpy Gus. Don't get your panties in a bunch."

"Who says I wear panties, Ryan? I didn't realize my drawers were so fascinating to you. I could just ask Stark to fly this rust bucket if you think it's beyond the scope of your abilities. Flying three ships is nothing for him, I'm sure."

Ryan sputtered protests, causing Link to laugh.

"Keep it together, you two. Just get into the air."

"Yes, sir."

"Got it."

Link took one last look at the empty terrain in front of him and pushed the buttons to close the hatch.

"Stark, put us on course to intercept the Pod, will you? I am uneasy about leaving the two of them out there alone."

"Don't worry, Genius Girl is saving the day."

"I don't doubt it."

Only later did he realize that was the first time he could remember having Stark advise him on something that was emotionally related.

Etheric Empire, Planet Lyriem, *Pod*

Phina sat thinking with her head tilted to the side. The slight burn of the stretch kept her thoughts focused. Braeden believed this would work, but pushing the energy in or trickling it in didn't work. Perhaps...

She released another trickle into the connection between them through her hands, but again, it felt like the energy evaporated. It seemed to hit something, then bounce off. It couldn't be anything physical.

Braeden?

Little sister?

Do you have any shields up? The energy isn't going into you. It bounces off of something.

Phina got the impression Braeden mentally mumbled curse words in Gleek. *A moment, please.*

Long before a moment had passed, she felt a sudden feeling of openness under her hands, though physically, nothing had changed. Weird. Making another attempt,

Phina discovered the energy didn't dissipate but felt like it entered Braeden's hearts. Gradually, Phina increased the amount of energy she sent and quickly realized she had to be extremely careful about how much and how fast it entered his body.

This is taking forever.

My apologies, little sister. It doesn't seem like anything can be done to speed up the process.

That's all right. It's just going to be rough for a while.

Phina didn't know how long she leaned forward with her hands on Braeden's chest. She lost track of everything except the energy flowing through the connections between them. When a hand covered hers, she opened her eyes and saw Braeden's bright green eyes.

I have enough energy for now, little sister. We can do more later if it is needed.

She took a deep breath and nodded, letting her hands slip away. She wasn't in pain, but for the first time in a long while, she felt really tired. That extra pulse of energy that drove her to constantly move was gone. Phina was both relieved and a little scared. Providing the energy for Braeden had been nothing short of amazing. That she had used so much of her energy and still Braeden moved slowly and cautiously showed her how very close to death he had come. She shook out her body, which had grown stiff from sitting in one position for so long.

Are you going to be all right?

Eventually. The amount of energy I had accumulated throughout my life will not come back quickly or easily. It will take time.

Perhaps when I have that excess energy accumulated again, I can give it to you.

Braeden gave her a small smile. *That would help both of us.*

Rather fortuitous, don't you think? Phina waggled her eyebrows.

Indeed.

So, what caused the drain on your body? Phina stood up and began to pace. Fudging crumbs. Already her energy had begun to replenish, giving her that annoying restless feeling, though it was far less than it had been.

Braeden's voice spoke with a slight rasp. *That is something I will need to talk to everyone about, and we will need the leaders of the Aurians, especially.*

Perfect. Everyone is waiting for you.

Phina and Braeden looked over to see Link standing in the doorway, his face showing both concern and amusement.

"How did you get here?"

He gave a light shrug. "The same way you did, I imagine. I came on board."

Phina walked over and leaned around him, seeing the cargo bay of *Stark* through the door of the Pod. "Huh. Apparently we missed that."

"You were occupied," Link agreed. He leaned close, brown eyes narrowing. "What did I tell you about rule number four?"

She rolled her eyes and gave him a scowl of displeasure. "I knew you were going to say something!"

"Don't mess with me today, kid. Rule number four."

"Always be ready to defend yourself," she recited in a monotone.

"That's right." He looked at her expectantly.

Widening her eyes innocently, Phina pressed a hand to her heart. "I was saving Braeden's life."

"Don't give me that. You can do both at the same time."

"Have you ever connected mentally to someone to hold onto their sense of self while you trickle energy into their body and monitor their health and well-being so you don't overload them in order to save their life?" She smiled sweetly.

"You know I haven't."

The smile and every spark of emotion dropped from her face. "Then stop criticizing. I had my attention split three ways. I couldn't handle a fourth one and knew Stark would have said something if we had a problem."

Link leaned his head forward, his eyes weary. "Stark can't warn you about everything. You have to be more aware because not everyone will have your back."

She shook her head thoughtfully. "That's not very trusting."

"That's called self-preservation."

Phina stared at him, then realized their faces were less than a foot apart, much closer than felt comfortable. As she eased away, still considering Link's firm statements, she caught sight of Braeden from the corner of her eye, sitting still to be unobtrusive. For a tall, lanky Gleek, that was quite a feat. Link still stood in front of her, seeming to dare her to make a follow-up comment. She decided not to call him on it...yet.

"Didn't you say they were waiting?"

. . .

Etheric Empire, In Orbit around Planet Lyriem, QBS Stark

She-Who-Mourns sat in a chair sized to make her feel like a child again and watched these unknown beings carefully. She knew what they called themselves and each other. She saw what they had done and how they acted. But their motivations were still hazy to her, which made her wary of what they wanted. The Skaines had used the pretense of being their rescuers to enslave them. She-Who-Mourns did not feel very trusting after that revelation, but the earnestness she had seen in the young female's eyes caused her to want to try again.

"So..." The female featuring in her thoughts of trust paused between bites. She scarfed down three nutrition bars but had slowed on her fourth. She had introduced herself as Phina and now waved her hand at the four Aurians. "Is dark hair a male thing and white hair a female thing, or is there something significant about the colors?"

After exchanging glances with He-Who-Listens, who was sitting next to her, She-Who-Mourns nodded at Phina. "It is, as you say, a male and female thing."

"That's a useful thing, knowing at a glance."

She-Who-Mourns remained silent since the comment didn't appear to need a response. She glanced at the three males with her, but their expressions made it clear they were even less inclined to speak. She bit back a sigh. Of course. Why put themselves out to be noticed when she could do it instead?

The other beings with the young female, the tall, thin

bald one they called Braeden and the shorter one with hair they called Greyson Wells, sat in silence on the other side of the table. It was clear the females would be facilitating the discussion at hand.

After another glance around the table, She-Who-Mourns decided she would just get it over with. Subtlety would be pointless right now, and these creatures seemed to favor being direct. "Could you explain why you helped us?"

Phina finished the last bite of her nutrition bar and licked her fingers clean before folding her hands together and speaking. She focused on She-Who-Mourns. "We, the Empire, choose to help those we encounter who need help, sometimes by fighting oppressors, liberating slaves, or providing food and shelter when needed. Our Empress has pledged to destroy the Kurtherians, who have done many terrible and unspeakable things in their quests for knowledge and power. In essence, we are the cleanup crew, trying to make the wrong they did right again while we search for them.

"We, as in our group, heard about your situation when I was able to translate the recordings that were made when our people visited your planet eight years ago and again three years ago. At the time, no one understood your language, and it only seemed to our people to be beautiful music. It wasn't until the last few weeks that I was able to understand the words and create a translation program with the help of one of my teachers. Once we realized that you were in trouble, we came as quickly as we could."

"I see." She-Who-Mourns wanted to rage and despair at the same time. She remembered when those groups had come, though not to the villages where she had been at the time. Visitors were not so frequent that news didn't spread about them fairly quickly. In the time since, thousands upon thousands of people had died.

Phina must have seen her distress since the young female leaned forward with sorrow and compassion in her eyes. "I'm so sorry about the lives that were lost. I wish we had figured it out sooner."

She-Who-Mourns raised a hand and shook her head. "It was not your responsibility. We are just grateful we were saved. Thank you for all you have done to help us."

Phina swallowed roughly and nodded. "Is there anything else I can answer about who we are or what we are doing here?"

"Not at the moment," She-Who-Mourns managed, though suppressed sobs formed an ache in her chest. "What are your plans for us?" The males on the other side of the table exchanged glances with Phina, which gave She-Who-Mourns an uneasy feeling. "What are you not telling us?"

"Oh, we aren't telling you a lot yet, but the main issue now is related to the reason your planet is dying. Braeden?" She turned to the male on her left. "Do you want to explain?"

The overgrown green-eyed male gave Phina a sideways glance, which caused her mouth to twitch. She-Who-Mourns had the strangest feeling there was some sort of unspoken communication between the two and cocked her head to pay more attention. He spoke in measured tones with a distinct and clear sound to them.

"Do you know what caused your planet to start dying?"

She-Who-Mourns froze, and her people shook their heads. "You know?"

His green eyes focused on her, causing her to feel uneasy. "I have suppositions based on what I felt. My body began breaking down and dying within minutes of landing on the planet."

Her eyes widened as she whispered. "So quickly?"

"Yes. It is only through a series of fortunate events that I am still alive."

He-Who-Acts fidgeted in his chair. She suspected he also felt uncomfortable with the chair proportions since he had an even greater sense of pride. "Well? Don't leave us in suspense!"

"I won't talk about the events that kept me alive, but I will share what I believe is happening. As I lay semiconscious, I became aware of a tug."

"A tug?" She-Who-Mourns tilted her head in puzzlement.

"Yes. A tug that pulled the energy out of my body toward a specific location on the planet."

Her heart sped up, and she swallowed roughly. Braeden's gaze sharpened, which gave her the sense that he had felt her sudden spike of fear. She shook her head, trying to push the absurd thought aside.

"A specific direction? Then you think the energy is going somewhere?"

"Correct."

"What could do that?" He-Who-Listens whispered.

"That is what we hope to find out." They heard the voice, though a quick glance around the room revealed no one to match.

Phina tilted her face to the ceiling with a huge smile on her face. "ADAM!"

The man next to her, Greyson Wells, sighed and leaned an elbow on the table.

"ADAM?" She-Who-Mourns leaned forward, curious.

Wells gave her an amused but irritated glance. "The Empire's eyes and ears. He's an AI."

CHAPTER TWENTY-TWO

Link was bemused by the confusion in the Aurians' faces, so he clarified.

"AI. Artificial Intelligence."

Apparently the Aurians hadn't advanced enough before their decline to know the term. The thought filled him with unease. Shouldn't other aliens have developed AI technology before now? Surely humans couldn't be the only ones. Pushing the thought aside to deal with the current problem, he turned to Braeden and leaned around Phina.

"What's your best guess?"

Braeden's hairless brow furrowed; the expression looked odd without eyebrows. "Guess about what could be causing the pull of energy? I assume the mechanism is technological, but that could be wrong. Just because we haven't come across anything biological that could have done it doesn't negate the possibility." He tilted his head in thought, the awareness in his eyes fading as his attention turned inward. "Though a biological anomaly would be an amazing discovery, wouldn't it?"

"And alarming."

The awareness shot toward Link. "Yes, of course. However, as it has grown increasingly rare for our people to come across an unknown in the universe, the possibility is intriguing."

Phina spoke, diverting their attention. "Anyone have a thought as to how we will be able to find this thing, whatever it is? Braeden, you said you could feel the pull. Does that mean you can follow it back to the source?"

"Yes, I believe I could if we descended into the atmosphere enough to feel it but not pull as much out of me."

His piercing eyes turned to Phina, giving Link the sense that he had asked her something privately. What would it be like to be able to speak mind to mind? Would it be similar to the implant with a private channel or different? Phina apparently agreed with his request since she nodded, though she looked concerned. That didn't bode well. What the hell were they up to?

Link cleared his throat and decided he would stick close to Phina for the time being. No telling what new danger she would rush into if he wasn't there to help. "Stark, could you go into the atmosphere and continue down gradually until Braeden tells you to stop?"

"You got it."

Link felt the slight press of inertia as Stark moved.

"ADAM, any thoughts or insights?"

"Not yet. Once we reach the area, I would like to be involved in the discussion about the next step."

"Stop." The word came out roughly. Braeden appeared to be trying to breathe through what he was feeling. The ship halted.

"Which direction, Braeden?" Phina asked softly.

"It feels half a world away. That way." Braeden pointed.

Stark acknowledged the direction, and the ship began to move again.

"What direction is that, Stark?" Link wondered if the location would be familiar to the Aurians.

"Northeast."

He-Who-Acts looked confused by the terms. "Toward the dark sun or toward the bright?"

"If you are referring to where they are in the sky, we are moving toward the dark sun. As Braeden said, it's half the world away from where we started. Braeden, tell me any change in direction or speed if you will." Link looked at the ceiling in surprise. Stark sounded different today, personable without hamming it up. Huh.

A camera view from the front of the ship was displayed on a wall screen.

"I will." Braeden closed his eyes, and his face drew in with concentration. He was breathing more heavily, and his chest was moving with greater frequency. Phina frowned in concern, placed her hands on Braeden's chest, and closed her eyes as she had in the Pod.

Not wanting to stare, Link turned to the Aurians, wondering if they knew anything about where they were headed. He-Who-Listens stared at the screen, not blinking, his face impassive. He-Who-Moves tapped his fingers on his palms, his face reflecting his feelings about what he was seeing. He-Who-Acts clenched and unclenched his hands, his eyes not leaving a spot on the table in front of him. She-Who-Mourns sat frozen in her chair, her face turned to the screen. Her expression was one of horror and fear.

She knew.

Phina opened her eyes and turned away from the landscape on the screen, which seemed to go on in endless desolation. Just knowing that all the life had been sucked out of this planet caused pangs of heartache. Better to occupy herself with the people in the room.

Braeden, having been replenished by Phina, sat with his eyes shut, listening to and feeling that tug of energy. If Gleeks sweated, he would be profusely perspiring since his face showed signs of strain and his body shook as they drew closer. Some unknown object sucked the life out of people and planets. Not that she was feeling depressed or bitter or angry about it.

Nope, no.

Her hands kept clenching and her jaw twitched, showing just how coolly and calmly she had taken everything so far.

With a shudder, Phina closed her eyes for a brief moment, then turned to Link so Braeden and the screen were behind her. Less to tempt her to rage.

Link hadn't changed clothes since their fight with the Skaines earlier, so they still bore dust and blood. This was the most disheveled she had seen the man since they met. She realized she had been staring at the man's torso for far too long, and just then Link's muscles visibly tensed. She glanced at his face.

As usual, the man showed little expression, though he was staring across the table. Phina followed his gaze to She-Who-Mourns. Phina thought the Aurians' names were intriguing, though unwieldy. The female wore an expression of dread and terror as she stared at the screen. A quick glance showed nothing they hadn't seen in the last ten minutes, so the strong feelings emanating from the female were puzzling.

Since Phina's energy was back to its usual level, she opened her mind toward Link and She-Who-Mourns to get a sense of what was wrong.

Link's thoughts were elusive and chaotic, allowing her little understanding of the problem since there was no one thought or emotion that popped out. Instead of his emotions being rigidly controlled as she had learned to do, Link had apparently learned to feel all the emotions but show very little on his face. Phina hadn't thought it possible.

Yet, through the chaos, a phrase kept popping up just out of her mental sight. Straining, she could just barely manage to understand it. "She knows. She knows."

Who knew, and what did she know?

Remembering that his gaze had been locked on She-Who-Mourns, she reached out for her and let go of all but a small awareness of Link. The female's mind had less chaotic thoughts, but that marked the end of her scan being easy. Her mind was filled with terror, reluctance, and shame. She didn't hear any words, but her emotions projected something along the lines of, "It's all my fault."

Making a logical leap, Phina thought She-Who-Mourns believed she was to blame for what had happened to the planet. But how? Phina began a series of logical processes, mental calculations, and intuitive leaps that led her to a conclusion she wasn't happy about.

Fudging. Pickled. Crumbs.

Lost in her thoughts, she almost missed it when Braeden stiffened. "Slow down. We are close."

"How close is close?"

The ship jerked to a halt so quickly the others swayed in their chairs.

"A little farther."

The ship moved forward slowly until Braeden called a halt. He shivered and trembled, his body straining. Phina felt his distress and leaned forward to place her hand on his arm in comfort. His body vibrated with effort, and she could feel the growing weakness within him. She glanced around and saw everyone else in the room growing alarmed and pale.

"Stark, take us straight up out of the atmosphere."

After a moment, which Phina registered with a part of her brain that decided Stark must have calculated and come to a determination about why she had made the request, the ship swiftly moved higher. Braeden visibly eased the farther they moved away from the surface of the planet.

Looking around, Phina realized the Aurians were all looking paler, their dark skin gray. A swift glance at Link confirmed her earlier conclusion.

"This is going to suck."

"What will suck?"

Link had swung around to face Phina, suspicion causing his eyes to lock on hers and his eyebrows to draw in with concern. The little she-devil was up to something again, and he knew he wasn't going to like it.

"Oh." She blinked her eyes twice, then casually looked around the room as if searching for a way out of explaining.

"Phina."

Taking a deep breath, she straightened her shoulders and looked straight at him, stubbornness in her eyes and determination firming her mouth. "Someone needs to go down and see what can be done with whatever phenomenon is pulling the energy. Braeden would die. The Aurians can't go as they are still weak from malnourishment and dehydration. Humans can't go as their bodies wouldn't withstand the energy pull this close to the source. You just had a taste of it and were already having problems. So, it must be me."

"You're human, so you can't go."

Phina gave him a sad smile. "I think after the last few weeks, whatever I am, we can safely say I'm no longer a normal human."

Out of the corner of his eye, Link saw the Aurians turn toward each other. Coincidence, or did they understand what was happening here?

"Still, that doesn't mean you're safe." Why did he feel like he held water in his hands every time he tried to argue with her?

"I have the best chance. My body creates excess energy now, and that's what this thing pulls."

"All the more reason not to go!" Why couldn't the stubborn woman see he was trying to protect her?

"Someone has to, and that someone is me!" Phina's eyes flashed with determination and pain.

What was going on in that damned woman's brain?

"It is the same. I didn't want it to be, but it is. It is the same place and the same device."

When the Aurian female spoke, Link jerked back and ran a shaky hand through his hair. Link tried to focus on She-Who-Mourns as she spoke; she was living up to her name. Her eyes appeared larger, and they were frightened and brimming with sorrow. She clutched her arms around herself, frail and delicate.

He-Who-Acts turned his head toward her in anger and disbelief. His arm pushed He-Who-Moves back into his chair so He-Who-Acts could see her face. "You are saying you knew about this? You are el'adron! Our last el'adron! Were you a part of this tragedy that destroyed our home?"

"No!"

She-Who-Mourns was shocked out of her private horror at his accusation. Her face showed dismay and shame. Link's assessing eyes took it all in, then he spoke his conclusions.

"You knew about it."

Closing her eyes, she nodded. Her confidence and poise had fallen away, revealing a regretful, haunted, shattered female.

"Yes," she whispered. "I knew."

He-Who-Acts blurted, "Why did you not say something? We could have fixed this, and our families and friends would not have died!"

The Aurian female flinched at his vehemence. Phina held up her hands. "Wait, please. Let's listen to what happened before we judge the actions that were taken."

"I agree. It's easy to speak in hindsight." Link nodded in approval while Braeden spoke, breathing and moving easier now that his body wasn't stressed from the energy drain.

Tears shimmered in She-Who-Mourns' eyes as she nodded before looking down, her white hair falling forward to cover her face. She spoke quietly but could still be heard.

"Before this began, I was pledged to one of the males in our town, which is a short distance from the place down below. He was named He-Who-Thinks because his mind never stopped. He always questioned and attempted to learn new things. He would travel to the surrounding towns and cities, looking for new devices or ideas for making them. He enjoyed figuring out what they could do, taking them apart, and making them better."

Link sagged back in his chair. He could see where this story was headed. She-Who-Mourns twisted her fingers around each other as she continued.

"After a time, he brought home a large broken device he was very excited about. He never did explain how he got it and was secretive whenever the subject came up. One day I overheard him talking about the device with a friend. He had been able to fix part of it because his hands were much smaller than those who had made it and previously owned it. When the friend questioned him about the previous owners, he closed up, saying they were no longer around to claim ownership."

She-Who-Mourns finally looked up, her expression still troubled. "I should have taken that as the warning it was. After that conversation, he became even more withdrawn and secretive about everything, not just the device. We no longer had conversations, and any time I attempted one, he became impatient. After weeks of this, I woke up one morning feeling strange and having lost time. I finally went to visit his workshop. He barely acknowledged me, racing around the device to check readings and such. I told him our pledge was in danger of being compromised, that he hadn't kept the promises he had made, and if things didn't change, I would have to leave. I felt sick anytime I was home, and being closer to the device made it worse." She hugged herself, rubbing her flesh as if to get warm.

"He said he had more important things to do, and if I couldn't see that, then I wasn't the female he thought I was. I got angry, but I was hurt that he placed higher importance on this device than he did for me, his pledge. I left the next day and returned to my family in a town not far away. A couple of weeks later, I had a sense of danger and foreboding. After the first people became ill, I suspected it was connected to the device that He-Who-Thinks had found. I knew this illness wasn't going to go away, and we needed to leave."

She looked up, her eyes streaming tears. "I tried to go back to break the device that had cursed us all, but illness overtook me, and I wasn't able to continue. All I could do was run away with whoever would come with me. Some believed me, but even with the su'adon, very few followed me. They could not understand the danger." She shook her head sadly.

"We had never experienced anything like it, so their belief that nothing like I described could affect them prevented them from accepting the truth. We stopped anywhere we found people and told them we needed to flee, usually only able to stay a few weeks before needing to leave again. We ran halfway across the world to escape from it."

Her tale ended in a whisper. Link narrowed his eyes, certain there was more to the story. "And what makes you believe the illness is connected to this device?"

She turned to look at him, and chills raced down his spine. Damn it. Those shattered eyes were starting to get to him. "Aside from my illness, you mean? When I visited his workshop, he kept muttering about energy readings and drawing energy in while examining the plants he had placed around the edges of the room. They were all dying."

Braeden made noises of intrigue and satisfaction as if his ideas had been confirmed. He-Who-Acts shook his head in confusion. "Why would you hide this? Were you afraid we would throw you out?"

She-Who-Mourns flinched but shook her head. "There was no point to knowing. It could not be changed, and the knowledge would do nothing but create a greater burden and make us lose hope." She sighed sadly.

"If you had said something sooner, we could have gone and found the device and stopped all this!" His words were full of loss and frustration. She-Who-Mourns shuddered but fell silent.

"You would have died long before you got there."

Everyone turned to face Braeden, whose eyes were fixed on the Aurians. They shrank back at that.

"She was right to keep silent. Once this device had been set in motion, I believe anyone approaching it would have died long before reaching the center where the device is located."

"Which is why I have to go and see what we can do to fix this."

Phina's declaration dropped into the room like a stone in a pool. At the burst of fear that he would lose her, Link felt the darker part of himself, the part he strove to suppress whenever possible, surge forward.

CHAPTER TWENTY-THREE

**Etheric Empire, Orbit around Planet Lyriem, QBS
Stark**

"Over my dead body."

Phina turned to Link, too shocked to react. After a moment, she twitched her mouth into a smile. "That seems a little excessive, don't you think?"

His tone was implacable. "No. I don't see why anyone should go down there. We'll find somewhere else for them to live."

"Actually," Stark cut in, "leaving this device or process in place is a bad idea. The amount of energy it's amassed is huge since it's the whole of the energy of the planet and its people. Without seeing the code, it's difficult to say what will happen, but the readings on my scanners are not good for the health of this star system, and it could very well affect those living on the other three planets. From the readings I've taken every hour, we have only days until it reaches a critical level."

Phina jumped in. "Then it needs to be checked out

immediately. Since I'm the only one who has a chance to make it through the energy drain, I need to go."

Link groaned in frustration. "A chance. And that doesn't concern you, that you might not make it back? Don't we have a right to want you safe?"

Phina sat back in her chair, putting more distance between them. This was the argument in the bar all over again. She needed to understand what was driving him. Reaching out mentally, she found out. Though nothing showed on his face, his anger inundated her, but under that lay fear, pain, and regret. She stiffened and closed her eyes.

When she opened them a moment later, her voice, soft with compassion, barely reached Link's ears.

"I know you want me to stay safe. I wish life allowed me to alleviate your concerns." She knew he wouldn't appreciate her commenting on his fear of losing her in front of the others. "The life we've chosen isn't designed to be safe. None of us have chosen safe lives. On the contrary, we put ourselves in danger all the time for the Empire and anyone who needs help. This is no different."

Link shook his head, his eyes stormy with emotion. "The hell it's not! You would be alone and in danger, with no way for us to get you back without losing people! You haven't the experience for a situation like this."

"She won't be alone."

Drk-Vaen, with Sis'tael behind him, filled the doorway. Phina felt a combination of relief that she wouldn't have to be alone and fear that they would die too. Her shoulders tensed. She couldn't do it.

"You can't come with me. No one is going to die."

Drk-vaen clicked his mandibles but didn't get a chance

to speak. He was pushed inside by Sis'tael, who then stepped around him.

Head held high, Sis'tael hissed in anger at Phina. "You are not going by yourself. I think we all are agreed on that. The energy pull doesn't have the same effect on us as it does on you soft humans."

She nodded at Braeden, who turned a reproachful eye on the female. "And Gleeks and Aurians. Our hard exoskeletons protect us from the effects. We talked it over with ADAM and Stark, and they agree it shouldn't affect us nearly as much."

Phina frowned. "But the effects aren't gone, and that means you could still die."

"So could you," the Yollin pointed out in turn, her arms folded across her chest. "You can't tell me it won't affect you because you would be lying, and friends don't do that to each other."

Phina started to protest again when Braeden put his hand over her wrist, stopping her mid-sentence.

"Phina, you want to protect your friends, and that's admirable. You aren't considering that by trying to protect them, you are preventing them from doing their job as well as doing their best to protect you in return. It can't be just one way. Relationships don't work like that."

Phina looked into his gentle eyes. "Is that what I'm doing?"

Yes. Braeden's voice spoke in her mind, and Drk-vaen and Sis'tael nodded.

She met Link's gaze next. It usually bordered on arrogance, but now it was soft with concern. He nodded as he spoke. "You're trying to control your relationships, my dear, so they are on your terms. I recognize the signs because I have tried to do the same thing. It doesn't work. Relationships can't be controlled and remain intact. They need to be accepted, felt, engaged in, and appreciated, but never controlled."

Stunned, Phina closed her eyes and dropped her head. *Had* she been trying to control her relationships? Not one to shirk facing herself when it was pointed out, Phina examined her past actions and what had driven them. She had to admit there was something to what they were saying.

Fudging crumbs.

It had gotten worse with the aggression and the heightened and tense emotions she'd felt after the changes had begun in her body. She had felt so out of control that she wanted to control *something*.

Anything.

Phina's shoulders dropped as she sighed.

"All right. The three of us will go."

"They can go without you. You don't need to subject yourself to that. I know it's painful for you."

Link's eyes flicked to Braeden and back to her, willing her to agree. Phina smiled wryly. "You can't have it both ways, old man. There will probably be coding I need to decipher."

His eyes acknowledged she was right, but she could tell he didn't like it. Too bad. "Again with the respect."

"I respect you just fine. It's your attitude that needs work."

His dark expression caused her to throw him a grin while his muttered curses cheered her right up.

. . .

Etheric Empire, Planet Lyriem, Pod

Sis'tael's armor-clad body sparked with excitement and concern. Mostly concern. Her clawed feet gently tapped a rhythm as her fingers played with the indents on the paneling on either side of her while her head swiveled, taking everything in.

Phina sat up ahead, reading the displays in the front of the Pod. Drk-vaen sat behind Sis'tael. The two were engrossed in their thoughts, leaving Sis'tael to ponder her own. She wondered what they would find when they reached the location.

"I can't believe this."

Phina's muttered words drew Sis'tael's attention. She craned her head to see what had caused the comment but couldn't view anything around her friend's head.

"Can't believe what?"

Phina absently ran her fingers through her hair, snagging on the braid. She pulled her fingers out and smoothed her hair, but the loosened strands still stuck out, giving her a disheveled and absent-minded look.

"I can't believe how much life on this planet was destroyed. It all withered and died, the life sucked out of it. Look at it! The Gleeks' planet is brown and dusty, but there are areas that are cultivated for farming. Even the Baldere's stark planet has more life than this one. The destruction is mind-boggling!"

Sis'tael put her hand on her friend's shoulder and squeezed gently. "Are you all right, Phina? It isn't your planet."

Phina's head bobbed up, startled. "No, but I feel responsible for helping them. They need it, and I think I can help, so I have to do so. Tell me you can't look at this destroyed planet, knowing thousands of Aurians have died, and not feel the need to do something."

Sis'tael leaned forward to view the screen that showed the scans of the terrain below. Just as Phina had said, the planet looked dry, dusty, almost brittle. Thinking about those thousands of Aurian bodies lying around that had shriveled up into dry, brittle skin and bones made her cringe.

"I get what you mean, at least a little."

"It's awful," Phina whispered and glanced at the display sharply. "I think we've found the epicenter of all this."

Drk-vaen placed a comforting hand on Sis'tael's shoulder. "Where, Phina?"

"Down there in the foothills of those mountains."

Sis'tael looked but couldn't see anything until they drew close enough for the mountain to fill the whole screen. To her mind, it was an empty, barren, cold place of doom.

"Damn it. We're going under that, aren't we?"

"Yes. We're going under the mountain."

Etheric Empire, Orbit around Planet Lyriem, QBS *Stark*

Link stalked down the corridor of the ship, steps determined, mind on nothing related to the people on board. What had made him think taking on a trainee was a good idea? It was a horrible idea. Now, instead of coolly going through his self-imposed assignments and pushing and poking other people's buttons, he was involved with crazy diplomatic machinations, weird alien shenanigans and intrigue, and a future replacement he had somehow lost all control of.

When the hell had that one happened?

When he reached the end of the corridor and turned on his heel, he couldn't help comparing and contrasting current events with those of even a year ago. After several minutes of pacing, he had to face facts. Greyson Wells, diplomatic superstar and spy extraordinaire, had been bored out of his mind back then.

Well, he wasn't bored now.

"Greyson Wells, stop wearing a track through the deck!"

Link jerked to a halt as Addison Stone came up the corridor behind him. The scowl he turned on her didn't faze the woman. Damn it, no one on this ship showed him any respect.

"What do you want?"

The look she gave him was withering. "I don't want anything from you. However, I need you to calm down."

Link stared at her. "You want me to calm down."

Addison upped the intensity of her gaze to scalding. "Weren't you listening? I said need, not want. Pay attention, man!"

He drew himself up, nearly crossing his eyes as he stared down his nose at her. "I assure you, I pay very close attention."

She put her hands on her hips and narrowed her eyes. "Then listen up, buttercup. You need to find something else to focus on before you stress yourself out or drive yourself crazy."

Link paused. He wouldn't acknowledge that the woman had a point.

"Are you offering me a suggestion?"

Link spoke in a congenial tone, but Addison looked wary all of a sudden. What bee had gotten into her bonnet?

"I wasn't referring to physical gymnastics if that's what you were asking."

He gaped, then spluttered, "What? Why would you... I would never suggest such a thing."

Addison's mouth twisted wryly. "Of course not." She started to move away. "And stop that stupid pacing! It's getting on my nerves!"

Like the woman had any room to talk! He continued pacing, though he added a circuit through the cargo hold for variety. His pent-up energy had to go somewhere. The others were busy helping the Aurians board the support ships that had finally shown up, and the ones who weren't occupied shied away from him. Pacing was the only thing he could do while he waited for his recalcitrant mentee.

No, he wasn't bored now.

If Link didn't know better, he would admit he was scared to death.

CHAPTER TWENTY-FOUR

Etheric Empire, Planet Lyriem

Phina paced forward, holding up her tablet for Stark to scan her surroundings more easily. The caverns inside these mountains were really amazing. Every step gave her a new view of the most fascinating hued rocks and crystals she had ever seen. Of course, it also brought her step by inevitable step closer to the alien machine set in place by a madman.

That was a sobering thought.

She pushed the unwanted reminder to the side where she didn't need to think about it too hard, on par with liverwurst and annoying brothers.

"Are we there yet?"

"No, Stark."

"You're right. Scans show a larger cavern directly ahead."

"There you go then. You didn't need me." Something glinted in the corner of her eye. Phina turned to shine the light on her helmet to her right. The display caused her to stop, open-mouthed in astonishment, while Stark kept talking.

Glittering jeweled crystals of varying hues and tones encrusted the rock walls and ceiling of the cavern. The largest of the crystals were cloudy spears that cleared toward the top. These were raw diamonds and gemstones of all types in this one cavern, if she had to guess. Her brain stopped working for a moment.

"See, that's what I've learned. Jokes and teasing don't work unless you involve someone else. So yes, I did need you."

Phina shook her head to clear it and moved forward as the Yollins stepped up behind her.

"Hey, Stark?"

"Yes, GG?"

"Could you mark this cavern on my right? It's important. It needs to be explored later."

"I can do that. Pick a numeric value between 7 and 9 and multiply by a factor of 262, and that's roughly how many tasks I can handle at one time. One is nothing. It's boring."

Phina rolled her eyes, pushed aside the bejeweled cavern for later consideration, and concentrated on recalling his previous comment as well as putting her feet in front of each other.

"So, you needed me to be the butt of the joke?"

"No, I needed you to be the recipient of the joke and a witness to its manifestation. If there is no witness, is there a joke?"

"Is this your version of 'if a tree falls in an empty forest, can anyone hear it?'"

"That was not my intention, but I can give you mathematical equations, laws of physics, and an exegetical and philosophical argument if you want the answer."

"Thank you, Stark. Maybe some other time."

"Really? When?"

"Sometime when I'm not exploring a creepy dark cave looking for a machine that kills people."

The cavern had narrowed, its walls now a few steps to either side of her. Phina sensed something ahead that felt heavy in her mind. She had been feeling that strange weight for some time, she realized; she had just ignored it, thinking it was the caves.

Since she had slowed down, her Yollin friends caught up.

"Does it feel strange in here to you?"

Sis'tael's voice seemed to come out of nowhere, making Phina start. "It does."

Drk-vaen stopped next to her. All three of them had halted without realizing it. That was alarming.

"I'm feeling an unusual sense of tiredness. Is it just me?"

Phina assessed her mind and body. "It's not just you, Drk. We need to keep moving."

"It's that machine, isn't it?"

"Yup." Phina didn't know what else to say. They needed to get this done quickly. No more playing around.

The trio began moving rapidly, but after a while, Phina realized they had slowed down. Step by step, she forced herself to keep moving forward. Mentally, physically, and emotionally, every step forward became a slog and a contest of will. Her focus narrowed to that one thought.

By the time the cavern opened into another one, Phina

had almost forgotten why they were there. Even if she hadn't, what she saw would have shocked their mission out of her mind.

The great cavern in front of her stretched into the distance. In the middle of the rocky cavern lay...a paradise. Phina alternately blinked and squeezed her eyes shut a few times, but the verdant natural wonder remained the same. Having a goal made it easier to continue her unsteady pace forward.

When she was steps away, Phina raised her hand, eyes on the shimmering air in front of her. She didn't understand that she had stopped until she realized her hand wouldn't go any farther. No, not just wouldn't, but couldn't. Something had stopped the motion.

Bringing her hand back, Phina felt detached from herself, as if she were viewing her actions from a distance. An alarm blared in the back of her brain, but the mystery in front of her was so interesting that it was easily shoved to the side. She brought her hand back and thrust it forward several times, trying to find a way through the barrier. She forgot what she was doing there, only remembering that she had to keep going.

As her motions grew more frantic, Phina realized applying greater force allowed her to move her hand farther. Force. Greater force. Testing one more time, her hand moved even farther. Her thoughts were consumed by the action. By the time she knew what she had to do, she had forgotten her own name.

Forcing herself to back up was the hardest thing she had ever done. She thought it was, anyway. She couldn't remember. After she had gone back as far as she believed she needed to, muffled shouts registered. Irritably clawing a hand to the side to get the annoying buzz to stop, the young woman focused again on that mesmerizing barrier in front of her. What was she doing again?

Right.

Entering paradise.

She shook her head to make the buzzing noises go away. She knew how to get to paradise, and she was going to do it.

She knew she had to be quick and couldn't hesitate.

With a final gasp, she thrust herself forward with every last iota of will and focus. She was going to make it. The shouts grew louder, but she didn't stop or even hesitate. She did what she had to do. With only a few feet left, she pushed forward and, twisting in the air to gain momentum, she dove bladed-hands-first like a diver into water.

Phina lost momentum when she hit the barrier, but her move allowed her body to pass through. When she felt no resistance, she sank to the ground and fell into a black well of unconsciousness.

But she had made it. She had reached paradise.

So this was what dying felt like.

Drk-vaen had had a bad feeling about the plan from the beginning. He just wished he had been able to think of something to do to change it.

The truth was that until they knew what they were dealing with, their hands were tied. They needed more information, and without someone on the ground, they had no way of knowing what had to be done. So, he'd said nothing.

Which he was now bitterly regretting.

When the walls opened to show a vibrant green forest in the middle of a cavern with some sort of forcefield around it, Drk-vaen realized they were in big trouble.

"Holy hell." Sis'tael spoke softly, awestruck as she took it in.

Clicking his mandibles, he turned to his love in amusement. "Holy hell?"

She chittered nervously for a moment, the sound dying as her attention went back to the patch of green in front of them. "It seemed to fit."

Drk-vaen looked at the life kept within the barrier surrounding it, lying inside a dry, dusty cavern littered with the mummified remains of various small creatures on a planet that was dying inch by inch. His amusement faded. "Yeah, it does."

Sis'tael gasped. "Look at Phina!"

Swinging his head around, Drk-vaen realized Phina had rested her hand on the barrier. As the Yollins watched, she poked the thing with varying amounts of force. She had to have some method to her madness, right?

"Phina, are you sure that's safe?"

Their friend's silence was concerning.

"What's wrong?" a new voice asked.

Drk-vaen shook his head. "Stark, we don't know. Phina seems to be in a waking trance. She's moving, but she's not responding to us, and we don't know what's going on."

"Give me a minute."

The large Yollin glanced at the female who gave him

their version of a shrug, then turned back to her friend. Drk-vaen sighed and rubbed the back of his hard, bony head. This trip hadn't turned out anything like they were expecting. What was that human phrase? *"The best-laid plans of rats and men?"* He pondered that while they waited and wondered if humans considered the rats to be as intelligent as humans since they were included in the saying.

Stark's voice broke the tension.

"Wells says to abort. Bring Phina even if you have to carry her and come back to the ship."

The Yollins exchanged glances. Sis'tael looked troubled. "I am not sure that's the best decision. Phina needs to get this done. She's going to be upset if we do anything to mess her up if she knows what she's doing."

Drk-vaen watched Phina as she began to shuffle backward. "That is something to consider. Maybe we should try to get her attention and see if she responds."

They moved toward her, yelling and trying every way they knew to get her attention short of grabbing her. Finally, Phina stopped and stood still, her gaze on the barrier.

Drk-vaen and Sis'tael halted when they saw Phina's face twist into a grimace while her left hand came up in a clawing motion. After the echoes had died down, Phina's face gave a twitch of satisfaction before all expression fell away.

Sis'tael's mandibles were completely extended, which showed how alarmed she was. "She isn't responding right, but that gesture looked like she wanted us to be quiet."

"I don't know. Perha…"

Phina moved forward in a stumbling run that grew

steadier as she gained momentum. Drk-vaen bellowed in protest, and Sis'tael ran forward to stop her. He wasn't far behind her. Phina had obviously gone mad.

Feet from the barrier, Phina leaped and dove into it. Sis'tael stopped in shock. Drk-vaen reached out to grab her and did his best not to trip over her legs as he came to a halt. They stared as their friend broke free of the force field inside the bubble and fell limply to the ground.

Then again, he had been told over and over that the young female was brilliant.

Moments passed, and Phina didn't move. There wasn't even a breeze to ruffle her hair. Drk-vaen's hand slid down Sis'tael's arm until he found her hand. Sis'tael grabbed his arm with her other hand. "Do you think…"

"She's going to be fine," he assured her.

If only he could begin to believe it.

CHAPTER TWENTY-FIVE

Etheric Empire, QBS *Valiant*

Braeden's eyes widened, his head turning in the direction the trio had traveled down to the planet. He was keeping tabs on Phina in his concern for her well-being while he helped the team pass out supplies for the Aurians. Phina's mental activity had suddenly decreased.

As he swallowed roughly, afraid for the worst, he felt a small hand on his arm. He looked down into the light-filled eyes of She-Who-Mourns, her expression grave. "You are concerned. Is it Phina?"

Braeden still felt weary from his ordeal, so he gave her a nod and gestured to a large, sturdy container full of bandages that sat off to the side. Since most of the Aurians' health issues were related to dehydration and malnutrition, the supplies for wounds hadn't been touched very often, but the containers worked just fine for makeshift seats. He and the female threaded their way past Aurians and those from the Empire helping them with food, water, medical treatment, cleanliness, and places for everyone to sleep.

"I am concerned about them, yes." Braeden shook his head as they sat down. "From what I can tell, they have found what they sought, but I think something is wrong with Phina. I am having trouble keeping the mental connection steady with my lack of strength. I wish there was more we could do to help them, but we can only wait and hope."

She-Who-Mourns sat straight, her body poised and elegant. She reminded him of Anna Elizabeth. She nodded thoughtfully. "Hope is important. It is what kept my people alive when all seemed lost."

Though he was concerned, Braeden couldn't repress his curiosity and leaned forward. "It has been some centuries since my people visited your planet. May I ask what the word 'el'adron' refers to?"

The small female clasped her hands together and looked up solemnly. "It means 'light of our hearts.'" It is sacred, a spiritual leader who is also a judge of others. Our word is law to our people. All who are el'adron have the su'adon." She gestured to her light-filled eyes. "You see that mine are the only eyes like this. All the rest of my people have violet eyes. The su'adon is influence, able to share comfort or peace, or hope, sometimes fear or pain. In my role as a judge, I also invoke the truth and bring it to light. It is a role we all take seriously, so it is hard for some, like He-Who-Acts, to see that I too make mistakes at times." She hesitated but continued, her eyes filled with sorrow. "It is considered highly improper, akin to abuse, to use su'adon on a pledgemate, but perhaps if I had, I could have prevented this tragedy." She bowed her head as tears fell from her eyes.

Braeden could see that many of the nearby Aurians were listening to their conversation, including the male in question. He was frowning but listening to the words the el'adron spoke. He-Who-Acts quietly came forward when She-Who-Mourns cried and crouched to put his hand on hers.

"I can't deny I was angry, but after hearing your explanation and thinking about it, I understand why you said nothing. You have always been careful to give us hope, and knowing the cause would have taken that away." He gently squeezed her hand and let go. "You did nothing wrong. You were more wronged than any of us. You are our el'adron, and I believe in you."

He stood and backed away as She-Who-Mourns looked up in surprise. Her tears fell faster as all the Aurians in the large room faced her and bowed their heads. "We believe in you, el'adron."

She-Who-Mourns stood and crossed her hands over her heart. "Thank you, my people. You honor me with your belief and trust." She bowed her head to them in return, then turned to Braeden with hope and determination.

"There *is* something we can do for Phina. We can ask the universe to aid her."

She closed her eyes, then sang one of the most gorgeous pieces of music Braden had ever heard. It spoke of love and duty. It spoke of justice and truth. It spoke of hope and trust.

By the time She-Who-Mourns finished, her eyes glowing with light, Braeden believed. Phina might struggle, but she would survive.

. . .

Etheric Empire, Planet Lyriem

Phina's body burned as if every nerve was on fire. She left the black realm of unconsciousness, knowing nothing but pain that seemed to go on forever. She tried to scream but couldn't push the sound past her throat.

Then it ended.

She lay still, panting for breath. Feeling disoriented, she made a few attempts to open her eyes, finally slitting them to look around. All she saw was green, a bright shade so vibrant it almost didn't look real. Where was she?

If she hadn't already had an experience where she had lost consciousness and didn't even know her name, she would have panicked. As it was, she knew herself. She just had no idea where she was or how she'd gotten there. Obviously, she was on a planet.

As her eyes gradually grew used to the strange radiating light, Phina was finally able to open her eyes completely. Numerous trees and plants bore fruits and vegetables. It looked like paradise.

Phina finally convinced her body to move from its sprawled state and slowly pushed up.

"Phina! We've been so worried about you!"

A relieved grunt followed, one that was too deep for the first voice.

Who could that be? She ran through the possibilities and came up blank. Body so tense she longed for a massage and still shaky, she finally gained her feet, picking her tablet up on the way, and turned around. The sight of the two Yollins thrust her most recent memories into the forefront of her brain, disorienting her for a minute. Right. Drk-vaen and Sis'tael. Her friends. They were helping her find and stop a crazy person. And there was something to do with a...cat? She shook her head in confusion.

"Are you okay, Phina? You looked like you were in pain."

Phina rubbed her face, attempting to dispel the lingering ache as well as stimulate thought. The effort was only marginally successful. "I will be. This stuff isn't exactly a walk in a park."

Drk-vaen and Sis'tael exchanged glances, then looked back in amusement. "Well..." Drk-vaen began.

"It kind of is." Sis'tael finished.

Phina looked up in surprise, then glanced at the green foliage. After a few moments, a smile graced her lips up. "I guess you're right."

"So, what's the next step?"

Phina avoided looking at her friends. "Maybe you two should stay there while I explore."

Drk-vaen took a step forward and stopped mere inches from Phina, separated only by the luminescent translucent barrier. "Not going to happen. Try again."

After staring at his fierce, determined face for a moment, Phina nodded. "Fine. Just don't say I didn't try to save you two from the crazy stuff."

He gave her a smile so fierce that if she didn't know him, she would have been frightened. "No worries, Phina. Crazy is what we Guardians and Marines run toward."

Shifting, Phina raised an eyebrow to Sis'tael. "Looks like he's been practicing his scary face."

Her friend grinned. "Oh, yeah. Mister Scary has come out to play."

Drk-vaen shook his head and rolled his eyes in mock

disgust. "You females sure know how to knock a male's ego down."

Phina playfully buffed her nails, then examined them, giving him a bright smile. "Just doing my part to keep males humble."

Drk-vaen grumbled as Sis'tael recovered from her laughter. "What I want to know is, how we are going to get in there without going through a similar painful experience?"

Phina considered scenarios in her head for a few seconds, then assessed her body. She felt much better, not as stiff as she had moments ago. She thought back over events and realized she had been massively and danger-ously depleted of energy just before plunging through the barrier. When her body felt like it was on fire, it must have been the quick pull of energy to replenish it once the drain was gone. She shook her head, not looking forward to the return to the ship.

"Phina?"

She looked up, revisited several ideas, and settled on the simplest and most likely to work based on her hazy memories. Phina braced herself, then thrust her arm forward with great force. She broke through the barrier, grabbed Drk-vaen's hand, and pulled the Yollin through. He stumbled, and his weight pulled at her as it met the resistance of the barrier. However, within seconds, her friend had come through. Without any ceremony, Phina dropped his hand, leaving him wobbling for balance, and moved over a couple steps to accomplish the same for Sis'tael.

She wobbled too as she shook off her disorientation. "Well, that's one way to do it."

Phina shrugged. "Me pulling you through seemed like it would have a better outcome than you doing it yourself."

Her friend gave her a shaky smile. "We aren't unconscious on the ground, so I guess I can't argue with that."

Drk-vaen put a hand out to help Sis'tael stabilize, though Phina suspected he needed the contact as well. Phina stepped into the foliage around them to give the two some space, pushing through the dense stems and branches. She looked at the plants and the translucent barrier that buzzed with energy.

"This looks like a forcefield that is generated by the machine to protect the area around itself. Drk, how wide would you say this unlikely natural wonder is?"

He thought for a moment. "Perhaps one hundred and twenty meters?"

"Maybe someone should have come looking by now?"

Drk-vaen became more alert, his eyes searching the area. "Now that you mention it."

"Hmmm." Phina took one more look around, hands on her hips near where her knives were sheathed. "Let's take a look closer to the center, but keep a watch. With foliage this thick, there could be dozens of people around without us realizing it."

Sis'tael jerked her head from side to side, her mandibles clicking in agitation. "Thanks for sharing that disturbing thought."

Phina gestured for the Yollins to spread out. It wasn't until they had moved several torturous meters through the jungle-like terrain that she remembered she didn't need to rely on her five senses.

She mentally reached out and found the minds of her friends, then expanded her search. It didn't take long to realize that only one other mind resided in this oasis.

Phina continued forward and pushed through a leafy curtain, then stopped dead.

An Aurian male stood in front of a device that pulsed and radiated light. It was wide enough that two of her could have barely touched fingers as they spanned the circumference. A thick rod reached up from the base toward the cavern's ceiling. Phina didn't know how high since her full attention now rested on the male.

He appeared ragged, his clothing worn. It stretched out from his center in strips and pieces. Though he seemed thin, he appeared to be vibrantly healthy. His hair had grown to twice the length of a normal male's, though it was uneven and the strands were unkempt and knotted.

Her perusal took her to his face. His jaw had dropped, and his bright eyes were wide with disbelief. He sputtered his shock before finally getting words out. "What? How did... Who are you people?"

Her Yollin friends turned to her with amused and expectant expressions. Phina gave them a glare they returned with innocence, inasmuch as a Yollin could convey that expression. She shook her head and decided to ignore them in favor of the crazy male...alien...person.

"We are part of a team from the Empire that came to save the people on your planet."

He drew himself up in astonishment. "Save them? From what?"

"From *that* is my guess." She nodded at the machine behind him.

If he'd had eyebrows, they would have lowered in anger and disbelief. "What do you mean by that? My shining one wouldn't harm anything! Can't you see what's around you? This whole area grew because my shining one caused it to!" His claim ended triumphantly.

Phina viewed him dispassionately. This guy seemed to have no idea of the harm he had caused. That put a different twist on things. She had expected either a dead guy or a cold-blooded murderer. Instead, they found a fanatical bumbler who didn't understand how many people had died because of him.

She sighed. "I hate to be the one to tell you, but your 'shining one,' as you call it, has caused thousands upon thousands of deaths."

He gasped. "How dare you say such a thing! My shining one causes life, not death!"

Phina pulled her tablet out. "Stark, bring up the video of the planet, would you? "

"Sure thing, boss."

She walked forward a few steps so he could see the screen, trying to ignore the hesitant steps he took backward until he couldn't go any farther. She stopped a few paces away, turned the tablet around, and held it up. He froze; his eyes were riveted to the screen, his gaze hungrily drinking everything in.

For the first few seconds. His ensuing shock turned into a mix of disbelief and anger. "What is this? This can't be Lyria! It's dry and barren. Lyria is green and full of life!"

Frowning, Phina ventured. "The other Aurians called the planet Lyriem."

"'Song of sorrow!' What would cause them to change the name so much?" the Aurian asked.

She raised her eyebrows and pointed at the stark, barren land on the screen. "That, I imagine."

The male stared at the screen with a scowl.

Phina sighed as if she weren't painfully aware that the fate of life on the planet rested on the shoulders of the male in front of her and her ability to convince him to help her figure out the device. "Believe or disbelieve what we say. It won't change what is."

His eyes narrowed, and he glared at her. He ignored Drk-vaen and Sis'tael, who had quietly taken up flanking positions. "How do I know you aren't showing me somewhere else and trying to trick me?"

She shrugged. "It's possible. I'm not, but you can't know for certain with me showing you a generic landscape. We are in a time crunch here, though."

The male, who was leaning protectively against the machine behind him, looked pathetic. "Well, I'm not giving you my shining one just because you tell me to! I'm a highly evolved, intellectually advanced being. I need proof! I need information! I need..."

Sis'tael muttered, "A life?"

"...facts and pictures! One video doesn't mean anything."

Phina eyed his thin face and body, likely a result of living within the energy-suffused forcefield for years. It wasn't until you looked into his eyes that you saw the frantic need that approached obsession. Those eyes aged the man far more than his body appeared.

"Stark?"

"Yes, Phina?"

The male cringed when he heard the voice through the tablet. Obviously, his time around tech the last few years had been rather limited. Shrugging, she steered her mind back to the issue at hand.

"If I give you a location, can you send the picture back to us?"

"Sure, boss."

Phina raised an eyebrow with an expectant look at the crazy Aurian. He shifted from side to side, biting his lip, wringing his hands, and avoiding her gaze. "What?"

"You asked for proof. We are trying to get it for you. Where did you live?"

He ducked his head rather sheepishly. "Ah. Right. We lived in Tre'falar." Thankfully the male saw her lack of understanding and moved on to describe the direction and distance. Phina turned back to her tablet.

"Stark, you got that?"

"Yup. Coming to your tablet in ten seconds." He counted down until the screen showed the ruins of a town. Astonishment washed over the Aurian's face.

"This…this can't be right." His voice was panicked. "No, no! This can't be all that's left. What happened to my family? All our neighbors? My pledgemate, She-Who-Shines? They can't all be gone!" He looked up, eyes frantic. "No, you're still tricking me! This could have been made to look like my home, but it's not! It can't be!"

Phina felt twinges of sorrow for him. He had lived for

years in ignorance, and the scales were now falling away from his eyes. Such revelations were painful. It would take someone with a heart of stone not to be affected.

Knowing it would be the final nail in the metaphysical coffin he had made for himself, she brought up the footage from within *Stark* that had been taken when his pledgemate described her escape and the ensuing disaster. The pained noises he made when he saw her face brought tears to Phina's eyes. After handing the tablet to him, she took a few steps back to be respectful.

The male sank to his knees in front of this infernal alien device. His expression changed from pain to disbelief, then horror, and finally acceptance. He continued watching his pledgemate while Stark played the scene. His face was visibly older when he finally rose and handed it back to her, now solemn and somber.

"I was such a fool." He shook his head, then looked up earnestly. "I didn't know. I did try to leave and find her every few years, but this force field kept me here." His eyes touched hers with quiet desperation.

"I know."

"But what can we do? It's too late to reverse the process. Perhaps when it first started it could have gone back to normal, but from what you said, it's spread across the planet." His anguished expression changed to consideration. "The amount of energy the device contains..." He looked at the device and then the energy field surrounding them. "It's incalculable."

Phina eyed the Aurian warily, not comfortable with what she saw on his face. As she watched him, she pinged

Stark on her tablet. "Stark, have you been following the conversation?"

"Yes indeed, Genius Girl."

"What are your thoughts on how we should handle the device? I'm guessing merely turning it off would cause problems."

The Aurian squawked in dismay as Stark gave a choking cough. "Problems. Yes. An explosion similar to a star going supernova would definitely be a problem."

CHAPTER TWENTY-SIX

Etheric Empire, Planet Lyriem

Phina paced on a small strip of cave floor that didn't possess a tree or machine. She had been brainstorming ideas about what to do with the device for the past hour with Link, Stark, Maxim, ADAM, and Braeden. ADAM had relayed communication between their group and a group on the *Meredith Reynolds* that consisted of Bethany Anne, General Lance Reynolds, and Dan Bosse, the General's right-hand man. Drk-vaen, Sis'tael, and He-Who-Thinks were either exploring or just trying to stay out of her way.

>>Bethany Anne says the Aurians have been failed badly enough already. She wants to know what it would take for us to save the planet. Is it possible?<< ADAM relayed.

"Wouldn't it be better to leave this place to its destruction and find a new spot for the Aurians to colonize? We need to get our people out of there." Link sounded irritated and anxious.

Phina shook her head. "We can't. I've been looking at

the coding and there are a few options, but most of them aren't good. We don't want to reverse the process since releasing the massive amount of energy contained in this field would cause an explosion that would destroy the planet as well as a good portion of this star system. However, something our Aurian friend here didn't realize is that there's a code at the end that will be triggered when the device has consumed all the energy of the planet. It doesn't make sense. My grasp of astrophysics could be better, but it looks like it will open either a black hole or a portal. From my calculations, it will reach that threshold in the next two weeks."

Link sighed. "You're right. Neither of those options sounds good."

"Are you kidding? They're horrible." Maxim was appalled.

She brought up the coding to scan it again. "I believe we can halt the process and put it into stasis without much trouble. I just want our digital friends to look it over to make sure my calculations and coding are accurate."

"I'll cautiously agree to that option." Link responded. "It looks like our best bet."

From ADAM came, "Agreed."

Braeden spoke up. "What will you do with this device once it is halted? I do not think it should just sit in the cavern."

"I've been thinking about that while you have been arguing about this." Phina expertly turned on her heel as she talked. "We have down here a large amount of what basically works out to be energy, correct? Energy that contains the essence of the life of the planet. Since we have it, we might as well use it to do some good instead of sitting around to potentially cause trouble later. What we need is a mechanism to spread that energy and infuse it back into the planet. We can use it to re-terraform the land."

"That sounds plausible." Link spoke slowly enough that Phina knew he was checking his tablet to see if it actually was.

"ADAM, don't we have a terraforming device we've used to repopulate a few planets?"

"We have, Phina, but without seeing the device there, I am uncertain if we can feasibly connect the two." ADAM sounded slightly stressed to Phina's ears. What would cause him to be so stressed that it affected his voice? The mind boggled, considering how stoic the AI always seemed.

"Well, hold on a minute while I do this...and this..." Phina paused to capture an image of the device and the energy field beyond it with the camera on her tablet, then walked closer to view the controlling mechanisms and the components. After making sure the pictures showed the proper views, she sent them to ADAM.

Moments later, ADAM responded, "From what I can see, it's possible, but it would require an additional device or mechanism to connect the two since they use different systems."

Phina nodded and resumed pacing, her solution at hand. "Braeden, the Gleeks appear to have a way to connect nature and natural energy with machines that I don't believe we have in the rest of the Empire. Is this something the Gleeks could help us with?"

Braeden's mental voice was comforting. *Only one of our people has that knowledge, but I believe we can accomplish this task. However, the method used would only be shown to one person outside of our brothers, and the one chosen cannot speak or share the specifics of what they learn with anyone. It is the only way my brothers would agree to it.*

Link sounded like he might protest, but ADAM cut in. "Bethany Anne thanks you, Braeden, and sends best wishes for the project going well."

Although he did not say anything, Phina could picture Braeden's head nodding in agreement during the pause that followed.

"So…" Link's voice sounded eager. "We came and found the planet and its people, we discovered the problem, located the source, and we now have a plan to resolve the issue. I believe it is time to return home to the *MR*. The Aurians can stay in guest housing there while we wait for the terraforming process to play out."

Phina stopped pacing and turned, her eyes catching those of He-Who-Thinks, who sat out of her way across the small clearing. Holding the eye contact, Phina swallowed before asking, "And He-Who-Thinks? Is he coming with us?"

There was silence for several moments before Link responded, "She-Who-Mourns just weighed in, and she's right. He made a grievous error, but we can't compound it by leaving him alone again or abandoning him to die. Bring him with you."

Phina nodded as He-Who-Thinks watched her anxiously. Taking the Aurian with them was the right thing to do.

. . .

Etheric Empire, Planet Lyriem

Phina stumbled but continued to put one foot in front of the other. They had put the machine into the holding pattern so energy would no longer be drawn into it and the life-suffused area surrounding it. They had also agreed to send a group of Marines and Guardians to make sure no one messed with the device before it could be used. Since the device wasn't taking in energy, it was safe for them to remain nearby.

Once they'd tested the system to make sure there wouldn't be a problem, they decided to leave. However, since they had left the barrier containing the energy, Phina had become more exhausted with every step she took.

"Phina? You all right?"

Phina blinked slowly and didn't answer the female voice. Rather, she tried to answer, but the words didn't make it from her brain to her vocal cords. It took too much effort when all the energy she had was put into taking one more step. Then one more. Where was she going again?

"We are almost to the ship, Phina. Just hang on. Stark, can you hear me?"

Right. The ship.

"Of course, Drk-vaen. I'm not hard of hearing."

"Can you ask the doctor to get ready? I think that thing you all were afraid would happen is happening."

Words, words, words. Why did they have to use so many words? And why were they talking about her and not to her? She was right here. One more step.

"You mean where GG's body is shutting down and she's going to die?"

That sounded bad. She wasn't going to die. She was going to make it to the ship. She shuffled her foot forward one more step.

"Yeah, that one." The voice didn't sound happy about it.

The other voice came back subdued and quieter, though it was no less urgent. "Doc says to double-time it. You are sixty-seven meters from the Pod. Get her here as fast as you can."

One more... The world blurred and swirled as she was picked up and the person began running, jostling her with the hurried pace over the uneven ground.

"Hold on, Phina!" the female voice called from her feet side. Foot side? Foot slide. Pool slide. Words were funny. She would have laughed at the thoughts in her head, but it was too much effort. Hold on? Hold onto what? "Just stay alive!"

Stay alive? She could do that. Phina was all over that. She just needed some sleep first. The voice faded, and she fell unconscious.

Etheric Empire, QBS *Stark*

Link paced the corridor, his coat swinging as he turned. His brown-and-gray-streaked hair was in tufts since he had been tugging on it for the past few hours. His shirt and pants were rumpled, having been worn for too long. The lines on his face appeared more prominent while his anxious eyes darted to a door down the corridor every few seconds. Beeping alarms kept being set off since Phina's vitals continued to spike and then crash. The stasis in the Pod-doc was the only thing keeping her alive.

Finally, Link lifted his hands to his hair, tugging and growling, "Stark, can't you go any faster?"

"Just as I told you the last twenty-seven times you asked, no. I am going the fastest that can be flown for everyone's safety. We have cut off a full twelve hours. We will be there by this time tomorrow."

Link turned to view the door, the shadows in his eyes deepening. He couldn't get out of his mind the sight of Phina's limp body carried by Drk-vaen. Sis'tael had been next to him, holding the almost forgotten He-Who-Thinks in her arms. The Aurian was loudly complaining that his position was undignified.

No one cared. All eyes were on the unconscious Phina. So much bravery and determination in one body that was failing. The doctor had said she might have died if they hadn't had a Pod-doc on board. He felt bleak at the thought that she might not make it and shook his head. "That may not be in time."

Stark remained silent for several moments, then briskly dropped his words over the ship-wide intercom. "Everyone has two minutes to use the facilities or grab what they need. Then buckle up, buttercups, and strap in. We are going home the fast and dangerous way. If we all don't die, we'll make it back in four hours."

Link closed his eyes, then opened them and ran, calling, "Thank you, Stark!"

"Don't thank me yet. We really could die. It's a good thing the Aurians left since they wouldn't have had reliable harnesses."

Link nodded as he reached the control room and his assigned seat. The team from the Empire had finished transferring the Aurians to the other ships while they waited for the group to return from their exploration. The doctor had been checking on the Aurians' health, and Alina had been sorting and passing out clothing, making adjustments on the fly.

Everyone had hurried back to *Stark* when they heard their friends were on the way and Phina was struggling. Shortly after they returned, Phina's body had crashed in a delayed reaction to her recent activity. Braeden theorized the energy from the machine in the cave had supplied what she needed, so the stores in her body weren't depleted. Once she had left the machine's sphere of influence, that store of energy had quickly been burned through, the toll on her body progressing too rapidly. She had come to with help and then gone into full-body muscle spasms and cramps, screaming in agony.

She had been taken into the medical chamber on the ship, Doctor April coming on board just in time. She had assured Link that Phina wouldn't feel much once she was sedated and placed in stasis in the Pod-doc, but clearly, pain wasn't the only concern since those damned alarms kept going off.

He scowled, hearing them again while he buckled himself in. He had hoped that whatever needed to be fixed could be done in the Pod-doc on the ship, but after some badgering, ADAM had finally told him that with how screwed up Phina's nanocytes were, only Bethany Anne's personal Pod-doc was capable of fixing them.

Regardless, Phina lay close to death due to one person. Link wouldn't rest until that person paid for their crime.

Etheric Empire, QBBS *Meredith Reynolds*, Receiving Hall

"Have you heard from Greyson about Phina?"

Anna Elizabeth strode down the corridor. She was wearing a ball gown, the royal blue at the shoulders fading to blue-gray at the hem of the wide skirt. Blue embroidered vines extended from the sweetheart collar and small off-the-shoulder sleeves toward the bottom, while icy lace extended up from the hem. Anna's face shimmered as she moved under the lights, with black, white, and hints of blue on her eyelids. The effect gave her an ice queen look that her silvered blonde hair accentuated, particularly with it held up by jeweled combs.

Jace turned toward her in his dashing black-tie ensemble. His face changed from slightly flirty as he spoke to a fellow student to all business as he responded to Anna Elizabeth, nodding. "Yes, still the same." The student rolled her eyes at the change and walked into the receiving hall. Jace didn't give her a glance.

The group had been back for a week. Phina was stable, but TOM, ADAM, and Doctor Keelson were analyzing her system to determine the best way to adjust her body to either adapt to or reject the changes. However, the most troubling thing to Anna's mind was that Phina had yet to wake up from the coma she had fallen into shortly before arriving on the *Meredith Reynolds*.

As Anna passed her mentee, she paused, her skirts

swishing from the sudden stop. She gazed at him in concern. "Are you all right, Jace?"

Surprised into halting as well, he turned thoughtful. "I'm concerned, of course. Phina and I had just come to terms with being friends. I hope she pulls through this soon."

"She has been through a lot." Anna nodded in understanding. Her and Greyson's friendship had started similarly. Speaking of... "Did Greyson mention if he would come to the event?"

Jace shook his head, which made Anna frown thoughtfully. She knew Greyson had hoped to make contact with a few people, and it had sounded urgent at the time. To have him forgo that opportunity... Well, it caught her attention.

Anna pulled herself out of her reflections to give Jace a faint smile. "Is everything handled? Barnabas has finished his scans of the senior diplomats?"

Jace nodded, his eyes showing satisfaction. "Yes, everything went just as you instructed, and Barnabas finished about thirty minutes ago. He said he would talk to you about the results tomorrow."

"He would have told us if there was an urgent concern to handle." Her eyes sparkled in amusement. "Well, then. I suppose all that's left is for you to enjoy your evening. Was that your date just now?"

Jace did a double-take, then glanced toward the receiving hall. "Er, yes. It was. I may be getting the cold shoulder tonight."

Anna raised her eyebrows. "I'm sure you won't have any trouble finding someone to spend time with."

Leaving Jace looking surprised and uncertain, Anna

Elizabeth glided into the receiving hall, her smile gracious and welcoming while her eyes moved from one guest to the next. She still found it amusing that Phina's solution had been to host an event designed for matchmaking as much as for celebration. While she hadn't considered the thoroughness of the young woman's solution before Phina brought it up, there was a certain elegance to it that pleased her.

It was, of course, one of the reasons she had endeavored to solicit solutions from the two trainees. It was all very well for Greyson to train Phina in his strengths, but Anna hoped to make sure the two most important positions in the Diplomatic Corp were filled with the best, most highly trained persons.

As the dean and the founding member of the Corps, she couldn't bear to do otherwise. Anxiety and sorrow filled her heart. She sincerely hoped Phina would wake up soon and be all right. Moving forward was how she coped with troubled times, so she continued through the room.

Her attention was captured by one of her senior diplomats gallantly flirting with the woman in front of him, possibly the person ADAM had matched him with. A brief glimpse of an artfully enhanced beautiful face caused her no surprise since Anna knew the man to value appearance more than the intelligence behind it.

As her gaze moved on, his smooth gallantry was in the minority. Anna couldn't suppress her amusement at the sight of her well-spoken senior diplomats being bashful, tongue-tied, and perplexed by the additional guests at their celebration event. She stored those glimpses in her memory to savor later and turned to proceed to her next item to complete.

"I wondered how long I would need to wait to get a word with you."

Anna Elizabeth turned in surprise, though nothing on her face betrayed her emotions. "Dan. I didn't expect to see you tonight."

Dan Bosse gave her a playful grin as he fingered a glass with bubbles, likely some form of champagne. "Am I too rough and tumble for your dignified event? Lady, you supply elegance and dignity to any event. There is no need to provide it myself when you are in the room."

"Nonsense." She narrowed her eyes as she examined his appearance and found no fault in the well-made suit that fit his large form. He stood taller than her even in heels and still had a military bearing that kept his posture straight and shoulders back. The small wrinkles in his face, the first signs of graying hair on his head, and the small beard on his square jaw were the only indications of a man just past his prime.

Dan winked at Anna Elizabeth, then turned to snag another glass like his from a tray as a waiter walked by. As he offered the glass to her, he casually commented, "Truth is never nonsense."

Anna searched the man's face and found what she had been looking for: sincerity and an artless openness. It was a refreshing change from her usual dance of intrigue and polite deception as the leader of the diplomats. As much as she loved her job, there were times she got so tired of pretense that she just wanted to chuck the whole lot in a bin and walk away. Perhaps she would once she got her trainee up to snuff.

Her mind turned to what that life after the Corps might be like. A picture of a small house on a lake rose in her mind, the house she had grown up in with her grandmother back on Earth. A pang of longing filled her. If such a place existed in the Empire, she would happily retire and live in peace. It might be lonely after so much activity, but living in a house in such a peaceful setting sounded like a little piece of paradise.

"Where have you gone off to now, Anna?"

Dan's voice snagged her back to the present. She let go of that vision with a sigh and pasted a polite smile on her face, then focused on the man to see him shaking his head with a frown, his blue eyes both gentle and weary. "Don't do that. You don't need to hide from me, Anna Elizabeth. We've known each other long enough that we don't need any pretenses, don't you think?"

Anna Elizabeth stared at him in confusion as the diplomats, their family members, and their dates moved around them, laughing and chatting. No one seemed to need her at the moment. She took time to really *see* Dan: his body language, his words, his expression, and what was in his eyes. She took a deep breath and let it out before quietly responding.

"What brought you here tonight?"

He assessed her carefully and apparently saw what he was looking for since he nodded. "You, Anna. I've been waiting for you."

"Me? I wasn't delayed long with Jace." Her brow furrowed in concern as she began looking around, seeing people she had meant to speak to and noting that the food needed to be refreshed.

Dan stopped her with a hand to her shoulder, drawing her attention back to him immediately. Her eyes were wide as they met his. They had known each other for almost thirty years, and he had never touched her before, not even to shake hands. His grip softened as he watched her, eyes searching.

"I don't mean just tonight, Anna. You've had important work to do and didn't seem to have room in your life for anything else. I've been waiting for you to feel ready to move to the next thing. I had about given up hope that there might be a time, but when I heard from ADAM, it seemed to be a sign."

Anna's eyes widen. "Heard from ADAM? What did he contact you about?"

Dan gestured around him with a small smile. "It isn't obvious? He matched us."

She only was able to control her surprise by drawing on her experience, though she had a feeling she wasn't fooling Dan. "I...I see. And our age difference doesn't bother you? Even the appearance of it?"

"Six years isn't such a gap after all this time, Anna." Dan eyed her carefully, and Anna could tell he was bracing himself for disappointment. "Are you even a tiny bit glad about ADAM matching us?"

Anna thought for a moment, shifting the pieces of her current and future life in her head. Could she fit someone within it? She remembered the view of the lake from the porch she longed for and how alone she'd thought she would be when she finally reached it. Would Dan fit there with her? Did she want him to?

She looked up to focus on his watchful eyes, which spoke volumes even though he stood silently. Her mouth twitched into a small smile. "How do you feel about porches and lakes?"

Dan's eyes lit up, warmth spreading as he smiled. The fingers on his glass relaxed, as did his body. "Is there fishing?"

Anna's smile stretched wider and her cheeks flushed, which hadn't happened in years. "I think we can figure something out."

CHAPTER TWENTY-SEVEN

Etheric Empire, Scientific Research Facility

Faith was standing at the table with a tablet in her hand when the door opened with a *swoosh*. Four armed guards walked in one at a time to secure the room and hold a weapon on the woman. Her eyes darted between them, her anger growing. She barked her words, irritated. "What is the meaning of this? I demand an explanation!"

Once the formation was complete, one guard advanced toward the woman, handcuffs in one hand. "Ma'am, I need you to come with us."

The woman's eyes glowed a deep red as her face sharpened, and she leaned forward with a snarl. The guard held his hands up, handcuffs dangling, to show he meant no harm. "Ma'am, I need you to calm down."

She snarled again and shifted her weight, then threw her tablet at him. His eyes widened and he ducked, not attempting to catch anything thrown with that much force. It clipped him on the shoulder, giving him a deep bruise.

He moved his arm, cringing at the pain of a possible fracture.

When the woman turned, her eyes fixed on him, about to attack, the other guards opened fire. She took another step forward, even with several projectiles in her, and was taking a third step when they shot her again. She shuddered, then dropped to the floor, her head making a cracking sound on impact.

The first guard winced as he viewed her heavily sedated body. His fellow guard walked up behind him. "I don't think she liked you calling her 'ma'am.'"

Wincing again and rubbing his shoulder, he nodded. "Yeah." He scanned Faith Rochelle's body again. "I don't think she did either."

Etheric Empire, QBBS *Meredith Reynolds*, Clinic

Doctor Keelson turned from the Pod-doc to the group that had crowded into the room behind her, gripping her tablet in one hand and putting the other on her hip. She edged back to give herself more room, but it didn't help. She glanced at the Pod-doc and its occupant and sighed.

"Basically, we have done everything we can: Pod-doc adjustments, genetic alterations thanks to our resident expert, and nanocyte coding changes. Her body is fixed and will be completely healthy—more than that, actually—for some time to come."

Link turned away from the Pod-doc. His eyes and face appeared weary, and stubble was visible along his jaw. His clothes were rumpled and creased as if he had spent far too long in them. When he spoke, his voice was agitated. "Why hasn't she woken up if everything is fine?"

Doctor Keelson pressed her lips together as she scanned the group. Red splotches and tears covered Alina's cheeks as she held on to Maxim, whose mouth was turned down grimly. He kept an arm around the young woman. Drk-vaen and Sis'tael stood in the back, both showing signs of distress as they fidgeted.

Link and Braeden stood closest to her. One was rumpled and weary but refused to leave to take care of himself. The other stood tall and silent as he focused on the Pod-doc, his gaze intent. She thought she saw someone in the outer room, but when she glanced that way, it was empty. She sighed again and rubbed the back of her neck with her hand.

"The problem is her mind. As far as we can determine, her brain is fine, functioning at peak capacity, yet she seems to be in a self-induced coma. We could force her body to wake, but without knowing what happened to cause her to put herself out, doing so might cause her lasting harm, or possibly even brain damage."

Sis'tael spoke up, her mandibles clicking. "None of us wants that."

The rest shook their heads, though Alina and Link had similar expressions of agony. Link just hid his a little better. It was always in the eyes. No matter how many times she gave good or bad news to family members, April always paid attention to the eyes since they showed the truth.

Braeden stirred, then turned to speak to the group at large, his movement less graceful than they had formerly been. "It is as the doctor says. I can reach Phina's mind, and it is present, with no brain damage. Everything has healed, and she has strengthened her mental pathways. I can even speak into her mind. However, it is as though she is both present and absent. Some part of her conscious self is missing from her body." He looked at the Pod-doc again thoughtfully.

"So, we just wait." Link spoke heavily.

Doctor Keelson and Braedon nodded slowly.

"I'm afraid so."

"However long it takes."

Etheric Empire, QBBS *Meredith Reynolds*, Bar

The waitress dropped a large mug of beer on the table and slid it over to Link, a few drops splashing over the side. She paused a moment as if waiting for something, her chest pushed forward to show off her tightly clothed body. Her efforts were wasted, though, since Link barely gave her a glance, not even handing over the usual tip. Realizing she would get nothing, she pursed her lips sourly and rolled her eyes as she stomped off.

Link's bloodshot eyes were only paying attention to his beer and the doorway, where he hoped to see his contact enter soon. He wouldn't have spared even this time, except that this person was one of his most trusted, and she never contacted him unless it would be of interest to one of his personas, she being one of the few to know about them. The only thing this contact didn't know was that Greyson Wells was just as much a persona as the rest.

Only Phina knew that.

He smacked his forehead twice with the heel of his hand. He had to get in gear. This was no time to be lazy or complacent, just because he was worried. He was running his hands through his hair when he heard a voice beside him.

"My, my, Greyson. This doesn't look good at all."

He turned to see Dorothy King and gave her his first genuine smile since Phina's collapse. He stood and bowed over the older lady's hand, kissing it. She blushed and pulled it away to lightly smack him in the chest. "Don't tell me you haven't found a girl who will look twice at you."

Link sighed with the same lightness. "Alas, fair lady, no one can compare with you."

She shook her head and stepped to the other side of the table to sit, her expression concerned. "I realize I'm old enough to be your mother, but really, Greyson. Don't put me in the position of having to chastise you for not taking care of yourself."

Link shrugged and looked mulish. "It can't be helped right now."

Dorothy's eyes narrowed as she nodded. "So, there *is* a girl."

He attempted a bland look but quickly relented since he didn't have the energy for it—a sign that he needed to take care of himself better. "My recruit. But not the way you're thinking."

She nodded as she assessed him. "I see. Something is wrong?"

Link barked a sarcastic laugh and took a drink of his beer before answering. "She's in a coma."

Dorothy's expression turned sorrowful. "I'm sorry to hear that, Greyson. I'll say a prayer for her."

He nodded, then cleared his throat and moved on to what had brought them here in an attempt to deflect the warmth he felt at her concern. He hadn't yet admitted to her that he regarded her as more his mother than his own had been. "You have something for me?"

Her eyes cleared and sharpened as she leaned forward, her hands resting on the table. "Yes, and let me tell you, young man, this will throw you for a loop. It definitely threw me for one."

Link straightened his shoulders and leaned toward her, as alert as it was possible for him to be. "Tell me."

Dorothy nodded. "I usually pretend to be almost deaf so those I work around will speak more freely. This time it didn't matter. They either didn't know or didn't care that I was there. I was cleaning the dock manager's office, the person who oversees all the spaceships passing through Ekeled station. As I cleaned the inner office, I overheard two males conversing about sending someone out for a job. I didn't hear much, only that it was religious in nature to the native species. What brought me to take the first transport over to see you was what he said as they left."

Link raised his eyebrows as she paused, looking down at her hands. "Well?"

She raised troubled eyes. "'Wouldn't that big shot of a spy get a kick in the pants to know the source of his headache is so close to him?'"

Link leaned back, his eyes blanking and his hands slack on his mug. "He's right. It's a kick."

She reached over and squeezed his hand, then let go

and stood up. She lingered for another moment, considering him before speaking. "There's something else."

He looked up, confused. "What?"

She raised her eyebrows. "It might just be these old eyes failing, but I could have sworn I saw a flash of green skin."

He stilled, his eyes fixed on hers as she nodded knowingly. Then she walked out. He took a deep breath to deal with the bombshell that had just fallen on him.

Damn it. This was gonna be bad.

Etheric Empire, QBS *Stark*

Braeden was watching a screen showing the planet below. It had taken time, but the Aurians had finally completed their re-terraforming process with the help of Gleek and Empire tech fused into a one-of-a-kind delivery system. The process had resulted in a beautiful and unique planet that appeared to be perfect for the Aurians.

It was habitable for humans as well.

That had gotten many on the upper levels of the Empire interested, Braeden had noted. After several meetings, She-Who-Mourns and her people had agreed to share their planet with a colony of humans. Since there were so few Aurians left, it would take a while to repopulate, so the two species would grow side by side.

Ryan Wagner turned with a grin. "It looks awesome! Why aren't we down there? What's the holdup?"

A laugh in a voice rich with age came from the other viewing screen. "Patience, Grasshopper." Addison Stone turned to the young man with a pleased smile. She had gotten to know the Aurians quite well and was very fond of them, even considering putting in for a transfer to the new human colony. "Good things come to those who wait."

"But there's nothing to wait for. The planet's been cooked and cooled and now has a sustainable atmosphere, so what's the holdup?" Ryan turned his palms up and shrugged at the look she gave him. "What? I listen. I can understand big words."

She shook her head with a wry smile. "The holdup, I think, is a name." She turned to the Aurians on the deck. They were looking at the viewing screens with awe and amazement. "So, have you chosen a name for the planet? Is it the same as before?"

She-Who-Mourns gave her a brilliant smile, the ancient look in her eyes now the only sign of the grief she had gone through. "Yes and no. We couldn't have done any of this without you and the others who could not come today."

Braeden nodded but remained silent, thinking about Phina with a heavy heart. She would have wanted to be here.

She-Who-Mourns continued, "Because of you, we have our home again. Because of Phina discovering and Stark giving us the location of a cavern filled with minerals you value for jewelry and decoration, we have a resource to trade with the Empire while we get back on our feet. You gave us renewed hope, so..." She turned back to the screen, her eyes filled with longing. "Our planet used to be named Lyria, 'planet of song.' It had become Lyriem, 'song of sorrow.' Now it will be Lyriasha, 'song of hope.'"

All the Aurians in the room nod solemnly. "Lyriasha."

"And along with the planet's name change, I am

changing mine," She-Who-Mourns continued, her eyes were fixated on the screen. "My name will no longer be She-Who-Mourns, but She-Who-Hopes."

"She-Who-Hopes," the Aurians chanted. He-Who-Thinks stood in the back, watching her with conflicted eyes. The Aurians hadn't quite forgiven him, and he'd had to agree to strict oversight for any future experiments, but the Aurian people had decided there had been enough death. His life was now devoted to finding ways to help the Aurians grow as a people and a culture.

The bond he had with his former pledgemate was strained too. She-Who-Hopes still had difficulty, but at least she was speaking to him now, which was more than he could have hoped for.

She-Who-Hopes nodded. "We will remember the past and mourn for those lost, but looking toward the future is what we need to do now."

Braeden gave an imperceptible sigh and turned to view the planet. Song of hope. Phina could use a song of hope just now. As the Aurians began singing and chanting in their language, Braeden turned off the translator and let the melody wash over him. It filled him with hope and made him realize he needed to share it.

He reached out to Phina, who was halfway across the Empire, with his powerful mind. As he connected, he recognized the curious present but absent state of her mind. So, nothing had changed since he had left weeks ago to facilitate the terraforming process between his brothers and the two volunteers from the Empire. That was both a relief and a worry. He took a mental step out of the way in the connection, allowing her to hear the song without his interpretation overlaying it.

After a few minutes of listening to the complex song, he tuned in to Phina again and almost dropped his staff in his surprise.

Half an empire away, Phina opened her eyes.

FINIS

THE STORY CONTINUES

Seraphina's story continues with *Diplomatic Resurgence*, coming soon to Amazon and Kindle Unlimited.

Claim your copy today!

We meet again! 😄 Thank you so much for reading Diplomatic Crisis and continuing to read our author notes! I really hope you enjoyed it!

Reviews

Awww! 😊 You guys are awesome! Thank you so much for your amazing reviews and responses to Diplomatic Recruit! I've become a compulsive Amazon checker looking to see if more ratings or reviews have been posted. 😄

I seriously can't thank you enough for all the support, encouragement, and excitement you all have given us for this series!

I read one review where the reviewer said they were mad that book two wasn't out yet. I called out to my husband Steve, "Yes! I've arrived as an author!" 😄 He was interested but understandably confused till I told him why.

I've always wanted to write stories people loved enough

to want more of and don't want to wait for the next book. I'm happy that dream is coming true!

Aurians

I mentioned in the author notes of Diplomatic Recruit that I thought this book, Diplomatic Crisis, might be my favorite.

There were several reasons for that, one of which was the awesome cover Mihaela Voicu has designed that I can't stop looking at! 😄

I think a lot of it is due to the Aurians in this book, their culture, and how Phina was impacted by them.

When the idea came up as to using music as language the first problem immediately presented itself- how was that going to work with the translation implant? 😕 It was almost scrapped several times. The scene with Phina and ADAM trying to figure out how to make it work was part of actually trying to think it through myself. 😄 I think we figured it out!

A lot of how the Aurians do things is a little strange but beautiful, and I am really happy as to how it all came together!

Greyson Wells

Greyson, Greyson, Greyson. When Michael and I began talking about what the series would look like after Last Adventure First, one of the first things brought up was that she had to have a mentor. She was a self taught spy who came to realize she still has a lot to learn and she isn't a conventional student. A mentor was definitely the best way to go.

Figuring out what that mentor would be like was probably one of the most fun parts of the brainstorming process! 😄 Michael had ideas about what her mentor should be like and it fit pretty well with where I was leaning too. There was a lot of back and forth as we threw in idea after idea as to how he would act or how his personae would work. Having his on station hang out located in the back room of the secret bar was a must, as well as his obsession with beer!

In the end, as her mentor took shape, the man himself became clear, even though at times it's really as clear as mud. The phrase "international man of mystery" could have been invented for Greyson Wells and he endeavors to fully live up to it!

Matching a name to his oversized arrogant filled persona was a trick easily solved as I looked over a list of names that were given to me when I asked in our Kurtherian Fans Write group at the time. I wanted something that sounded English since he had worked there a lot in his previous life, a little lyrical, a bit pretentious, and definitely memorable. Kelly O'Donnell had listed several and that one popped out immediately!

I would say that Link/Greyson is probably one of the more fun and consistently interesting characters to write. But then some characters are indelibly etched in my head and he's one of them! I really never know what he's going to say until he says it. Don't worry, he likes it that way! 😉 He's happiest when he keeps people guessing.

Btw, have you wanted to slap him at any time during this book? You aren't the only one! 😄 Quite a few comments from our beta readers were that Greyson was overboard with the attitude and it needed some help. Well, that attitude was on purpose. Mostly. Some of it was toned down and some explained a bit more as to why he reacted a certain way. Hopefully it's a good mix now. Even if you still want to give him a good slap. 😊

Diplomatic Resurgence

You will understand Greyson's actions and attitude even better after the next book. The past is coming back to haunt Phina and Link in a big way! Phina finds out she's been lied to her whole life. When the truth is revealed Phina has to pick up the pieces.

Did you catch the hint that someone new is coming onto the scene in the next book? There's a lot more in store for Phina in book three and the secrets are only the beginning. 😄

I can't wait for you to see what happens!

Until next time!

Thank you for not only reading this story, but back here to the author notes as well!

It has been a while since I worked with a brand-new author. One who had never released a book. Had never bitten their nails waiting for the reviews to come in.

'Are they going to be good? Are they going to say horrible things? *What if no one reviews the book at all?*"

I am not suggesting that I am totally beyond checking out reviews on books (I am human, after all), but I will say that after so many of my books going out, I don't sit on my laptop religiously clicking the enter key to refresh the page.

So, the opportunity to experience the situation again (if only vicariously through Sara) is a touch of fun and a whole lot of nostalgia for me. Obviously, the experience is WAYYY better when you, the fans, provide support in the reviews!

The other situation is akin to talking your collaborator

out of jumping off the kitchen table. It might not kill them, but it could be painful.

So, thank ALL OF YOU for not only reading (and often reviewing) Sara's book. But also supporting a brand-new author. You have allowed me to bless Sarah's life by bestowing the title 'Professional Author', and therefore I am blessed as well.

May you, the readers, realize the joy you give us every day!

Ad Aeternitatem,

Michael Anderle

CONNECT WITH THE AUTHORS

Connect with S.E. Weir

Website: http://seweir.com/

Facebook: https://www.facebook.com/sarahweirwrites/

Connect with Michael Anderle

Website: http://lmbpn.com

Email List: http://lmbpn.com/email/

Social Media:

https://www.facebook.com/LMBPNPublishing

https://twitter.com/MichaelAnderle

https://www.instagram.com/lmbpn_publishing/

https://www.bookbub.com/authors/michael-anderle

BOOKS BY S.E. WEIR

The Empress' Spy
Diplomatic Recruit (Book 1)
Diplomatic Crisis (Book 2)
Diplomatic Resurgence (Book 3)

Lightning Source UK Ltd.
Milton Keynes UK
UKHW041912030722
405290UK00001B/354